"This morning the police had a call from...
runs a boarding house next door to Miss Whittier's
home."

Claudia nodded.

"Miss Whittier was an early riser," Vivian said. "At
nine o'clock this morning, her blinds were still closed,
and her newspaper was on the sidewalk. Her neighbor
phoned to check on her, but nobody answered, so she
called 911. The police found Miss Whittier in her living
room. She'd been shot. They think it happened last
night, as long as ten or twelve hours before they found
her body."

"Tell me it it isn't so!" Claudia said, unwilling to believe
what she'd heard. Miss Whittier had done so much
good for Oak Hill. She'd helped start the shelter for
battered women and the soup kitchen for the down-
and-out, and she'd aided scores of individuals, young
people mostly, finding them jobs or money for college.
"Who'd do a thing like that?"

"Ray thinks it may have to do with drugs."

———————————— ★ ————————————

SIFTING THROUGH SECRETS

ELIZABETH HAWN

WORLDWIDE®

TORONTO • NEW YORK • LONDON
AMSTERDAM • PARIS • SYDNEY • HAMBURG
STOCKHOLM • ATHENS • TOKYO • MILAN
MADRID • WARSAW • BUDAPEST • AUCKLAND

Recycling programs
for this product may
not exist in your area.

SIFTING THROUGH SECRETS

A Worldwide Mystery/June 2012

First published by Alabaster Book Publishers

ISBN-13: 978-0-373-63632-7

Printed in U.S.A.

For F.C. and Emily Lester, who taught me that books, friends, and useful work were all the wealth I'd need; for Gertrude Lester, who loved God, people, and a good story; and for Grace Gougler, who is still the world's best mother-in-law at age 97.

ONE

Nestled in the rolling hills of central North Carolina near the town of Oak Hill, Pleasant Valley Retirement Center provides gracious living for seniors in a worry-free atmosphere.

From the brochure, "Pleasant Valley Retirement Center Welcomes You"

IDA MAE POINDEXTER OPENED her front door a crack and peered out at the other brick duplexes on the cul-de-sac. Good, not another living soul in sight! She didn't want to shock her neighbors, who always wore their daytime clothes, and nice ones at that, whenever they set foot outside their homes. Grasping the front of her pink-flowered housecoat so it wouldn't gap open, she scurried down the walk, her slippers flapping on the concrete, to pick up her morning paper.

Halfway back to her door, she stopped. In the flowerbed in front of her apartment, a cluster of headless sunflower stalks swayed in the early morning breeze. How had that happened? Had squirrels done it? Those pesky creatures raided the bird feeder in her backyard daily, aggravating her no end. Looking up at the branches of the oak tree beside her apartment, she spotted one of the little devils scampering along a limb. What she wouldn't give for a forked stick and a piece of rubber from an old inner tube! When she was a girl, she'd been mighty good with a slingshot and with her daddy's rifle, too. Fried squirrel with gravy and biscuits had been a real treat back then.

But maybe it wasn't squirrels. Maybe somebody was trying to enforce the rules of Pleasant Valley Retirement Center, the ones in the booklet she'd been given when she moved in. *Flowers may be planted in a space of no more than three feet in front of each duplex and should be no more than three feet in height,* it said. *Vegetables may be grown in backyards only.* Ida Mae grinned as she imagined one of her elderly neighbors sneaking into her yard at night, measuring her sunflowers, and lopping off their heads.

For two cents she'd move back to Wendley Street and plant what she pleased. But the house where she'd lived for sixty years wasn't hers to go back to. When her nieces Norma and Betty Jo caught her on a ladder cleaning out her gutters, they ganged up on her, saying she had no business trying to take care of a house at her age. Not that she was complaining. Norma and Betty Jo had been generous, chipping in big chunks of their own money so she could move into Pleasant

Valley instead of the apartment building for seniors down by the railroad tracks.

Shaking her head over the decapitated sunflowers, Ida Mae went back into her half of the duplex. It was cool inside. Thanks to the fresh air that had come in the windows during the night, she didn't need to turn on the air conditioning yet. Her nieces would have a fit if they knew she left the windows open, the same kind of fit they had every time they found her front door unlocked. The way they carried on, you'd think Oak Hill was New York City or some other crime-ridden place. She knew better than to mention the open windows. She'd learned a long time ago not to share everything with the younger generation.

Ida Mae gave her living room an approving look. It was neat and clean, the way she liked it, with fresh white walls and a beige carpet that matched the vines in her blue-flowered sofa. A painting of a flower garden, a housewarming gift from her nieces, hung over the sofa. Thanks to Betty Jo and Norma, she had this nice apartment to live in. She wasn't going to waste any more time fretting over a few sunflowers.

No, siree, she was going to sit right down and read the obituaries. She always read them first—"Just to make sure I'm not dead," she liked to tell people. Then she'd fix her breakfast, read the rest of the paper, and do the crossword puzzle.

Ida Mae went through the arch that separated her living room from the dining area, put the newspaper on the table, and went into the kitchen. Moments later she was back with a mug of coffee. When she sat down at the table and unrolled the paper, a black-and-white photo halfway down the page caught her eye. She stared at the picture, which showed a necklace in a man's hand. The caption read, "Necklace with blue glass beads, found with skeleton, is displayed by Oak Hill Police Detective B. Wayne Henley."

Ida Mae gasped. Then she read the inch-high headline at the top of the page, "Bulldozers Unearth Skeleton," and the article beneath it. According to the newspaper, heavy equipment working on the new interstate highway near Oak Hill had unearthed bones that appeared to be human. The bulldozer operator called the police, who found the necklace near the bones.

"We hope the necklace will help us identify the skeleton," Detective Henley had told the newspaper. "Anyone with information about it should call the Oak Hill Police Department right away."

Ida Mae read the article again. Then she slowly rose from the table and went to the kitchen, where she looked in the "Help at Your Fingertips" section at the front of her phone book.

When she punched the number into her phone, a

female voice on the other end of the line said, "Oak Hill Police Department. How may I help you?"

Ida Mae's eyes filled with tears. She wasn't ready to do this yet.

"Wrong number," she said in a croaky voice.

IN THE APARTMENT NEXT door, Claudia McNeill finished her first cup of coffee of the day. Not ready for breakfast yet, she rinsed out the cup and went to her living room, where she pinched a yellow leaf off her philodendron and ran a finger along the edge of the bookshelves, checking for dust.

Claudia smiled at the framed photographs that stood on top of the bookshelves. Here were her children, her grands, and her great-grands, in academic robes, military uniforms, and their Sunday best. Dark eyes shone from faces of varying shades of brown and tan, all with the McNeill look of determination.

The phone rang. Claudia felt sure it was a member of her family, calling before setting off for work or school. Each morning one of her children or grandchildren phoned. "Just thought I'd call and say hello" was the usual message—as if she couldn't figure out that they'd made a schedule, a secret from her, of course, to insure that someone checked on her every day. She didn't mind. She loved them for it.

She picked up the phone, wondering which family member it was today.

"Hello, Claudia?"

It took her a second to recognize the voice of the white woman who lived in the other half of the duplex. She'd heard Ida Mae agitated before, but never this upset.

"I was wondering if you'd like to come over for a bite of breakfast," Ida Mae said. "I have bacon and eggs, and I've put on water for grits."

"Why, that sounds lovely," Claudia said. Bacon, eggs, and grits would taste good, even though they were the kind of breakfast her doctor told her to avoid. But she would have gone to see her neighbor without the offer of food. Ida Mae's voice had a note of deep-down distress, the kind that meant she needed to talk something over with a friend.

Before moving into Pleasant Valley, Claudia had never lived next door to a white person. In fact, there'd been only a few of them in her lifetime that she'd classify as friends, as opposed to acquaintances. She hadn't met Ida Mae before entering the retirement community, but the day Claudia moved in, Ida Mae appeared at her door to invite her over for coffee and cake. It hadn't taken long to find out that Ida Mae was friendly and good-hearted, the kind of neighbor Claudia had been hoping for. Three months, hours of talk, and many cups of coffee later, Claudia considered her a friend.

"Want me to come right over?" Claudia asked, glancing at her watch.

"Yes—no, give me fifteen minutes. I'd better put some clothes on." Ida Mae gave a hoot of laughter, sounding more like her usual self. "Law me, Claudia, I'm in such a tizzy I forgot I'm not dressed."

KRISTIN GRANT SAT AT her desk at the *Oak Hill Sentinel,* reading the article about the bones that had been found at the highway construction site. It was a story she'd love to cover. A skeleton was definitely more interesting than last night's city council meeting. With a sigh, she put the newspaper down and began puzzling over her notes from the meeting. A rezoning vote had been postponed for the third time. Was that routine or did it mean something?

At previous city council meetings, several of Oak Hill's citizens had spoken about the issue, which involved rezoning an area on the east side of town from residential to commercial use. "A key part of Oak Hill's economic development," one of them had called it. "Wanton and tragic destruction of a historic community," someone on the other side had said. Why was it so important to them? She suspected she was one of the few people in town who didn't know.

After two years of writing engagement and wedding stories for a big newspaper in Raleigh,

Kristin had jumped at the chance for a reporter's job at a paper in a much smaller town. Her first six months at the *Sentinel* had been heaven. Bill Caldwell, the newspaper editor, had let her write feature stories. Finding subjects to write about had been easy. Apparently, everybody in Oak Hill and the surrounding county wanted to be in the paper. Kristin was besieged by would-be local celebrities—a farmer who'd grown a giant pumpkin, a woman who'd taught her cat to flush the toilet, a female Elvis impersonator. Before long she thought she knew all there was to know about her new hometown.

But when Bill asked her to start covering city council meetings, Kristin realized how much she didn't know about Oak Hill. With a little help from Steve Jacobs, the reporter who'd handled that assignment previously, she'd managed to write two articles, but she couldn't keep asking Steve to bail her out. Worse yet, yesterday Bill had told her— with a big smile, as if it were news she'd be glad to hear—that he was thinking of having her cover the county commissioners' meetings, too. Kristin knew even less about Yarborough County politics than she did about the issues in Oak Hill.

She was about to ask Steve to explain the rezoning vote when her phone rang.

"This is Ida Mae Poindexter," the caller said. "You wrote a story about me for the newspaper."

That narrowed it down to what—two hundred people? Kristin jotted down the woman's name and tried to remember who she was.

"I won the Valentine's Day contest. Remember, the paper wanted people to send in romantic stories? I sent one about my late husband, Odell, and me. You and the photographer came to my house. I was living on Wendley Street then. You ate some of my pound cake."

Oh, yes, the pound cake. Kristin remembered it perfectly. Not the bland, crumbly stuff sold at the grocery store, palatable only if covered with strawberries and whipped cream, but a rich, moist cake with hints of lemon, warm from the oven. She and Matt Trexler, the *Sentinel* photographer, had each eaten two big slices of it.

"Of course I remember you, Mrs. Poindexter," Kristin said.

"I want to talk to you about that skeleton, the one in this morning's paper. But I can't do it on the phone. Can you come to see me?"

The article about the skeleton had been written by Steve Jacobs, who handled all the stories having to do with the police or crime. Kristin briefly considered referring the caller to Steve. But her reporter's curiosity—or was it the thought of Mrs. Poindexter's culinary skills?—made her say, "I'll be right there."

By the time Ida Mae had explained how to find

her apartment, Kristin had her purse and keys in her hand. The city council article could wait. A woman who made such scrumptious cake certainly merited another visit.

Claudia was peering through the blinds in Ida Mae's living room when a little red car pulled up to the curb in front of the duplex.

"She's here," Claudia said. She turned to Ida Mae, who was seated on the sofa, fanning herself with a magazine. Claudia could see that stress had taken a toll on her friend. Several of Ida Mae's tightly permed white curls were sticking out at strange angles from her head, and the elasticized waistband of her navy-and-red top had ridden up, exposing a half inch of white nylon underwear above her navy blue pants.

"You sit still and compose yourself," Claudia said, "and I'll answer the door."

"I'm composed," Ida Mae said. "I'm just worn out from washing those dishes like we were going to a house afire. I swan, Claudia, I thought I was the workingest woman I knew, but you beat all."

Claudia smiled. In the three months they'd known each other, Ida Mae had never let her do so much as carry an empty coffee cup to the kitchen. This morning Ida Mae had called the newspaper reporter while the remains of breakfast were still on the table and then had launched into a frenzy of table-clearing and dishwashing. Claudia had suggested that they put the dirty dishes in the dishwasher, but Ida Mae replied that washing them by hand would take only a jiffy. When Claudia pitched in to help, her friend hadn't objected.

No, Ida Mae clearly wasn't herself this morning. During breakfast she'd been cheerful one minute and teary the next. Claudia had tried to convince her that finding the necklace near the bones didn't necessarily mean anything bad. Maybe the bulldozer had dug up part of an old family cemetery everybody had forgotten about. Maybe the necklace hadn't been on the skeleton at all, but had been dropped there by someone else. But Ida Mae hadn't been convinced.

As Claudia watched from the window, a young woman left the car and started up the walk. With her long blond hair, sandals, and flowered skirt that almost reached her ankles, she reminded Claudia of one of those hippie girls in the '60s. She was skinny, and she looked about fourteen. But so did Claudia's grandson Michael, and he was a neurosurgeon.

"You must be the reporter from the *Sentinel*," Claudia said with a welcoming smile as she opened the door.

"Mrs. Poindexter?" The reporter looked puzzled. Claudia realized she must have been expecting a white woman.

"I'm right here," Ida Mae said, getting up from the sofa. "This is my friend, Claudia McNeill, who lives next door." She gestured toward the table in the dining area. "Why don't we sit over there? We've just finished breakfast, but it would be the easiest thing in the world for me to fix you some bacon and eggs and grits."

Claudia smiled. Ida Mae, who loved to feed people, was beginning to sound like herself again. She probably thought the reporter needed to gain a few pounds. Claudia and Ida Mae didn't hold with all the dieting people did these days. They agreed that most of the actresses on TV looked just plain scrawny.

"Oh, no, I've eaten," Kristin said.

"Some coffee? And a slice of pound cake? I made the cake yesterday afternoon, so it's good and fresh, and I started a pot of coffee right before you drove up."

The reporter's face broke into a smile. "Thanks. That sounds good."

As Ida Mae bustled off toward the kitchen, Claudia took a closer look at the young woman. Her hair color seemed real, but you could never tell these days. She wasn't from around here, unless Grant was her married name. The Grants in Yarborough County, the white ones anyway, were tall people. There was no wedding band on the girl's left hand, so she must be single. Even if married women called themselves Ms. and didn't take their husbands' names, they still seemed to want rings, Claudia had noticed.

A FEW MINUTES LATER, Kristin was seated at the table with a steaming mug of coffee and a generous slice of pound cake in front of her. She still wasn't sure why she was here, but if the cake was half as good as it looked, the visit wouldn't be a total loss.

Ida Mae brought mugs of coffee for herself and Claudia, along with a blue pottery cream pitcher that matched the sugar bowl and salt and pepper shakers already on the table. Then she tried to persuade Claudia to have a piece of cake, too.

"I couldn't eat another bite," Claudia said. "That breakfast you fixed will last me all day."

The cake was even better than Kristin remembered. "This is wonderful," she told her hostess.

"Ida Mae makes real good pound cake," Claudia said, nodding in agreement. "Now me, after close to sixty years of feeding my family, I'd almost rather eat store-bought food than cook, but Ida Mae enjoys it."

"Cooking calms me down," Ida Mae said. "Like this morning, I was mighty upset. But after I stirred up some breakfast for Claudia and me, I knew what I should do, which was call you." She pointed to the headline in the newspaper that lay on the table, and her eyes brimmed with tears.

Kristin had rarely encountered tears on her job, so she didn't know what to do. Before she could decide whether to pat Ida Mae's hand, offer her a tissue, or wait until she calmed down, Claudia took over.

"She's scared those bones they found are her sister's. The one who disappeared."

Kristin didn't remember an elderly woman disappearing in the six months she'd been in Oak Hill. Maybe it had happened earlier. "Your sister is missing? How long has she been gone?"

Ida Mae took a tissue from her pocket and dabbed her eyes. "Since 1946."

Kristin's eyes widened. That was—how many years ago? How old would Ida Mae have been then?

"She has proof," Claudia said. "Show her, Ida Mae."

Ida Mae went to the china cabinet in a corner of the dining area, took something out, and brought it to Kristin—a necklace of blue beads interspersed with silver links, a duplicate of the one in the newspaper picture.

"My husband gave me this," she said. "My sister Vonda thought it was so pretty, I bought her one like it for her birthday, right before—" She shook her head.

"Before she disappeared?"

"From the face of the earth." Ida Mae wiped away a few more tears. "Not a phone call, not a Christmas card. But we never gave up hope."

"Have you told the police this?"

"Oh, we're going to do that," Claudia said, "but we wanted to talk to you first."

"Me? What can I do?"

The two older women looked dumbfounded.

"Why, you can put it in the paper, of course," Ida Mae said. "I'll tell you everything you need to know. Do you have something to write with?"

Kristin suppressed a grin. She should have known. In Oak Hill, neither triumph nor tragedy would be complete without being written up in the *Sentinel.* She pulled a pen and notebook from her purse. "I have everything I need. But after I interview you, may I drive you to the police station?"

"You won't have to do that. They'll come here. Claudia's going to call them while I talk to you."

"In that case," Kristin said, spearing the last bit of cake with her fork, "let's get on with the interview."

Twenty minutes later Kristin was on Ida Mae's sofa, talking to Bill Caldwell on her cell phone. Ida Mae and Claudia were in the kitchen, where they'd retreated when Kristin said she needed to call the newspaper editor. Kristin explained to Bill that Ida Mae's sister Vonda had disappeared in 1946. The family thought she'd eloped with a man named Harvey Dawkins, but they hadn't seen her since then. Ida Mae was afraid the bones unearthed at the site of the new highway were her sister's.

"She showed me an entry in the family Bible and some old photos, so I know the sister existed," Kristin murmured into the phone. "Ida Mae has a necklace that looks like the one in the paper, and she says her sister had one that was identical. The sister took a suitcase when she left, and the story in the *Sentinel* said that hardware, probably from a suitcase, was found near the skeleton."

"Sounds like a front-page story for the paper," Bill said.

Kristin held her breath. This was the point where he'd say he wanted Steve to write the article. Instead he asked, "Can you handle it, Kristin?"

"Sure," she said, beaming. "I'll need Matt to take photos. Ida Mae and her necklace will make a great picture."

"You'll need to include the law enforcement angle, too. Do the police think the bones are the remains of Mrs. Poindexter's sister? Are they treating it as a suspicious death? That sort of thing."

"The police are on their way here now. I'll try to find out all I can."

As she hung up, Kristin heard voices outside. She looked out the front window and saw two men in dark suits, white shirts, and dark ties. Unless they were Mormon missionaries, they had to be cops.

When Ida Mae invited them in, one of the men, a stocky blond with a buzz cut, gave Kristin a suspicious look.

"I'm Detective Henley," he said.

Apparently he expected her to identify herself, too. "Kristin Grant," she said. She extended her hand, not planning to tell him she was a reporter.

"I'm Detective Ray Shelton," his companion said with a smile, shaking the hand Henley had ignored. Detective Shelton was tall and broad-shouldered, with deep brown skin and close-cropped hair. His suit looked more expensive than Detective Henley's and was far less rumpled.

"Kristin works for the *Sentinel,*" Ida Mae said, dashing Kristin's hopes of keeping her profession a secret. "She's going to write this up for the paper."

Detective Henley frowned. "This is a police investigation, Ms. Grant. We can't have a reporter here."

"We'll be glad to talk with you after we've interviewed Mrs. Poindexter," Detective Shelton put in smoothly. "I imagine she'd prefer to speak with us in private."

Kristin felt sure she'd learn more if she listened to the detectives' conversation with Ida Mae. She turned to her hostess for help.

"I want Kristin to be here. Claudia, too." Ida Mae's shoulders slumped, and she wiped her eyes with a tissue. "This is rough on me. I need them here for support."

"Ida Mae's having a hard time, Ray," Claudia said to Detective Shelton. "If she wants Kristin here, let her stay."

Detective Shelton gave Claudia an affectionate smile. "All right, Grandma, you win." He turned to his partner with a sheepish grin. "I've never disobeyed my grandmother in my entire thirty-two years, and I'm not about to start now."

Kristin bit her lip to keep from smiling. Grandma? No wonder Claudia and Ida Mae were so sure they wouldn't need to go to the police station. Claudia had clout.

Detective Henley's frown deepened, and his face took on a reddish tinge. Kristin could see the man was upset. Did he hate the press, she wondered, or was he ticked off at being outranked by a grandmother?

Ida Mae gave her eyes one last swipe. Then her face brightened. "Why don't we all sit down? And Wayne and Ray, wouldn't you like a slice of pound cake and a cup of coffee while we talk?"

TWO

Our mission is to provide news to the citizens of Oak Hill and Yarborough County in a fair and accurate manner, giving special emphasis to local issues and events. And though some may disagree, I think we do a darn good job of it.

Bill Caldwell, editor of the *Oak Hill Sentinel,* in a speech to the Oak Hill Rotary Club

Skeleton May Be Remains of Local Woman
by Kristin Grant, Staff Writer

Bones found when woods were cleared to make way for a new interstate highway may be the remains of an Oak Hill woman missing since 1946. Ida Mae Williams Poindexter, a resident of Pleasant Valley Retirement Center, believes the necklace found with the skeleton is the one she gave her younger sister, Vonda Louise Williams, in the spring of that year.

"It broke my heart when I saw the picture of the necklace in the paper," Poindexter said yesterday. "I don't want to believe those bones are my sister's, but I don't know what else to think."

Williams disappeared in July 1946 at age 17. At the time, her family believed she had left town with a boyfriend. None of the family has heard from her since then.

Poindexter says the necklace pictured in yesterday's *Sentinel* is identical to one she owns. She received her necklace as an anniversary gift from her husband in 1945.

"Vonda liked mine so well that I saved up to buy one like it for her birthday the next year," Poindexter said. Both necklaces were purchased at Wentworth's Jewelry, a store then located on Main Street in Oak Hill.

"Mr. Wentworth had to special order Vonda's necklace," Poindexter recalled. "He told me Vonda and I were the only ones in town who had that kind of necklace."

At the time of her disappearance, Williams lived with Poindexter and her husband, the late Odell Poindexter, at 822 Wendley Street. Williams had come to Oak Hill in December 1945 to work at Treadwell Manufacturing, Inc., a local hosiery company that has since gone out of business.

Williams and her two sisters grew up on their family's farm near the Sneed's Cross-

roads community in southeastern Yarborough
County. All three came to Oak Hill in the
1940s and worked in hosiery manufacturing. The oldest of the sisters, Arlene Williams
Burton, is deceased. Burton's daughters,
Norma Burton McMurray and Betty Jo Burton Carmichael, live in Oak Hill.

"Mama never gave up hope that Aunt
Vonda would come back," said Carmichael,
who is retired from teaching English at Oak
Hill High School. She is the proprietor of
Betty Jo's Craft Gallery in downtown Oak
Hill. Her husband, Carson Carmichael, is an
electrical contractor.

"I'm glad Mama didn't know her sister was
dead," McMurray said. "It would have just
killed her." She is the owner of McMurray
Realty. Her husband, Lloyd, operates a local
insurance agency.

"YOU WERE ABLE TO TALK to the nieces? That's
good," said Bill Caldwell, peering over Kristin's
shoulder at the story on her computer screen. "Did
you have to break the news of their aunt's death?"

"No, thank goodness. Mrs. Poindexter called
them as soon as the two detectives left. She
thought her nieces would want to be quoted in
the paper—and she was right."

"They talked to you on the phone?"

"No. She told them they needed to come to her apartment right away because something bad had happened. It worked. They arrived in less than ten minutes, looking scared to death. They were probably relieved to hear that the news was nothing worse than the death of an aunt they'd never known."

"Did you find out much from the police?"

Kristin shook her head. "Almost nothing. Detective Henley was angry I was there and tried his best to kick me out. Detective Shelton didn't tell me anything, either, but he was much nicer about it."

Bill grinned. "Shelton and Henley play good cop/bad cop without even trying. I'm not surprised they wouldn't tell you much. After those drug stories we did, the police won't give us the time of day."

A few months before, the *Sentinel* had published a series of articles by Steve Jacobs about illegal drug traffic in Oak Hill, and Bill had written an editorial implying that lax local law enforcement was part of the problem. The chief of police responded with a blistering letter to the *Sentinel,* accusing the newspaper of exaggerating the town's drug problem and insulting the Oak Hill police force.

"There's a rumor going around town that one of the road construction guys saw a hole in the back of the skull the bulldozer unearthed," Bill said. "Possibly a bullet hole. Did you hear anything about that?"

Kristin shook her head. "Mrs. Poindexter asked about the cause of death, but the detectives said they couldn't reach any conclusions until they'd heard from the state medical examiner."

"Steve couldn't convince them to confirm or deny the rumor about the skull, either. He's gone out to the construction site to see if anyone there can tell him anything. Do your best to pry some information out of the police. I'd like a separate article on the police response, with a quote from the chief, if you can get it."

Kristin reached for the phone. Why not start at the top? She dialed the police department, identified herself as a reporter from the *Sentinel,* and asked to speak to Chief Cates. A bored female voice told her the chief wasn't in.

"When do you expect him back?"

"I have no idea," the woman said before plunking down the phone.

Undeterred, Kristin decided to walk to the police station, which was only a few blocks from the newspaper office. If she couldn't find the chief, maybe somebody else would give her a statement. Besides, Myrtle's Grill was on the way. If she stopped there for a quick lunch, Chief Cates might be back in his office by the time she reached the police station.

A few minutes later, Kristin was sitting in a booth at Myrtle's, looking over the handwritten list of the day's meats, vegetables, and desserts, which was paperclipped to the printed menu. Should she order a vegetable plate to make up for the fat and calories in Ida Mae's pound cake?

Myrtle Swaim, the restaurant's owner, ambled over to Kristin's booth, smoothed back the strands of auburn hair escaping from her upswept hairdo, and took an order pad from her apron pocket.

"I'll have a chopped barbecue sandwich," Kristin said, giving in to temptation. She agreed with her colleagues at the *Sentinel* that Myrtle's Grill served the best barbecue in town, generous servings of sliced or chopped pork with the tomato-vinegar-and-secret-spices sauce unique to central North Carolina.

"You want any fries or hushpuppies with that?"

"Just the sandwich," Kristin said, feeling virtuous. Ten blissful minutes later, she wiped barbecue sauce from her chin, took a last sip of strong, sweet iced tea, and went to pay for her meal.

Myrtle was at the cash register, a copy of that morning's *Sentinel* on the counter beside her. "Big news, those bones being found," she said, nodding toward Steve Jacobs's article.

Kristin smiled. Tomorrow the paper would

carry even bigger news—her story about Ida Mae Poindexter's necklace and the skeleton's identity. Then she had a twinge of unease. She'd heard that the Oak Hill grapevine worked fast. By the time the paper came out, would everybody in town already know that the bones were the remains of Vonda Williams?

"The paper doesn't say it, but I heard there was a bullet hole in the skull," Myrtle said. "That makes it murder, I guess."

"I heard that, too," Kristin said, "but I don't think the police are ready to call it murder yet."

Myrtle's laugh was scornful. "A skull with a bullet hole in it? That's a mighty good sign of murder, if you ask me. I'll have to tell Billy Wayne Henley that, the next time he's in here."

"Billy Wayne is Detective Henley?"

Myrtle nodded.

Kristin grinned. Billy Wayne, huh? She'd have to remember that.

When Kristin reached the police station, a fifty-ish woman with hair the same deep burgundy as her nails was seated at the receptionist's desk, absorbed in a *TV Guide*.

"I'm Kristin Grant from the *Sentinel*," Kristin said. "I wonder if I could speak with Chief Cates."

"He isn't in," the woman replied without looking up.

Just then a burst of male laughter came from behind a closed door marked *Chief of Police*. Kristin gave the receptionist a skeptical look.

"I mean he's not available right now," the woman said, showing no signs of embarrassment at having to change her story. "You can call tomorrow and see if he's free."

"Is there someone else I could talk to? We're doing a story about—"

"Didn't you get enough information earlier?"

Kristin turned and saw Detective Henley frowning at her.

She gave him her most winning smile. "Could you answer a few questions for me?"

He turned and began walking away.

Kristin followed him. "What did you think of Ida Mae Poindexter's story? Could the skeleton be her sister's remains?"

Henley picked up his pace.

"Since there was a bullet hole in the skull, are the police treating the case as a murder?" Kristin asked, jogging to keep up with him.

He suddenly stopped, and she almost collided with him. He glared at her, his face reddening. "Like we already told you, we have to wait till we hear from the state medical examiner."

"Will it be difficult to investigate a crime that old?" she asked as he opened a door marked *Detectives' Office*.

He didn't answer.

"Is that a 'no comment'?"

He shut the door in her face.

"Hey, Tammy, bring me another beer."

"Get it yourself, you lazy bum."

Kristin pulled the pillow over her head to shut out the sound of her neighbors' voices. The walls at York Towne Apartments were paper-thin, and Tammy and Darren Loflin's living room was next to her bedroom. The Loflins were night owls. Their angry shouts and the blare of their TV kept Kristin awake almost every night. When she'd first moved in, she'd spent anxious moments with her hand on the phone, ready to call 911 if she heard thuds, screams of pain, or gunshots. But before long she came to the conclusion that the Loflins' violence was only verbal. Thank goodness they were the only neighbors she heard. Her apartment was on the end of the building, and the elderly man who lived below her was very quiet.

When Kristin came to Oak Hill, she hoped to find a garage apartment behind an antebellum home where her windows would overlook a tree-shaded lawn and well-tended flowerbeds, and she'd be lulled to sleep by the scent of magnolias. In this fantasy, her landlady, an elderly widow, would ply her with home-cooked food and introduce her to all the eligible men in town.

In reality, the only apartments available in Oak Hill were the modern, multi-unit type. Kristin's windows looked out on an asphalt parking lot where music blared, tires screeched, and motors roared day and night. Her landlord was probably a big corporation with cheaply constructed apartments like York Towne all over the Southeast. As for eligible men, she hadn't had a date since she moved to Oak Hill.

As she tried to tune out the Loflins, Kristin thought about the events of the day. She felt sure the bones were the remains of Ida Mae Poindexter's sister. Steve had found several construction workers who swore there was a hole in the skull. If they were right, Vonda Williams had been murdered, even if the police weren't ready to admit it yet.

Kristin let herself dream a little. Maybe this murder would be a major career breakthrough for her. Maybe she'd write a series of articles about Vonda Williams's death, revealing facts the police didn't know. The series would win an award, and Bill would give her a huge raise, and—

"That's what *you* think!" Darren roared on the other side of the wall.

—and she'd move to an apartment with thicker walls, where she could get a good night's sleep. Yes, that would be the first thing she'd do. But to merit a huge raise, she'd have to do something spectacular, like uncover the identity of the killer. After sixty years? Who was she kidding? The murderer could have been a drifter, somebody who killed Vonda and then moved on. Even if the killer had been a local person, he might be dead by now. If he were alive, he'd be—she sleepily did the math—at least eighty.

Kristin thought about the people she'd met when she did a story on the craft show at the Oak Hill Senior Center. It was hard to imagine the man who built bluebird houses as a murderer. Or the woman who made teddy bears, or the little old lady who painted those sweet flower pictures, or—

"Shut up!" Tammy shouted.

"Excellent idea," Kristin muttered. She repositioned the pillow over her head and concentrated on going to sleep.

THE NEXT MORNING, KRISTIN took the shortest way to work. Sometimes, relishing her escape from the bumper-to-bumper traffic she'd dealt with in Raleigh, she chose a roundabout route through Oak Hill, navigating narrow roads lined with small frame houses, many with backyard vegetable gardens. Other mornings, she chose wider, tree-lined streets with the kind of spacious, well-kept older homes that might have her coveted garage apartment in back. But today her priority was coffee, better coffee than she'd find at the *Sentinel* office.

She parked in the newspaper's lot and checked her watch. There was plenty of time to walk to

Myrtle's and be at work by eight. When she arrived at the restaurant, the breakfast rush was in full swing. Sounds of conversation and clinking crockery filled the room. The aromas of bacon and sausage convinced Kristin that she needed more than coffee.

"Help you?" Myrtle asked as Kristin approached the cash register.

"A large coffee and a sausage biscuit to go."

As she waited for her order, Kristin looked around the room. The majority of the breakfast customers were men, most of them in open-necked shirts and jeans. Those who wore jackets and ties were probably lawyers from the offices that ringed the Yarborough County courthouse a few blocks away.

From a booth at the back of the restaurant, Detective Shelton waved to her. As Kristin raised her hand to return his greeting, his companion turned to look her way, and she found herself waving at Detective Henley. Billy Wayne, she thought with a grin. The name suited him. She pictured him at age eight, a chubby, belligerent schoolyard bully with a red face and a blond buzz cut.

A few minutes later, Kristin was at her desk, eating her sausage biscuit and sipping coffee as she checked her voice mail. The first message was from a teacher, asking her to speak to a fourth-grade class about her job. School? In the summer?

Then she remembered that Oak Hill's elementary school was experimenting with a year-round schedule. Sure, she'd do that.

"Community involvement is part of your job," Bill Caldwell had told her when she was hired. She'd already spoken to a high school journalism class and flipped hamburgers for charity at a street fair. Talking to fourth-graders should be a breeze.

The next message was from the Pleasant Valley Retirement Center. "We're having a talent show, a fundraiser for our residents' association. We'd like an article promoting it, with pictures." Kristin jotted down the caller's name and number.

"This is Ida Mae Poindexter," the third caller said. "I guess you aren't at work yet. I get up early, and I forget that the rest of the world doesn't. Law me, I'd better get to the point before this thing beeps on me. Can you come and have breakfast with Claudia and me Saturday?"

Kristin decided to return Ida Mae's call first. It wasn't just the thought of breakfast, though she was sure it would be excellent. If she wanted to investigate Vonda Williams's death, she needed to talk to Ida Mae. Kristin smiled. So what if the police wouldn't talk to her? She was going to have breakfast with the murder victim's sister.

ON SATURDAY MORNING, Ida Mae's table was loaded. Kristin looked in amazement at orange juice, fresh strawberries, scrambled eggs, country ham, grits, honey, three kinds of jam, biscuits, and a bowl of something Claudia identified as red-eye gravy. How could three people eat all this? Neither Ida Mae nor Claudia was much over five feet tall, and though you couldn't call them slim, they weren't seriously overweight, either. Surely they didn't eat this way all the time.

"Let's hold hands while I ask the blessing," Ida Mae said.

Ida Mae's hand was in easy reach, but Claudia was on the other side of the table. Kristin's arm was aching by the time Ida Mae had asked God's blessing on the food, her guests, and their families and friends. When Ida Mae invoked the deity's favor on the police "in their investigation into the death of my dear sister, Vonda," Kristin was reminded that her purpose for being here was not just to eat a huge breakfast. She was formulating her first question for her hostess when Ida Mae finally said, "Amen."

But before Kristin could ask anything, Ida Mae urged her to fill her plate. "Don't be shy. Eat all you want."

"Everything's wonderful," Kristin said when she'd taken a few bites.

"My nieces have been after me to get those Meals on Wheels or eat in the Pleasant Valley dining room," Ida Mae said, "but why should I do that when I can cook?"

Ida Mae's reference to her nieces was the opening Kristin had been waiting for. "Tell me about your family," she said.

"Well, now," Ida Mae said, setting down her fork, "my people have lived around Sneed's Crossroads for over 150 years. Papa's great-great-granddaddy came down from Virginia in 1837."

Too late, Kristin remembered that for many people she'd interviewed in Yarborough County, "family" began several generations back. As Ida Mae wended her way through the nineteenth century, chronicling the progress of the Williams family and their kin, the reporter wondered how she could fast-forward the saga to Vonda.

When Ida Mae paused to take a bite of scrambled eggs, Claudia asked, "Are your people from around here, Kristin?"

Kristin explained that she'd been an Army brat, growing up in four different states and one foreign country.

"After my father retired from the Army, he went to work for an electronics company, and we moved to Raleigh. My parents were killed in an automobile accident while I was in college," Kristin said, bringing the story to a quick close in hopes of steering the conversation back to Ida Mae's sister.

"You're an orphan?" Ida Mae asked. "There

aren't as many of those as there used to be. I knew several, growing up."

"You have no family at all?" Claudia asked with a look of concern. "No sisters or brothers? No aunts, no cousins?"

"An uncle and some cousins in Oregon, but I don't know them well. We didn't see much of them when I was a child."

Claudia shook her head over Kristin's lack of family ties. "My oldest was thirty years in the Air Force. Went to Germany, California, Texas, all over. But he came back to see us every chance he got, bringing his family with him. I sure would have hated it if I'd missed seeing my grands grow up."

"No grandparents?" Ida Mae asked Kristin.

"They died when I was a child."

"My, my," Ida Mae said. Then her face brightened. "We have plenty more breakfast here to eat. Who wants ham? Or grits?"

Kristin's plate was still hidden under mountains of food. "Maybe a little later," she said, slathering jam on a biscuit.

"A car just stopped in front of your apartment, Ida Mae," said Claudia, whose chair offered a view of the window. "Do you know anybody who drives a big Cadillac?"

"I know of a few who do, but I doubt any of them would admit to knowing me," Ida Mae said with a chuckle. She slid her chair back from the table and went to the window to look out. "No, I've never seen her before."

Claudia joined Ida Mae at the window. "Doesn't look like anybody I know, either. But she's headed this way."

Kristin put down her fork. Evidently curiosity wasn't frowned on here. Besides, she'd met several hundred people in her six months in Oak Hill. Maybe she could identify Ida Mae's visitor. Joining Ida Mae and Claudia at the window, Kristin saw a midnight-blue car parked at the curb and a small woman in oversize sunglasses and a tangerine pantsuit heading up the walk.

"She's at the wrong apartment, I'd judge," Ida Mae said when the doorbell rang. "I'll set her straight, and then we can finish our breakfast."

Kristin and Claudia hovered at the edge of the living room while Ida Mae went to the door and opened it.

"Ida Mae?" the visitor asked.

"Yes, I'm Ida Mae Poindexter. What can I do for you?"

The woman took off her sunglasses. "I'm your sister Vonda," she said.

THREE

Strong families were the firm foundation on which our town was built.

From *Memories of Old Oak Hill*
by Isabel Rowland Everhart

For a few seconds, all four women stood completely still. Then Ida Mae gasped, put her hand over her heart, and stumbled backward. The others rushed to keep her from falling.

"She needs to sit down," Claudia said. They backed Ida Mae across the room to the sofa, where she sank onto the cushions.

"Can I bring you anything, Ida Mae?" Claudia asked. "A glass of water?"

Ida Mae shook her head. She blinked a couple of times. Then she frowned at the newcomer. "You can't be Vonda. Vonda's dead. They just found her bones. It was in the newspaper."

"That's just it, Ida Mae," the woman said. "I read that, too, in the Atlanta paper. When I saw that you thought I was dead, well, I knew I had to come back here and set things straight."

The wire service, Kristin thought. It must have

picked up the story from the *Sentinel,* and this woman had read it in Atlanta. Could she really be the long-lost sister? The newcomer was short, like Ida Mae, but much slimmer, and she looked much younger. Her face, which was carefully made up, had far fewer wrinkles, and though Ida Mae's hair was snowy, the other woman's was pale gold. Could dieting, a good hairdresser, and a skilled plastic surgeon work this magic?

"Ask me something, Ida Mae," the other woman said. "Something about our past, so you'll believe I'm really me."

"All right," Ida Mae said, looking at her speculatively. "What was the name of the little branch behind our house?"

"Moore's Creek? No, that was the one that ran beside the road. The one behind our house was called Little Moore."

"What was our milk cow's name?"

"Molly."

"You broke something I got for my eighth birthday. Do you remember what it was?"

The newcomer nodded. "A little teapot. Doll-size. It came with a set of little cups and saucers."

Ida Mae gave the newcomer a long, hard look. "You're Vonda, all right," she said. "But what I want to know is, where in the world have you been all these years?"

Kristin stepped closer, eager to hear the answer, but Claudia had other plans for her.

"Why don't you and I clear off the table and put the food away?" Claudia said to the reporter. Then she turned to the newcomer. "Unless you'd like something to eat? Or a little coffee?"

"Nothing, thanks," Vonda said.

To Kristin's regret, Ida Mae didn't insist that they all stay and finish breakfast together. Kristin tried to pick up bits of conversation from the living room as she helped clear the table, but she could make out only a word or two here and there.

When the leftovers were in the refrigerator and almost all the dirty dishes were in the dishwasher, Ida Mae called from the living room, "Claudia and Kristin, you all quit working and come in here. I want to introduce you to my little sister."

The two women were seated side by side on the sofa holding hands. Kristin scrutinized them. Yes, she could see the family resemblance. Both women had blue eyes, round faces, and short, up-turned noses.

"You'll have to forgive me for forgetting my manners," Ida Mae said. "Vonda showing up like this put me in a tizzy. Vonda, this is Claudia Mc-Neill, who lives next door, and Kristin Grant, who works for the newspaper. Kristin wrote the story that was reprinted in your paper, the one that made you decide to come back to Oak Hill like you should have done sixty years ago." Ida Mae gave her sister a fierce look. "I could just shake you for staying away. I could just turn you over my knee and paddle you. If you couldn't come home, why didn't you call us? Or write us a letter?"

Vonda seemed unperturbed. "As I've been telling Ida Mae," she said to Claudia and Kristin, "I left Oak Hill to marry Harvey Dawkins. I didn't find out till too late that he was married to somebody else, somebody he met in Norfolk while he was in the Navy. After Harvey Junior was born and we were living in Raleigh, Harvey started running around on me. When I told him I wanted a divorce, he said, 'No need to divorce me, honey. We're not legally married.' I was humiliated, of course. Infuriated, too. I took Harvey Junior and bought a ticket for the next bus out of town. I ended up in Atlanta and found a job working for—"

"Whoa there, Vonda," Ida Mae interrupted, holding up her hand to stop the flood of words. She turned to Kristin, who'd been listening, transfixed, to the newcomer's story. "You need to write this down so you can put it in the paper."

As soon as Kristin had her pen and notebook in hand, Vonda picked up the tale where she'd left it. She'd taken a job as a secretary to Parnell Hatcher, a contractor, telling him that she was a widow from out of state with no living relatives.

"Parnell made a fortune building those little-bitty houses that the veterans bought after the war. He was a deacon in the church and a member of the Chamber of Commerce and an officer in the Lions Club. I was afraid he wouldn't marry me if he knew that Harvey Junior was—well, that he might not be legitimate. And once we were married, I was afraid he'd divorce me if he found out I'd lied to him. Anyway, Ida Mae," Vonda said, turning toward her sister, "for all I knew, Harvey Dawkins might have come back here. If he found out I was married to somebody with money, why, there's no telling what he might have done. Blackmailed me, I suppose."

To Kristin, Vonda's reasoning sounded believable. In the 1940s having a child out of wedlock must have been a scandal, as it probably was today in the minds of many people in Oak Hill. She wondered how much of this story Vonda really wanted to see in the newspaper.

"Parnell adopted little Harvey," Vonda said. "He paid his way through college and law school." She added that her husband had died ten years before, and her son was now a lawyer in Atlanta.

"A lawyer! Think of that!" Ida Mae said. "Do you have any grandchildren?"

This question triggered another flood of words. Vonda told them about Harvey's marriage to "a fine girl, a doctor's daughter, very pretty and sweet," who produced three children. But a midlife crisis drove Harvey into the arms of another woman, and his wife took the children and fled to California. Vonda had no use for her new daughter-in-law, a former cocktail waitress half Harvey's age. Vonda was furious at her son, which was part of the reason she'd decided to reunite with her family in Oak Hill and let the world know his origins.

"He won't like it a bit when this hits the news. I never told him much about his father, just that he was in the Navy and died after the war. But it'll serve him right. He and that new wife of his shouldn't have tried to make me sell my house and go into a home."

The other three looked at her blankly.

"Rest home. Retirement community. A place like this. Not that there's anything wrong with living in a place like this. But I have a lovely home that Parnell built, filled with beautiful memories, so why should I leave it?"

As Ida Mae and Claudia nodded sympathetically, Kristin changed the subject. "What happened to your necklace, the one your sister gave you?"

Vonda looked down at her hands and twisted one of the ornate rings she wore. The large blue stone at its center was the shade of the beads in

Ida Mae's necklace. Kristin thought it might be a sapphire.

"I sold it," Vonda said. "I needed the money for Harvey."

Ida Mae nodded in approval. "You needed money for the baby after you left his no-good daddy."

Kristin hated to spoil this image of motherly concern, but her reporter's instincts got the better of her. "Do you mean Harvey the baby or Harvey the baby's father?"

Vonda was silent.

"When did you sell the necklace?" Kristin asked.

"Tell the truth, Vonda," Ida Mae said, her tone sharper now.

"Right before Harvey and I left Oak Hill."

"Who bought it?" Kristin asked.

"Somebody I met at a little store outside of town. Harvey and I stopped there one day when we were out for a ride in his car. She admired it, and I asked her if she'd like to buy it. What difference does it make now?"

"Use your head, Vonda," Ida Mae said. "Whoever you sold it to was probably the person whose skeleton was dug up by the bulldozer."

Vonda blinked. "Well, I don't know who she was. I was trying to raise a little money so Harvey and I could leave town. She wasn't from around here. I didn't dare sell it to anybody I knew. I was afraid you'd hear about it, Ida Mae."

There was silence for a few moments. Then Ida Mae turned to Kristin. "Do you want a picture of Vonda and me for the paper?"

"Sure. Let me call the photographer."

"I'd better call my nieces first," Ida Mae said. "They need to hear about Vonda before the news spreads all over town. Besides, they'd hate it if you didn't put their pictures in the paper, too."

A FEW MINUTES LATER, CLAUDIA left for her own apartment. "You need family time together," she told Ida Mae. "I'll run along."

Once she was home, Claudia knew she should go directly to the phone. The return of Ida Mae's sister—somebody who'd been given up for dead—was big news. Claudia's children would never forgive her if she knew a story that good and didn't tell them, but what she really wanted to do was sit down and catch her breath. The goings-on next door had just about worn her out.

Claudia rested on the sofa for a while, but when she heard a car door slam, she went to the window, knowing that her family would want a full report. Looking out, she saw a woman in a denim jumper, her silver-gray hair tied back with a ribbon—Betty Jo, Ida Mae's niece who owned the craft shop downtown. Then Ida Mae's other niece arrived—

Norma, the one who sold real estate. Norma's hair was short and a deep chestnut color—dyed, according to Ida Mae. Her lime green jacket, white skirt, and heels meant she'd been at work when Ida Mae phoned her.

To look at them, Claudia thought, you'd hardly know they were sisters. But they were united when it came to Ida Mae. Daughters couldn't have treated her better. This was the second time in a week Betty Jo and Norma had come running when their aunt called them.

As Claudia watched from the window, another car drove up. The driver, a man with a camera, headed for Ida Mae's apartment. He was the photographer from the paper, Claudia supposed. He didn't stay long, and Kristin left soon after he did. That left nobody but family next door, with sixty years to catch up on. Claudia could just imagine the chattering going on. Ida Mae loved to talk, and the nieces were no slouches at conversation, either, but Vonda beat them all. Claudia smiled when she remembered how her late husband would have described someone like Vonda: "She can out-talk a Baptist preacher who does auctioneering on the side."

Ida Mae and Vonda—now those two were a pair! Claudia could see that Vonda was the county club type, reed-slim and glossy, while Ida Mae was as down-home as collards and cornbread. But both women were strong-minded and opinionated. If Vonda stayed around long, there'd be fireworks next door, Claudia was sure. Ida Mae, for all the welcome she'd given her sister, had good reason to be angry with her. Claudia could imagine what her children would say if one of their sisters or brothers came sashaying home after sixty years of silence, expecting bygones to be bygones!

The thought of her children reminded Claudia that she'd better start making phone calls to fill them in on the developments next door. If they read the story in the newspaper before they learned about it from her, they'd never let her forget it.

IN THE APARTMENT NEXT door, Vonda, Norma, and Betty Jo were all talking at once, bringing each other up to date on marriages, births, and deaths, and exchanging pictures of children and grand-children. Ida Mae's hearing wasn't what it used to be, especially when several people were talk-ing, so she tuned the other three out and let her thoughts drift a little.

Her baby sister was right here in her living room, after all these years! Ida Mae still couldn't quite take it in, and she couldn't understand why Vonda had stayed away so long. She'd broken Mama's heart and Papa's, too, disappearing the way she did. Ida Mae would have given anything if her sister Arlene could have lived to see Vonda come back to Oak Hill.

Had Vonda stayed away because she was ashamed of her family? The Williams sisters had grown up poor. They'd improved their lives by leaving their parents' farm and taking jobs in the hosiery mill, but when Vonda married Parnell Hatcher she'd moved up quite a few rungs on the social ladder.

Ida Mae pushed these thoughts from her mind. No matter why she'd stayed away, Vonda was here now, and the whole family needed to get together so they could meet her. That meant a meal, and Ida Mae, being the oldest, should be the one to fix it. She waited until there was a gap in the conversation and jumped in.

"I want you to come here for supper with Vonda and me tonight," she said to Betty Jo and Norma. "You and your husbands and Heather and Brian and Amy and Kevin and—"

"My goodness, Aunt Ida Mae, how are you going to fit all of us in here?" Norma interrupted. "Let me fix dinner after church tomorrow and invite everybody. Amy and her family are already coming, so—"

"It would be better to come to our house," Betty Jo broke in. "We have more room."

The squabble ended with an agreement that the nieces and Carson and Lloyd, their husbands, would come to supper at Ida Mae's that night. Then the whole family, including Ida Mae and Vonda's great-nieces and their husbands and children, would gather at Norma's house for Sunday dinner.

"But you'll have to promise to come to our place soon," Betty Jo said. "You're going to be in town for a while, aren't you, Aunt Vonda? We have extra bedrooms now that our children are grown, and we'd love to have you stay with us."

"She'll stay right here," Ida Mae insisted. "I have a spare bedroom, too, you know."

"I'll stay with Ida Mae," Vonda said, "but just for one night. I noticed the Oak Hill Inn on the way into town. I thought I might stay there for a while if—well, if you were glad to see me."

"Glad to see you?" Ida Mae felt a rush of affection for her sister. "Why, I've wanted to see you for sixty years."

Kristin was rarely at her desk on a Saturday afternoon, but this story had to be perfect. It was going to be the most-read article in tomorrow's paper, she knew. Of course, she wasn't going to include everything she'd heard from Vonda, whose story had changed slightly by the time she repeated it for the benefit of Betty Jo and Norma. In that telling of the tale, Vonda hadn't mentioned being angry with her son, the Atlanta attorney. She told her nieces she'd come back to Oak Hill to let her family know she hadn't been murdered and to reunite with them. That was the version of the story Kristin would put in Sunday morning's *Sentinel*.

As for Harvey Dawkins, the man with whom Vonda had left Oak Hill and produced a child, Kristin had decided, on Bill's advice, not to mention him in the newspaper. She couldn't take Vonda's word that he was a bigamist, and the Dawkins family, or Harvey himself if he happened to be alive, might object to having him labeled as one. In fact, if Harvey Dawkins lied, and his marriage to Vonda was legal, then Vonda herself was a bigamist. Or Vonda could be a colossal liar, and the whole story of her leaving town with Harvey could be a fabrication. Kristin was going to say only that Vonda left town with a boyfriend, just as she had in her previous article.

"His name will get around town anyway," Bill assured her. "Never underestimate the power of the Oak Hill grapevine."

When her story was the way she wanted it, Kristin headed back to her apartment, ready to enjoy what was left of the weekend. She planned to be up early Sunday morning to read the newspaper. Bill had assured her that "Missing Sister Returns" would be the front-page headline.

AFTER NORMA AND BETTY JO left, Ida Mae offered to fix lunch for her sister, but Vonda said she was too tired to eat. Ida Mae helped carry Vonda's suitcases from the Cadillac to the spare bedroom. Then, while her sister napped, Ida Mae made a quick trip to the grocery store. By suppertime, she'd fixed a roast, oven-fried chicken, four vegetables, a relish tray, and a peach cobbler. Those who didn't want cobbler would have to make do with leftover pound cake and ice cream. She set her table with her good china and best tablecloth. Then she picked flowers from her yard and arranged them into a centerpiece for the table, wishing she had a sunflower or two to put with them.

While Ida Mae put the finishing touches on the meal, Vonda took a long bubble bath and spent an even longer time fixing her face and hair. She came out of the bedroom in a pale green dress that showed off her trim figure. Ida Mae was amazed at how good her sister looked. She could pass for ten years younger than she really was, maybe more. In the old days Vonda had been the beauty of the family, with wavy brown hair, bright blue eyes, and a smile that could turn your heart around. Now her hair was a soft gold that made her eyes look even bluer. She was slimmer than she'd been in her teens, and her face had hardly a wrinkle. She must have discovered the Fountain of Youth down there in Atlanta.

At the dinner table that evening, Carson and Lloyd ate heartily, while Norma, Betty Jo, and

Vonda kept up a constant chatter, and Ida Mae urged everybody to take second and third helpings.

"Aunt Vonda, you're the guest of honor," Norma said when the last bite had been eaten. "You and Aunt Ida Mae go sit down while Betty Jo and I clean up."

Vonda trotted into the living room, but Ida Mae had never been one to let others work while she sat idle. As she helped her nieces clear the table, she caught scraps of conversation from the living room. Lloyd and Carson were talking baseball. They were Atlanta Braves fans, and Vonda was telling them how much she'd enjoyed going to the home games with her late husband, Parnell.

Hearing them, Ida Mae was reminded of days long ago when she and Odell used to hear Vonda in the living room or on the front porch talking to one of her boyfriends. As clearly as if it had happened yesterday, Ida Mae remembered a time, not long before her sister disappeared, when Harvey Dawkins came by in an old Ford to take her for a ride. Vonda had worn a blue checked skirt, a white blouse, and the necklace with the blue beads that matched her eyes. Was that when she sold it? Ida Mae pictured her sister handing the necklace to someone and pocketing a few dollars in return. But who was the woman who bought the necklace—and died wearing it?

FOUR

We rejoice with Ida Mae Poindexter, Norma McMurray, and Betty Jo Carmichael, who have been united with a family member who was lost to them for many years. What a joyous time this must be for them!

The Reverend Scott Farley,
pastor of Oak Hill United Church of Christ

THE NEXT DAY Ida Mae woke up at six-thirty, feeling like a kid on Christmas morning. Her sister was back, and she could hardly wait to see her. It was hard not to bang on the door of the spare bedroom and wake Vonda up, but she knew her sister wanted to sleep late.

"I need to recover from all the excitement," Vonda had said the night before. "I'll skip church, if you don't mind, Ida Mae."

Ida Mae, who never skipped church unless she was sick, had considered staying home, too. She wasn't sure how long her sister would be in town, and she wanted to have plenty of time to visit with her. But she knew that word of Vonda's return would have spread all over town by time for the

Sunday morning service, and everybody would want to talk about it. Ida Mae could go to church and answer their questions or stay home and have the phone ring off the hook for the next week. She opted for church.

By seven o'clock, having heard no sounds from the guest bedroom, Ida Mae tiptoed to the front door and went out to retrieve the morning paper. Vonda's story was on the front page, titled "Missing Sister Returns." Ida Mae read the article twice while she ate her breakfast, nodding her head in approval. Kristin had done a good job. Then she scrutinized the photograph that accompanied the story. Betty Jo and Norma looked good, and she didn't look so bad herself, considering the age she was. Vonda, who was beaming like she'd won first prize at the county fair, looked almost as young as her nieces.

By nine o'clock Ida Mae hadn't heard a peep out of her sister, so she started a fresh pot of coffee and set some boxes of cereal and a loaf of bread on the kitchen table. She left the newspaper on the table, too, with a note saying that milk, orange juice, butter, and jam were in the refrigerator. It wasn't much of a breakfast to offer company, she thought, but as skinny as Vonda was, that was probably all she ate.

Ida Mae pulled into the church parking lot fifteen minutes before Sunday school was scheduled

to start. As she'd expected, mo[...]
goers had heard about Vonda's reap[...]
were hoping to meet her. Since Vond[...]
there, Ida Mae was the next best thing. She[...]
busy answering questions until well past time [...]
Sunday school to begin. During the eleven o'clock
worship service, Reverend Farley mentioned Vonda's return and gave thanks for her reunion with
her family in one of his prayers.

After the service, Ida Mae was besieged by people who wanted to hear all the details. Some of
the older church members claimed to remember
Vonda, though Ida Mae doubted they really did.
At the time Vonda disappeared, she and her sisters still went back to the country every Sunday
to attend their home church, Big Hickory Baptist,
with their parents.

By the time Ida Mae had dealt with all her
friends' questions, it was past time to go to Norma's. She had to push the speed limit a bit on
her way home. Surely the police wouldn't arrest
a churchgoer on a Sunday morning, she thought,
and if they did, they ought to be ashamed of themselves.

When Ida Mae reached her apartment,
Vonda was sitting in the living room in another
expensive-looking outfit, ready to meet the rest
of the family.

"I'll drive to Norma's," Vonda said.

ice to ride in a car
le along every day.
upholstery and gad-
s old Chevrolet had
d through the streets
attles and bumps that
rips through town.

When the family gathered around the dinner table, Ida Mae was so happy she had to dab away a few tears. Betty Jo's daughter, Heather, was there with her husband and baby daughter, and so was Norma's daughter, Amy, with her husband and their two children. The only ones missing were Betty Jo's son, a law student in Chapel Hill, and Norma's son and his family, who lived in Asheville. When the others asked about Vonda's family, Ida Mae felt sad for her sister, who was estranged from her son and whose grandchildren were off in California.

On the way home from Norma's, Vonda said she was going to call the Oak Hill Inn to see if they had any rooms available.

"No need to do that," Ida Mae said. "There's plenty of room for the two of us in my apartment."

"Then I'll stay for tonight, anyway," Vonda said.

The rest of the day passed quietly. After a supper thrown together out of leftovers from the day before, Ida Mae did the crossword puzzle in the Sunday paper, and Vonda took a walk. That night,

Ida Mae drifted off to sleep thinking how lucky she was to have her sister under her roof.

But the next day her doubts began. Vonda slept late again, so Ida Mae had to tiptoe around the apartment for several hours. Then a reporter from the Greensboro paper called to ask if he could interview the sisters. Ida Mae was inclined to say yes. Who wouldn't want to be written up in a big-city paper? But she thought she'd better ask Vonda's opinion. When Ida Mae tapped on the bedroom door and repeated the reporter's question, her sister asked if he wanted pictures. Ida Mae trotted off to the phone and came back to say that he did. When Vonda heard this, she insisted he'd have to wait until she could visit a beauty parlor.

"You look fine to me," Ida Mae said. Her sister's hair was tousled, but a comb could remedy that.

Vonda looked in the mirror and shook her head. "I can't have my picture in the paper looking like this."

"I doubt you can get an appointment on such short notice."

"Don't worry. I have good luck about these things," Vonda said with an airy wave of her hand.

A few minutes later, Vonda breezed into the kitchen wearing a turquoise caftan. She asked Ida Mae for the name of the best hairdresser in town.

That didn't happen to be something Ida Mae

knew. She went once a week to Ruby Sandler, who fixed hair in her home. Ruby had done Ida Mae's hair in the same style for twenty years. Her work suited Ida Mae just fine, but she was sure it wouldn't please Vonda.

"Who's the most expensive?" Vonda asked. "The expensive stylists are usually the best."

Fortunately, Ida Mae had heard that Connie at the Cut'n'Curl charged ridiculous prices. This information pleased Vonda no end. She was even happier when she called Connie and learned she had a cancellation for two o'clock that afternoon.

"That'll give me plenty of time to make a chicken pie for our lunch," Ida Mae said.

Vonda frowned. "A salad is all I want. Let me see what you have."

After rummaging through the refrigerator and the kitchen cabinets, Vonda announced that she would have to shop for salad ingredients. While her sister was out, Ida Mae made a pitcher of the unsweetened tea Vonda preferred and made sure she had plenty of the sweet kind in the refrigerator for herself. An hour later Vonda was back with olive oil, spices, and some odd kinds of greens that Ida Mae had barely heard of, much less eaten.

The salad wasn't bad, but hardly an adequate meal, Ida Mae thought. Vonda turned down dessert, citing the dangers of sugar and saturated fat. By the time her sister left for her hair appointment,

Ida Mae was ready for her to move to the Oak Hill Inn, and the sooner the better.

MONDAY WAS BUSY at the *Sentinel* office, and it was almost two o'clock before Kristin could break for lunch. Once she was outside, the steamy summer air wrapped around her like a hot, wet towel. By the time she reached Myrtle's, her hair was damp, and her sandals were sticking to her feet. She sat down at a table near the front and let the air conditioning wash over her.

Today it had to be a vegetable plate. "Sliced tomatoes…squash…corn…and banana pudding," she told Myrtle. You had to love a restaurant that counted desserts as vegetable choices, Kristin thought. Someday she was going to order a vegetable plate consisting of one real vegetable, banana pudding, strawberry shortcake, and peach cobbler.

"Sweet tea and cornbread," Kristin added. Sometimes she thought she'd been a native North Carolinian in a former life. She liked all the local specialties, including turnip greens and black-eyed peas.

Kristin's gaze wandered to the window at the front of the restaurant. Across the street was a small brick building with a sign saying *Wilton Treadwell, Attorney at Law*. The name sounded familiar. Hadn't some Treadwells owned the mill where Vonda worked? Kristin wondered if the lawyer was a member of the same family.

As Kristin looked out the window, a massive black automobile, twenty-five years old at least, began to maneuver into a parking place in front of the restaurant. She watched with admiration as the driver skillfully positioned the big car in the small space. Then an elderly African-American woman emerged from the auto and began putting coins in the parking meter. Gray-haired and tall, with perfect posture, she wore a beige linen suit and a high-necked blouse in spite of the hot weather.

The woman looked familiar, and as she crossed the street and went into the law office, Kristin tried to remember who she was. Then her food arrived, and she turned her attention to the cornbread, vegetables, and tea.

"Mind if I join you?" a gruff voice inquired.

Kristin looked up. Wayne Henley was standing beside her table, looking ill at ease. The expression on his face was—well, an optimist might call it friendly. Since he wasn't scowling, Kristin gestured for him to sit down.

"I read your article in the Sunday paper," he said after giving Myrtle his order for a barbecue plate. "Looks like you had it all wrong in your first story, when you identified the skeleton as the remains of Vonda Williams."

"I just reported what her sister told me. I didn't have any way of knowing that it—"

"Okay, okay," the detective interrupted. "But tell me this. When this Vonda person, a supposed murder victim, showed up in Oak Hill, how come you didn't bother to let the police know?"

Let the police know? It had never crossed Kristin's mind. Her only concern had been to finish her story before the deadline for the Sunday paper.

"The *Sentinel* is always complaining that we don't solve crimes," Wayne said, his face reddening. "But you had information that could help us, and you didn't pass it on. I guess we were supposed to read it in the paper like everybody else."

This sounded like the Billy Wayne Henley she'd met before. She decided that the best response was silence. To avoid his angry gaze, she looked out the window and saw another tall, well-dressed, elderly woman push open the door of the lawyer's office. This one was white, with snow-white hair. Like the first woman, she was rather formally dressed for a summer afternoon in a small southern town. Did Wilton Treadwell specialize in elderly female clients, or was the Oak Hill AARP chapter meeting in his office today?

"Are you going to stay on that skeleton story, or is Steve Jacobs taking it over?" the detective asked as Myrtle set his food in front of him.

"I'm handling it," Kristin said, looking enviously at his barbecue, hushpuppies, slaw, and fries.

"Then maybe we ought to cooperate." He took a big forkful of barbecue, washed it down with a gulp of tea, and looked around. Myrtle was watching them from the cash register. He lowered his voice. "We have the report from the medical examiner. The victim was a young woman, possibly African-American. You can put that in the paper."

"Did the report say she was murdered?"

He nodded. "Death was probably from a gunshot wound to the back of the head."

"Humph," said Myrtle, from her post at the cash register. "I could have told you that."

He frowned at her. "You shouldn't be listening. This is official police business."

"Then you shouldn't be talking so loud."

"So it's still an open case?" Kristin asked, trying not to smile at his discomfort.

"Of course."

Wondering what to ask next, she glanced out the window. The same elderly white woman she'd seen before was coming out of the lawyer's office. The other woman's car was still in its parking space. Did Oak Hill have an unusually large population of old ladies, or did it just seem that way because she'd been spending so much time with Ida Mae and Claudia?

The thought of Claudia made Kristin realize

something. "I bet you didn't have to wait for the Sunday paper to learn about Vonda's return. Claudia McNeill probably called Detective Shelton right after she left Ida Mae's apartment."

He reddened again. "His grandmother told Ray's mother, who told him. But it was still your duty to let us know."

Kristin resisted the impulse to roll her eyes in disbelief. What would her journalism professors have said about that theory? Then she realized that if she wanted to learn anything from the police, she'd better try to build rapport with this guy. She did her best to look contrite. "I'm sorry. I just didn't think. Let me tell you what I know."

In the next few minutes, Kristin told the detective all she'd learned from Vonda. She wasn't giving away any secrets. He probably knew the whole story already, from Ray.

Then it was Kristin's turn to listen. Wayne gave her a mini-lecture on the drug problem in Oak Hill, with emphasis on the good work of the police force. He explained that they were hampered by the fact that the major drug dealers lived outside of town, in the jurisdiction of the county sheriff.

"Bill Caldwell complains because we only arrest street-corner dealers, but what does he want us to do? Stop catching bluegills because we can't hook a twenty-pound bass?"

"Nice figure of speech," Kristin murmured,

ready to bet her banana pudding that the man was a fisherman.

"Huh?"

"I said if you aren't going to eat those hushpuppies, could I have one?"

He looked at her skeptically. Then he surprised her by laughing and pushing his plate toward her. "Sure. Eat 'em all."

He leaned back in his chair and smiled. "I get a little wound up when I talk about the newspaper. Hope you don't take it personally."

Claudia made sure Vonda's Cadillac was gone before she started next door.

"Come in. It's not locked," her neighbor called when Claudia rang the doorbell.

Claudia shook her head as she went into Ida Mae's apartment. "Your nieces would have a hissy if they knew that door was unlocked."

Ida Mae winked. "That's why I keep the blinds open. I always check to see who's out there, and if it's Norma or Betty Jo, I pretend to unlock the door. Vonda's been after me about it, too. She says it's not safe. She doesn't think I ought to leave my windows open at night, either. Seems to me the woman thinks she's still in Atlanta."

Claudia held out a plate covered with aluminum foil. "I brought you some of Vivian's chocolate cake. She always sends me home from Sunday dinner loaded down with food. I thought maybe you and your company could use it."

Ida Mae grinned. "No use to save it for Vonda. She doesn't eat enough to keep a chickadee alive. All we had for lunch was a little bit of salad. Let's you and me have a piece of that cake, and I'll pour us some tea to go with it."

In a few minutes they were seated at the table, each with a large slice of chocolate cake and a glass of iced tea.

"Your sister's gone?" Claudia asked.

"Yes, but not far and not for long. She went to have her hair fixed. She's been talking about moving to the Oak Hill Inn, but I reckon she likes Pleasant Valley too much to leave." She shook her head. "I tell you, that girl hasn't changed a bit!"

Claudia tried to think of an appropriate response. "I suppose she wants to stay with you awhile, renewing old ties."

Ida Mae snorted. "Renewing old ties? She's more interested in making new ones." She laid down her fork. "I guess you know we weren't exactly in the upper crust, back when Vonda left Oak Hill. But Vonda's been running with the big dogs down in Atlanta, and it looks like she's going to do the same in Pleasant Valley."

Claudia looked at Ida Mae expectantly. There was more to this story, she was sure.

"Sunday night she went for a walk. She said she

needed the exercise. She goes to a gym twice a week in Atlanta, and she has one of those treadmills in her house to use on other days. That's why she looks so good, I guess."

That and a good plastic surgeon, Claudia thought. She waited for her friend to continue. Ida Mae often meandered off on side trips when she told a story, but the destination was usually worth the time it took.

"While she was out walking, she met a gentleman taking a walk of his own. A Mr. Frank Rowland, she said, like the name wasn't familiar to her—though I doubt she'd forgotten that the Rowlands were the biggest bugs in Oak Hill outside of the Treadwells when we were growing up. Vonda told me that Frank Rowland—a widower, she was quick to find out—was delighted to hear that she played bridge. He said he might be calling her, because his bridge club sometimes needed somebody to fill in."

Claudia kept silent, wondering if this was all.

"He told her about the cultural events at Pleasant Valley. That's what he called them, *cultural events*." Ida Mae chuckled. "I guess that includes the lady singer you and I went to hear, the one who screeched so. Give me old-fashioned gospel singers anytime, instead of that. Anyway, now Vonda is dead set on going to the talent show Friday night. I reckon it's the reception afterward she's most interested in, since Mr. Rowland said he hoped to see her there."

Ida Mae took a sip of tea and a bite of cake, a sure sign that her story was winding down. Then the phone rang, and she left the table to answer it.

"Vonda won't be back till three-thirty, and there's a newspaper reporter coming then," Claudia heard her say. "But you can come, too. The more the merrier."

"That was the Greensboro TV station," Ida Mae said when she hung up. "They want to put Vonda and me on the news. I guess she won't mind, since she'll be all prettied up by then."

"My, my!" Claudia said. "Be sure to let me know what time you two will be on TV. And don't let Vonda hog the camera. I want to see you, too."

Ida Mae laughed. "Vonda's the one they'll want to show. She always was the pretty one in the family, and she's the one who's at the Cut'n'Curl, getting ready for the photographer."

LATER THAT AFTERNOON, when Claudia was back in her own apartment, her grandson Ray phoned to ask if she remembered anyone disappearing from Oak Hill in the late 1940s.

"The state medical examiner says those bones belonged to a young woman, maybe African-American," he said. "She was apparently killed by a gunshot to the head. If Vonda's sister sold her necklace in July of 1946, our murder victim must have died some time after that."

Claudia sucked in her breath. A young life ended, and in such a terrible way. Then she put her mind to her grandson's question. "A black girl who disappeared? In the late 1940s? That was a long time ago, Ray."

"I know. Just think about it, and call me if you remember anything."

"I will," she promised.

A few minutes later Claudia sat down on the sofa and let her thoughts go back through the years. In 1946 her husband, Layton, was back from the Army, commuting to college in Greensboro in an old rattletrap car and janitoring in a hosiery mill at night. She and Layton lived with his parents in the country outside Oak Hill. There was a lot of coming and going in those days—people returning from the service, people marrying, people moving north.

She and Layton had grown up poor, like Ida Mae and her sisters. Even after Layton started teaching at the high school, there hadn't been much money. He and Claudia had scrimped, saved, and prayed to send all five of their children to college and two to graduate school. Claudia thanked God daily that her children and grandchildren had a better life than she'd had, and that the world she grew up in was gone. Not totally gone, she knew. There were still hardheaded and hard-hearted white folks around. Some of her grandchildren liked to lecture her about racism like they were the first to have discovered it. Well, she'd known it, she'd lived with it, but, praise God, she and her family had persevered in spite of it.

Claudia smiled when she realized how far her thoughts had strayed from what Ray had asked her to do. Her mind had a habit of doing that when she had time to sit and think. Someone who'd disappeared and had never been heard from again? She'd do her best to remember.

FIVE

With its small-town atmosphere and low crime rate, Oak Hill provides a safe, secure environment for business and family life.

From the Chamber of Commerce brochure, "Introducing Oak Hill"

THE NEXT MORNING Ida Mae called Claudia to say that Frank Rowland had invited her sister to his bridge club that afternoon.

"He said one of the members couldn't be there, so he wondered if she'd mind filling in." Ida Mae chuckled. "Wild horses couldn't stop her. She's gone to have a facial so she'll be pretty for Mr. Rowland. I thought only movie stars had those things."

"My, my," Claudia said. Ida Mae's sister had latched onto one of the richest men in Pleasant Valley—and she'd already been married to a wealthy man. All those years her family had worried about her, Vonda had been doing just fine.

"Vonda was always good with men," Ida Mae said, as if reading her friend's mind. "Him a widower and her a widow. Who knows what will happen?"

They were silent as they pondered the possibilities.

"You looked good on TV last night," Claudia said. "I stayed up till eleven o'clock to watch you."

Ida Mae laughed. "Don't you mean Vonda looked good?"

"You did, too," Claudia said. She thought Ida Mae looked the way a person their age ought to look, not all dieted, dyed, tucked, and lifted like her sister. What was wrong with having a little meat on your bones? As for hair, Claudia's was gray, and she hoped someday it would be pure white, like Ida Mae's. Wrinkles? Maybe she didn't have as many as Ida Mae, who said her face had more lines than a city street map, but the ones Claudia had, she didn't mind.

"I've been thinking about those bones the bulldozer dug up," Ida Mae said. "Most likely they belonged to the person who bought the necklace from Vonda. I've pressed her to try to remember the person she sold it to, but she says she put Oak Hill out of her mind when she left, except for Mama and Papa and Arlene and me…though I don't believe she gave us much thought, either."

Claudia felt sure Vonda hadn't been pining for her family all those years she was away, but she wasn't about to tell Ida Mae that. Instead, she said, "Ray called me last night. He said the bones were from a young woman, maybe African-American—and she was murdered."

"I'll tell Vonda that, though she may have heard it by now. She was supposed to stop at the police station to talk to Ray and Wayne before she had the facial." Ida Mae sighed. "I guess she couldn't work the police into her schedule any earlier, what with having her hair fixed and flirting with Frank Rowland and talking to the news media and all."

"Ray asked me if I remembered a young woman disappearing around that time," Claudia said. "After your sister sold the necklace, I mean. I couldn't think of anybody. Young women went away, but as far as I can remember they all wrote letters home and came back for visits."

"Maybe her people didn't tell anybody they hadn't heard from her. I didn't tell Mama and Papa about Vonda at first. With Harvey Dawkins being gone, too, Odell and I figured Vonda had run off to get married and would be back before long. We were going to let her do the telling, because we knew Papa would be mad. We weren't much, but Harvey Dawkins was even less, and a pretty girl like Vonda could have done better."

The two women were silent for a moment. Then Claudia sighed. "Whoever that poor murdered girl was, it's a tragedy, a life being cut off like that."

Ida Mae nodded. "I've been thinking…even if

the dead girl wasn't from around here, even if she was just passing through, her killer could have been somebody from here. Maybe somebody we knew. Maybe somebody who's still living in Oak Hill."

"More than likely the murderer's dead by now. Or mighty old."

"Yes, mighty old," Ida Mae said with a smile, "if he's as old as you and me."

LATER THAT MORNING, Claudia's doorbell rang. Peering out the front window, Claudia saw her daughter Vivian on the doorstep. Her expression was grim. A band of fear tightened around Claudia's heart. Something bad had happened.

"What is it, baby?" she said, opening the door.

"It's none of the family, Mama."

"Thank God for that. Who, then?"

"Let's go sit down." Vivian put her arm around her mother's shoulders and led her to the sofa. When they were seated, the younger woman took her mother's hands in hers.

"It's Daphne Whittier," Vivian said. "She's dead. I wanted you to hear it from me first."

"Miss Whittier? But she seemed so healthy. Was it her heart?"

"No, Mama. She was murdered."

"Murdered?" Claudia stared at her daughter in disbelief. Daphne Whittier had been a teacher at

Carver High when Layton started working there, and later she was its principal. She became the assistant principal of Oak Hill High when segregation ended and the town's two high schools were combined into one. Later she was elected to the city council. How could someone like that have been murdered?

"Ray called to tell me about it a little bit ago. I know you watch *News at Noon,* so I wanted to be here before you saw it on TV," Vivian said. "This morning the police had a call from a woman who runs a boarding house next door to Miss Whittier's home."

Claudia nodded. Tabor Street, where Miss Whittier lived, had once been a neighborhood of teachers, ministers, and doctors, the African-American elite of Oak Hill. But now most of the homes were in disrepair, and all except Daphne Whittier's had been turned into boarding houses or apartments.

"Miss Whittier was an early riser," Vivian said. "At nine o'clock this morning, her blinds were still closed, and her newspaper was on the sidewalk. Her neighbor phoned to check on her, but nobody answered, so she called 911. The police found Miss Whittier in her living room. She'd been shot. They think it happened last night, as long as ten or twelve hours before they found her body."

"Tell me it isn't so!" Claudia said, unwilling to

believe what she'd heard. Miss Whittier had done so much good for Oak Hill. She'd helped start the shelter for battered women and the soup kitchen for the down-and-out, and she'd aided scores of individuals, young people mostly, finding them jobs or money for college. "Who'd do a thing like that?"

Vivian put her arm around her mother. "Ray thinks it may have to do with drugs. Miss Whittier had just about succeeded in running the dealers out of her neighborhood, and she was after the police to shut the big suppliers down. One of them may have decided she was causing too much trouble."

"Wasn't somebody living with her? A relative?" Claudia thought she'd seen a young woman with Daphne Whittier at church.

"Yes, her great-niece. She's a graduate student, staying in Oak Hill while she does research in Greensboro this summer. She wasn't at the house this morning. Ray's on his way to Greensboro to look for her."

Claudia squeezed her daughter's hand. "I'm so glad you're here. You're right, I watch the noon news almost every day. It would have been lots worse, hearing this alone."

"Gotta look after my mom," Vivian said. She kissed her mother's cheek and stood up.

"Do you have to go back to work now?" Claudia asked, trying not to sound disappointed. She was proud of her daughter's position in the county's social services department, but she hated to see her leave.

"No, I said I wouldn't be back right away. How about we go in the kitchen and make us some lunch?"

AT NOON, KRISTIN WAS at her desk, working on an article about Daphne Whittier's murder. Earlier in the day when Bill told her about the crime, she realized once again how little she knew about Oak Hill. She vaguely remembered Daphne Whittier's name from a city council meeting where the woman had spoken against something the council was considering, but Kristin had no idea how important she'd been.

"She was an educator, she served two terms on the city council in the 1980s, and she's been on almost every board and commission in town," the newspaper editor told her. "I'll do a story on her life, sort of a front page obituary. I want you to cover the crime angle. See what you can find out from the neighbors. Talk to the police."

"Won't Steve want to handle this?" When she'd written the stories about Ida Mae, Kristin had wondered if the other reporter thought she was intruding on his territory.

"Steve's tired of trying to wring information

out of the Oak Hill police. He says he'll do anything, even cover the junior high soccer games,
if somebody else will take the crime beat." Bill
grinned. "Maybe you'll have better luck. I hear
you're Wayne Henley's lunch buddy."

Kristin blushed. Word of her meal with the detective had found its way back to the *Sentinel* office, and somebody must have mentioned it to the
editor.

"You've seen Daphne Whittier at city council meetings," Bill continued. "She's been there a
lot recently, either talking about drugs or opposing the rezoning of her neighborhood. She's written letters to the newspaper about both issues. It
was Daphne Whittier who prompted our series on
drugs. She wanted the police to start going after
the big drug suppliers, not the teenagers selling a
few ounces of marijuana to their friends."

"The bass and not the bluegills?"

"What?"

"Just an expression I heard. Where did Daphne
Whittier live? I'll go there right away."

FIFTEEN MINUTES LATER, Kristin was in a neighborhood that had seen its better days. Spacious
homes built as single-family dwellings now had
peeling paint, unkempt yards, and signs advertising rooms for rent. It wasn't hard to pick out the
Whittier house. It was the only one with flower-

beds, neatly trimmed shrubbery, and crime scene tape. A large white sedan was parked in front of it.

"That looks like the car the detectives drove to Ida Mae's," Kristin said to Matt, the *Sentinel* photographer, who had come with her. "They're probably inside the house."

"You won't have any trouble finding neighbors to talk to," Matt said, nodding toward the houses nearby.

There were people on every porch. Dozens of pairs of eyes followed Kristin and Matt as they got out of the car, walked to the nearest house, and introduced themselves. Everybody was willing to have their pictures taken and be quoted in the newspaper, as long as they were saying how shocked they were by the crime or were singing the praises of its victim.

"They don't make 'em like her anymore," a middle-aged, dark-skinned woman said. The people around her murmured their agreement.

"I heard Daphne Whittier was trying to drive the drug dealers out of this neighborhood," Kristin said.

This brought affirmative answers and words of approval, but when Kristin asked if they thought Miss Whittier had been killed because of her fight against drugs, nobody wanted to venture a guess.

"She was against rezoning this neighborhood,"

Kristin said. "Do you think that made any ene-
mies for her?"

The question brought blank looks. Zoning issues didn't seem to be of much interest here, Kristin realized. She wondered if Daphne Whittier
was the only person who cared that these big old
houses might be torn down to make room for a
shopping center. New stores meant new jobs. For
most people in this neighborhood, that probably
outweighed the fact that they'd have to find other
places to live.

"Nobody saw or heard anything last night?"

"I did," said a skinny blond boy who looked
about eight or nine. "I saw a car stop in front of
her house."

A pudgy white woman in a tank top clamped
her hand on the child's shoulder. "You hush, Kyle."
She turned to Kristin. "He has a big imagination.
He was in the house watching TV. He didn't see
nothing."

Kristin wanted to ask the boy some questions,
but now he was looking down at his feet. The
woman still had a firm hold on his shoulder.

"I understand Daphne Whittier's great-niece
was living with her," Kristin said. "Do you know
if she's there now?"

"Yonder she is," an elderly African-American
woman said, nodding in the direction of the Whittier house. A young woman had come out the front

door, followed by Detective Henley and Detective Shelton. She wore a white sleeveless blouse and jeans, and her feet were in sandals. Her face, surrounded by beaded braids, was expressionless. Kristin hurried toward the detectives and the young woman, but before she reached them, the threesome drove off in the white sedan.

A few minutes later, Kristin headed back downtown, afraid she'd missed her chance to talk to the police. But when she reached the *Sentinel* office, Kristin learned that the police chief had called, ready to give the newspaper a statement.

"He's waiting for you to call him back," Bill said. Seeing the reporter's look of surprise, he added, "Chief Cates will be under a lot of pressure to find Daphne Whittier's killer. He needs all the good publicity he can get. He's going to tell you that her death was a great loss to the town. He'll say that the police will be working day and night to apprehend her killer. And then he'll say that any other information about the crime will have to be kept confidential so as not to jeopardize the investigation."

Bill was right. That was exactly what Chief Cates said.

"Now wasn't that good?" Vonda asked when she and Ida Mae finished eating their salad.

"Very tasty," Ida Mae said, stretching the truth

in the interests of family harmony. In her opinion, today's salad was a lot like the one they'd had the day before—tolerable, but definitely not worth the effort Vonda put into making it.

Vonda checked her watch. "I'd better start getting dressed for the bridge club."

Dressed? Her sister looked perfectly fine to Ida Mae. Vonda's lilac pantsuit with matching sandals ought to do for any social event in Oak Hill, except maybe a funeral. Her hair was perfectly in place, and her skin looked dewy-fresh.

When Vonda trotted off to the bedroom, Ida Mae grinned. She was almost as excited over the bridge club invitation as Vonda was. She could hardly wait to have a few minutes to herself. Once Vonda was out of the house, she was going to have a thick roast beef sandwich, made with the leftovers from Saturday night's supper. Then, if Vivian's car was no longer parked next door, she'd call to make sure her neighbor was all right. Claudia had a heart condition, and when her relatives visited at odd times, Ida Mae feared the worst.

After that, if Claudia was fine, Ida Mae planned to weed the flowerbed in front of her half of the duplex. In hot weather she liked to do her gardening in the early morning, but since Vonda's arrival everything was out of whack. By the time Ida Mae had eaten her breakfast, fixed some coffee and toast for Vonda, and listened to her sister talk, half the morning was gone.

Ida Mae decided to watch the last few minutes of *News at Noon* while she waited for Vonda to leave. She turned on her TV just in time to hear the announcer say, "Join us at six for further updates on the brutal murder of Oak Hill educator and civic leader Daphne Whittier."

Ida Mae stared at the screen as the logo and theme music for the news show came on, followed by a commercial for denture cleaner. Sometimes her ears played tricks on her. Could she have misunderstood? Claudia would know. She always watched the noon news. Ida Mae went to the window and looked out. Vivian was walking toward her car, and Claudia was with her. Ida Mae hurried out to learn what had happened.

Vivian verified the bad news, and the three women spoke about it for a while. Then Claudia said she was going to spend the rest of the afternoon at the home of her granddaughter Lisa, who had a new baby.

"Lisa could use the company," Vivian said. "I'm going to take Mama over there and pick her up after work."

Ida Mae felt sure it was Claudia, not Lisa, who was Vivian's main concern. A visit to a new great-grandchild would help take her mind off Miss Whittier's murder.

As she walked back to her apartment, Ida Mae was troubled. She hadn't known the murder victim personally, but everybody in Oak Hill knew who Daphne Whittier was and how much she'd done for the town. If Daphne Whittier could be murdered, was anybody safe?

SIX

Freed from many of life's stresses, the residents of Pleasant Valley Retirement Center find that their days are filled with friendship and fun.

From the brochure, "Pleasant Valley Retirement Center Welcomes You"

CLAUDIA WAS GIVING HER kitchen a thorough scrubbing. She'd emptied the cabinets, and now she was scouring them with hot water and disinfectant—though they didn't need cleaning. Was she doing housework to keep from thinking about yesterday's horrible crime? If that was her plan, it wasn't working. Daphne Whittier's murder was the only thing on her mind.

She was almost ready to start returning things to the shelves when the doorbell rang.

"How's my favorite grandmother?" Ray asked when she opened the door. He leaned down to give her a hug and a kiss. "You wouldn't have any iced tea in your refrigerator, would you? It's a real scorcher outside."

Before Claudia could stop him, her grandson

strode toward the kitchen. He halted abruptly when he saw the dishes, canned food, and pots and pans piled on the countertops.

"Have you found it yet?" he said.

"Found what?"

"Whatever you're looking for," he said with a teasing smile. "My house would never look like this unless I'd misplaced something pretty important and was trying to find it."

"Oh, you! I'm cleaning. But I guess you've never heard of that," she said, well aware that the accusation was untrue. Ray had bought a house last year, and he kept it spotless.

Ray found two glasses, dropped a couple of ice cubes in each, and filled them with tea from the pitcher in the refrigerator. Then he carried them to the oval maple table in the dining area.

"When are you going to find a wife for that nice house of yours?" Claudia asked when they were both seated. "I hear the new soloist at your church is mighty pretty."

Ray smiled. "You hear too much." He took a clear plastic envelope from his pocket and held it so Claudia could see the photograph inside.

"Do you recognize this woman?"

The photo looked old. It was wallet size, but the picture was a studio portrait, and its subject was carefully posed. She was a young woman, African-American Claudia thought, but with a light complexion. Her hair, which seemed brown rather than black, was in a style that reminded Claudia of the movie stars of the 1940s. The words *Love, Leonora* were written across one corner of the picture in a looping script.

Claudia studied the photograph. She'd known many people in her lifetime, and this woman, if alive today, might look quite different. But Leonora? She didn't think she'd ever known anyone by that name.

"There's something familiar about her," she said, "but I don't know who she is. Where did it come from?"

"We found it on Daphne Whittier's living room floor this morning."

Claudia reached for the picture, looked at it, and nodded. "That's why she seems familiar. She looks like Miss Whittier. Or like Miss Whittier used to look, back when I first knew her. This Leonora woman is probably one of her relatives."

"I showed the picture to Stacy, Daphne Whittier's great-niece, who's been staying with her for the summer. She said she'd never seen the picture before and had no idea who it was. I talked to her in Greensboro yesterday. She's doing research there this summer, working on her doctorate in history."

"She wasn't at Miss Whittier's house when— when it happened?"

"She spent the night in Greensboro at a friend's apartment."

"Is she a suspect?" Claudia had lived long enough to know that sometimes people killed their own kin, but she didn't want to think this had happened to Daphne Whittier.

"No, not at this point. I spoke with several people who saw her in the university library the evening of the murder, and I talked to a friend of hers who says she spent the night in his apartment."

Claudia raised her eyebrows. "Her boyfriend?" She wasn't surprised that the young woman spent the night with a man. She knew that happened frequently these days. But she couldn't imagine Daphne Whittier approving of it.

"He's just a friend, not a boyfriend, they both say. Maybe so. The sofa had a rumpled blanket, sheet, and pillow on it, so she probably slept there, not in the bed with him." He grinned. "I probably shouldn't have told you that. Guess I just wanted to show my grandma what a good detective I am."

"I already know that, honey," Claudia said, looking at him fondly.

Ray stood up and held out his hand for the photo. "I'd better be on my way. Thanks for the tea."

Claudia gave the picture a long, careful look before she handed it back to him. "Miss Whittier wasn't from around here, you know. She came from Boston. This woman may never have lived in Oak Hill or even in North Carolina. But if she was a relative, somebody in the Whittier family should know her."

"Stacy's parents and brother are arriving today. I'm planning to ask her father about the picture. You know the funeral's tomorrow afternoon?"

Claudia nodded. "Your mother said she'd take Ida Mae and me."

To Claudia's way of thinking, tomorrow was mighty quick for the funeral. Most people waited a little longer, especially if relatives needed to come from out of town. Apparently Daphne Whittier had very little family. This morning's newspaper listed only her nephew, his wife, and their two children. According to the paper, there wouldn't be the usual visitation at the funeral home. Instead, the family would greet people in the fellowship hall of the church after the funeral.

At the front door, Ray hugged his grandmother again. "Promise me you'll be careful, Grandma. Keep your doors locked, and don't let anybody in you don't know. Somebody just killed one old lady, and I don't want you to be next."

"Watch who you're calling old," Claudia said. Then, seeing Ray's serious look, she added, "Don't worry, I'll be extra careful."

A FEW HOURS LATER, IDA MAE was standing at the door of her spare bedroom, watching Vonda fold her clothes and slap them into the suitcase that lay open on the bed.

"There's no call for you to get on your high horse just because I told your son you were here," Ida Mae said. "I've never been one to lie, and I'm not about to start now."

"Well, you didn't have to hand the phone to me. If you'd told me who it was, I wouldn't have spoken to him."

Ida Mae snorted. If Vonda hadn't wanted to talk to her son, she could have hung up right away, instead of arguing with him for a half hour before slamming down the phone. "I don't see why you're so mad at him. He was a real gentleman when he talked to me. Naturally he was upset that you took off without telling him where you were going. It had to be a shock to him, reading in the Atlanta newspaper that you were in North Carolina with a family he never knew you had."

Vonda stuffed a pair of high-heeled sandals into a satin bag. She gave Ida Mae a withering glance. "That *gentleman* who impressed you so much didn't care the slightest bit that I'd left home. He tracked me down here to talk about his favorite subject, selling my house, which I am *not* going to do." She slammed the suitcase shut. "Now if you'll step aside, I'll take my bags to the car and be on my way."

Ida Mae didn't move away from the doorway. "Are you going back to Atlanta?"

Vonda sniffed. "I can't tell you, can I? Because if that *gentleman* should call to inquire where I am, you'd tell him in a heartbeat."

Ida Mae had never seen her sister pitch a fit like this. It must have been a skill she'd picked up while she was away. If she'd thrown this kind of tantrum as a child, Mama or Papa would have taken a hickory to her for sure.

Ida Mae grinned. "What if some other gentleman should call? Frank Rowland, for instance. You want me to keep your whereabouts a secret from him, too?"

Vonda tossed her head and tried to pick up the suitcase.

"Come on, girl, let me help you carry that bag," Ida Mae said. "It's too heavy for you." She knew Vonda wasn't going far. She'd overheard her calling the Oak Hill Inn and making a reservation there.

Not long after Vonda drove off, the doorbell rang. Ida Mae wondered if her sister had had a change of heart. But when she looked out through the blinds, she saw Kristin on the doorstep.

Talk about perfect timing! The reporter had a reason for dropping by, Ida Mae felt sure, but if Vonda were here talking non-stop, Kristin wouldn't be able to get a word in edgewise.

"Come in and have a glass of tea with me," Ida Mae said. "We didn't have much chance to visit the other day, with Vonda turning up and all. Let's sit in the kitchen. The table in there is too little to be much use, but we can see out the window."

When they were seated at the kitchen table with glasses of iced tea and a plate of homemade oatmeal cookies, Kristin looked out into the backyard. "What beautiful flowers! And are those tomato plants?"

"Oh, yes. That's all there's room for. I planted some lettuce and radishes in the spring and a few tomatoes and beans this summer. I miss the big garden I had on Wendley Street. I had corn, squash, cantaloupes, field peas, you name it. I'll give you some tomatoes when they start coming in."

"That sounds great," Kristin said.

Ida Mae wondered if the girl had ever eaten real tomatoes. They'd be a treat after those cardboard-tasting things sold in the supermarket. She would have offered her a mess of beans, too, but she figured Kristin was a city girl who wouldn't know how to cook them. Even Norma and Betty Jo bought most of their vegetables canned or frozen these days.

"I came to Pleasant Valley to interview the activities director about the talent show," Kristin said. "She made it sound so good, I bought a ticket."

Ida Mae nodded. She and Claudia were going to the talent show, and Vonda had planned to go with them. But now, who knew? Would Vonda's nose still be out of joint on Friday night?

"I've been thinking about the woman who was murdered," Kristin said. "Not Daphne Whittier. The other woman, the one we thought was your sister. I don't think the police are going to spend much time trying to figure out who she was or who killed her. They'll concentrate on finding Daphne Whittier's killer."

Ida Mae nodded again. She and Claudia had said the same thing.

"I'm going to look into the earlier murder," Kristin said. "You were in Oak Hill then. Can you remember anything that might help?"

So that was why she was here! If the girl was going to investigate one of the murders, Ida Mae was glad she'd chosen the old one. Whoever killed Miss Whittier was probably still in town, and if Kristin started poking around, she could be in trouble before she knew it.

"Claudia and I have been thinking about it," Ida Mae said, "but we haven't come up with a thing. Neither one of us remembers anybody disappearing. Anybody but Vonda, that is."

"I've been wondering about the place where the skeleton was found. What was it in the 1940s?"

"Just woods. It was part of the Treadwell home-place, the farm where old Mr. Asa Treadwell grew up."

"The same Treadwells who owned the mill where you and Vonda worked?"

Ida Mae nodded. "But that doesn't mean much, the bones being on Treadwell property. The Treadwells owned most of the town and a good part of the county back then."

"I'm going to look at the newspapers from 1946. We don't have the microfilm that far back at the *Sentinel* office, but they have it at the library. It shouldn't be too hard. The paper came out only twice a week in those days."

Ida Mae didn't want to discourage Kristin, but she doubted the newspaper would be much help. Vonda's disappearance hadn't been in the paper. The other young woman's disappearance probably hadn't been, either. The police seemed to think the murdered woman was black, and there wasn't much about black people in the paper back then, if Ida Mae remembered correctly.

"Can you think of anyone else who might be able to help me?" Kristin asked.

"Daphne Whittier would have been the one to ask. If that girl had gone to the school where she taught, she would have known her." Ida Mae shook her head. "I can't believe Miss Whittier's gone. She always stood up for what she believed. I saw in the paper that she was still trying to keep Buddy Daniels from selling her neighborhood to Big Mart."

Ida Mae was surprised to see a blank look on Kristin's face.

"You wrote the article," she told the reporter. "Remember, the city council postponed the rezoning vote? Buddy Daniels has been buying up property near Miss Whittier's house. Big Mart wants to put a store in Oak Hill, and he wants to sell them the land for it. He's been trying to convince the city to rezone that neighborhood, but Miss Whittier kept going to the city council and arguing against it."

Kristin looked puzzled. "I was at the meeting, but I didn't hear a word about Big Mart. Just somebody wanting some property rezoned and somebody speaking against it."

"Well, no, they wouldn't come right out and say it in front of everybody. Now where did I hear that? I guess it was my niece Norma who told me. She's in real estate."

"So this Buddy Daniels has been buying land to sell to Big Mart, but Daphne Whittier was standing in the way?"

Ida Mae hesitated. "I suppose you could put it that way. Norma told me Buddy went out on a limb borrowing money to buy up property around Tabor Street. If he can't get the area rezoned, he may lose his shirt."

"Do you think he could have killed Daphne Whittier?"

"Buddy?" Ida Mae couldn't have been more shocked if she herself had been accused of the murder. "Oh, no. Buddy may be a little sneaky, but he's no murderer."

"Is he in the phone book?"

"Bryson Daniels. His office is on Maple Street." Ida Mae offered this information reluctantly, wishing she'd never mentioned Buddy Daniels or Big Mart. The reporter was acting like a dog that had scented a rabbit. Buddy Daniels wasn't a murderer, but he wasn't anybody to mess with either.

"If I were you, I'd leave Buddy Daniels alone," Ida Mae said. "And for goodness' sake, don't put those things I told you in the paper."

"Don't worry, I won't involve you," Kristin assured her.

That didn't make Ida Mae feel a whole lot better. She knew Kristin had a phone in her purse. The girl would probably be talking to Buddy Daniels before she was a block away from here. And that could mean trouble.

BY EIGHT O'CLOCK THAT night, Claudia was tired. She'd been busy all day, cleaning one thing and another around her apartment. She sat down on the sofa with the newspaper and looked at the TV listings. There was nothing that interested her. She didn't enjoy watching folks act silly and make jokes about sex, like they were eight years old and had just found out about it. There were some crime shows on, too—definitely not the kind of thing she wanted to see tonight.

Many evenings she sat in her living room letting her thoughts run free, reviewing the events of the day or revisiting things that had happened a long time before. Memory was a wonderful thing. She could do without her eyesight or the use of her legs if she could just keep on remembering. Of course, memories could break your heart, too. She still had a stab of pain every time she thought about Layton. He'd died too young, not long after he retired. But it would be worse if she couldn't remember him at all.

Her mind drifted back to the early days of Layton's teaching career. When he'd started teaching math at Carver High, Daphne Whittier had already been there a few years, teaching English. Back then, people weren't sure how to take Miss Whittier. When the Boston-bred educator first came to Oak Hill, she'd seemed proud, prissy, maybe a little stuck-up, and her clipped speech had been foreign to North Carolina ears. But as time passed, her differences faded along with her accent, and the community, even the white community, came to respect her.

As Claudia's thoughts traveled back through time, she was only half aware that night was falling outside. Her living room was becoming dimmer, but she was in no hurry to turn on the lights. She didn't mind the dark. There was something peaceful about it.

When the doorbell rang, she felt a twinge of apprehension, remembering Ray's warning. She realized that her blinds were still open, but since it was dark in her apartment, maybe whoever was outside couldn't see in. Claudia slipped over to the door, flipped on the outside light, and peered out through the peephole. The tall, skinny person on her stoop must be a teenager. Who else would wear baggy shorts that were almost sliding off his hips? His head was turned so she couldn't see his face. After what had happened to Miss Whittier, Claudia wasn't about to open the door to a stranger. She tiptoed to the window and peeked out.

"Jamal! Come in!" she said, opening the door to her youngest grandson. When she saw his face, she knew something was seriously wrong. "What's the matter, honey?"

"You remember Troy Bandry, my friend from elementary school?"

"Sure, I remember Troy. You two were inseparable back then."

When Jamal was in elementary school, he'd stayed at Claudia's house until his parents picked him up after work. Troy, who lived a block away, was usually there, too.

By the time the boys reached middle school, Jamal's mother, Claudia's daughter Francine, had been promoted to loan officer at the bank, and his father began commuting to a management job in Charlotte. They moved out of the old neighborhood and put Jamal in an after-school program at the YMCA.

About the same time, Troy's parents split up and his father left town. The boy and his mother moved into a run-down apartment, and Francine began discouraging her son's friendship with Troy. A few years later, when Troy was arrested for selling marijuana to an undercover police officer, Claudia wondered if her daughter had been right, or if, on the other hand, a friend like Jamal might have kept Troy out of trouble.

"I think the police are going to arrest Troy for Miss Whittier's murder," Jamal said. "They picked him up for questioning yesterday afternoon. Miss Whittier was the one who sicced the cops on him that time he was arrested, so they probably thought he had it in for her. But he didn't, Grandma. In a weird kind of way, he was grateful to her. He didn't get any jail time, and he had to keep his grades up as part of his probation. He's back on the baseball team, and he's doing great. Troy thought Miss Whittier pulled some strings to make sure he didn't go to jail. So see, he wouldn't have hurt her."

Claudia nodded. Daphne Whittier had helped many a young person find the right path in life. But she wondered if Troy's story of gratitude to the elderly woman was true or just a tale he'd spun to impress his law-abiding friend.

"Racist cops!" Jamal said. "Somebody's killed, and they arrest the first young black man they see."

"Jamal, that's your cousin Ray you're talking about." Claudia's voice was soft, but her gaze was stern. "Troy isn't under arrest, is he?"

"No, but—"

"Then he's okay, Jamal. They have to talk to everybody. That doesn't mean they think he did it. If the police thought he had something to do with Miss Whittier's murder, he'd be behind bars now. Does he have a lawyer?"

"Grady Wallace was his lawyer when Troy was in court before. I think Troy's mom called him yesterday."

"Grady's a good man. He'll look out for Troy."

"Grandma, will you talk to Ray? Tell him there's no way Troy could have done this."

"I will, honey. Sure, I will. But don't you worry. Troy's going to be all right."

Reassuring her grandson came naturally to Claudia. She didn't like seeing him upset and angry. She invited him into the kitchen for a bowl of ice cream, and in a few minutes he was telling her a funny story about his high school physics teacher. His worries about his friend were apparently forgotten.

But Troy was still on Claudia's mind. She knew that young people didn't always succeed in turning their lives around. If Troy had appeared at Daphne Whittier's door the way Jamal had shown up at hers tonight, Miss Whittier would have welcomed him in. Claudia shivered as she thought about what might have happened next.

SEVEN

The Oak Hill Inn offers an innovative menu in elegant surroundings. Located in the town of Oak Hill, it is somewhat off the beaten path, but those who make the trip will be rewarded with a meal to remember.

From Fine Dining in the Piedmont

KRISTIN WAS CONVINCED Buddy Daniels had something to hide. Otherwise, why hadn't he returned her call? It had been almost twenty-four hours since she phoned him. Didn't businessmen check their messages regularly and return them promptly?

Kristin had called Daniels right after she learned that he stood to profit from Daphne Whittier's death. The recorded voice she'd heard was male and self-assured, with a strong Southern accent. It informed her that the speaker was Buddy Daniels and instructed her to leave a message. Kristin identified herself as a *Sentinel* reporter, left her name and phone numbers, and said she'd like an opportunity to talk to him. Judging from his telephone voice, Kristin pictured Daniels as overweight and sixtyish, with a hearty laugh, a bone-crushing handshake, and a tendency to call women *honey*—annoying, maybe, but not sinister. She felt sure she could handle him.

At home that night, though, with more time to think, Kristin had developed strong qualms about interviewing Buddy Daniels. If he'd murdered an elderly woman to protect his investment, he'd certainly kill a reporter to cover up the crime. Ida Mae had urged her to leave him alone, and Ida Mae seemed to know a lot about what went on in Oak Hill.

The more Kristin thought about it, the more uneasy she became, so much so that a late-night shriek from the apartment next door sent her cowering under the covers. Then she realized it was only the Loflins, engaged in their nightly battle over which TV show to watch. Apparently Darren, "the stupidest jerk I ever knew" in Tammy's high-decibel description, had just swiped the remote from his wife.

The next morning, in the newspaper office with its bright lights and friendly faces, Kristin dismissed her fears of the real estate developer. After all, she was only going to ask the man a few questions, not accuse him of murder. By mid-morning, when he still hadn't returned her call, her only feelings toward him were annoyance and suspi-

cion. Was he too busy to call her because he was
tracking down Daphne Whittier's heirs to make
them an offer on the murdered woman's house?
Or was he afraid to talk to her because he had
something to hide?

Because Buddy Daniels was her only suspect in
Daphne Whittier's death, Kristin decided to turn
her attention to the earlier murder. She told Winnie, the *Sentinel* receptionist, that she was going
to the library to do some research. She set out on
foot for the main branch of the Yarborough County
Public Library, three blocks away.

Once she was there, a helpful library assistant explained that all the issues of the *Sentinel*
for 1946 were on one reel of microfilm. Kristin
threaded the film onto the machine and spooled it
forward until she reached the month of July. Her
plan was to begin with that month and work her
way to the end of the year. It was slow going. She
skimmed through the articles, skipping the na-
tional and international news. It was hard not to
be distracted by the amazingly low prices in the
advertisements and the accounts of Oak Hill's social life. The paper included reports of club activities, family reunions, and birthday celebrations.
Kristin found herself reading descriptions of the
food served at meetings of the Baptist Ladies Mis-
sionary Society, the Tuesday Morning Book Club,
and the Oak Hill Rotary Club.

She saw some familiar names, families who still lived in Oak Hill. The Treadwells were particularly prominent. The July and August issues of the paper featured articles by a Will Treadwell. He and a friend were traveling across the country by car. Had Will Treadwell later become Wilton Treadwell, Attorney at Law?

After an hour, Kristin had reached the middle of August and had found no references to the disappearance of Vonda Williams or anyone else. Thinking she'd done enough for one day, she returned the microfilm. On the way to the door she stopped at a display of new books and picked out two mystery novels, hoping they'd inspire her to solve Oak Hill's real-life crimes.

As she was leaving the library, she saw a black Lexus in the no parking zone in front of the building. As she came nearer, the window on its passenger side glided down.

"Ms. Grant." The voice from the car window was making a statement, not asking a question. While Kristin was wondering how to respond, the driver got out and came around the car to meet her. He had a trim build, was of medium height, and wore a pale gray linen sport jacket over a black T-shirt and well-pressed black jeans. Though his hair was the same shade as his jacket, his unlined face suggested that he was no more than forty.

"Buddy Daniels," he said, extending his hand.

His eyes were hidden behind sunglasses, and his face held no hint of a smile. "I think you want to talk to me."

This was Buddy Daniels? Kristin had seen him before, at the most recent city council meeting. He'd been in the audience during the discussion of rezoning Daphne Whittier's neighborhood. At the time, Kristin thought he looked interesting. Right now, *interesting* wasn't the adjective she would have chosen. *Intimidating* seemed more appropriate. Since she suspected him of murder, she supposed she would find him intimidating even if he were smiling.

Kristin tried to put a confident note in her voice. "Yes, I wanted to talk to you about—"

"Let me take you to lunch," he interrupted. "Would the Oak Hill Inn suit you?"

The invitation was so surprising that Kristin had no idea what to say. If he paid for her lunch, would that be a conflict of interest? Maybe so, if he were the subject of her investigation. On the other hand, if she didn't ask any probing questions, would he think she was helping herself to a free meal under false pretenses? Before she could sort this out, Kristin found herself in the Lexus, zooming toward the outskirts of town.

"Have you eaten at the Inn before?" her host asked.

"No, not yet." The Oak Hill Inn wasn't the kind

of place you went by yourself. When she arrived in Oak Hill, back in the days when she thought the town might have some social life to offer her, Kristin had envisioned herself going to dinner there with a date. But no one in Oak Hill seemed to think she was date material.

"The place was built as a private residence in the 1890s. Quite spectacular, considering what the rest of the town looked like then. The present owners spent a bundle putting it back in good shape, but it's a real money-maker now."

The rambling three-story building had a tower at one corner. A porch ran along most of the front and continued around one side. Wooden spindle-work decorated the porch and the eaves. Victorian, Kristin thought. Then, remembering the interview she'd once had with a historical preservationist, she decided it might more properly be called Queen Anne.

As for the interior of the building, she could only call it very, very nice. In the wainscoted dining room, tables covered in pale pink linen held bouquets of summer flowers. The menus were large and leather-covered. Piano music blended with the subdued voices of the diners. One look around convinced Kristin there was nothing wrong with letting Buddy Daniels buy her lunch. While they were eating, she might be able to extract some useful information from him. If she had to consume an elegant meal to accomplish that, well, there were worse ways to earn a living.

"How did you know who I was?" she asked when they were seated. "And how did you know I was at the library?"

He took off his sunglasses. His smile, the first one he'd offered, was disarming. "There are no secrets in Oak Hill. I've seen you at city council meetings scribbling in your notebook, and I've read your articles in the paper. You wrote one about my Uncle Clayton's license plate collection, as a matter of fact. Winnie, the receptionist at the newspaper, told me you were at the library. She was probably breaking the rules, but Winnie and I go way back. She knows I'm harmless."

When a waitress in a pink dress and a ruffled white pinafore came to take their order, Kristin chose a shrimp and pasta dish. While her host questioned the waitress about other menu offerings, Kristin looked around the room. She was surprised to see Vonda Hatcher at a table by the window, deep in conversation with a slim, elderly man with wispy white hair.

"Tell me what you've heard about me," Daniels said when the waitress left, "and I'll tell you if it's true."

The first thing that came to mind was Ida Mae's description of him: "A little sneaky, but no murderer." Kristin knew she shouldn't repeat that to him, so she tried something more innocuous. "I heard you bought property in Daphne Whittier's neighborhood to sell to Big Mart, but you weren't able to sell it because she fought the rezoning."

Her host's smile faded. "It's true that I own most of the land in her neighborhood. It's also true that the new interstate highway will come near there, which means that it will be an ideal location for stores, fast food restaurants, and gas stations. Daphne Whittier was a great lady who did a lot for this town, but she was way off base if she thought that her neighborhood would ever be restored to its former glory. It was going to continue to go downhill. The city council didn't want to offend her, but they knew that rezoning the area for business was the right thing to do. It would have happened even if she hadn't died."

"But now that she's gone, it'll be easier to have the area rezoned," Kristin said. She took a deep breath. "Do you need her property in order to have enough land to sell to Big Mart? It doesn't sound as though Miss Whittier would have been willing to sell. Do you plan to buy it from her heirs?"

His expression grew icy. "Are you saying that I'll benefit from Daphne Whittier's death—or implying that I had something to do with it? Bill Caldwell isn't stupid enough to let that kind of nonsense appear in the newspaper. But if you so much as hint at it—well, I have good lawyers, Ms. Grant, very good lawyers."

Kristin swallowed hard. He hadn't mentioned broken legs or cement overshoes, but he was definitely making a threat.

There was a long silence. Then his smile returned, and he began asking her questions about herself. By the time their food arrived, Kristin had begun to relax. She ventured a few questions of her own.

She learned that Buddy Daniels had grown up in Oak Hill. "Definitely not on the right side of the tracks," he said with pride in his voice. "All that I've accomplished, I've done on my own."

He told her he'd started out as an electrician's helper. He'd taken evening classes at the local community college and eventually had become a contractor. He talked with relish about building, buying, and selling houses and commercial property. Making money was clearly this man's overriding goal, Kristin thought. Could it have led him to murder?

When she refused dessert, he looked at his watch. "I need to be on my way, anyway. I have a funeral to attend."

Kristin gulped. She'd forgotten about the event Bill had asked her to cover that afternoon. She had a funeral to attend, too.

Daniels chatted in a friendly manner during the

ride back to town, but when he stopped the car in front of the Sentinel office, he said, "Be careful when you write about me in the paper. Be very careful."

She looked to see if he was smiling. He wasn't.

IDA MAE LOVED A GOOD funeral. She'd been to a great many of them, and from what she'd read in the paper, Daphne Whittier's was going to be one of the best. A full slate of preachers and local dignitaries would be there to give Miss Whittier the sendoff she deserved. But even if it had promised to be a pokey little funeral in the smallest chapel of the funeral home, Ida Mae would have attended. She wanted to pay her respects. To her way of thinking, we were put in this world to help others, and that's what Daphne Whittier's life had been about.

She was also going to the service to support her neighbor. She knew the murder had been hard on Claudia. Ida Mae had known Daphne Whittier only by sight and reputation, but Claudia had known her personally. Ida Mae knew her own spirits would be lifted by the funeral, and she hoped Claudia's would be, too.

"I knew there'd be a crowd, but I didn't know people would be here so early," Vivian said when they neared Mount of Olives United Methodist Church. Forty minutes remained until the service was supposed to start, but the parking lot was full, and cars were lining the street.

"Why don't I drop you off here?" Vivian said, letting the car idle in front of the church. "You can wait for me in the lobby, where you'll be out of the heat."

"With this many folks here, I think we'd better go in and find a seat," Claudia said. "We'll save one for you."

As the two women started up the front steps, Ida Mae wondered why churches were built so high. Her own church had installed a ramp—not that Ida Mae had any need for it yet. There didn't seem to be one here, and climbing all these steps in the hot sun couldn't be good for Claudia's heart. Ida Mae slowed her pace so as not to hurry her friend. As far as she knew, her own ticker was all right, but her knees ached by the time she reached the top.

It was blessedly cool inside. An usher gave Ida Mae and Claudia programs and led them to a pew halfway to the front. They put their purses in between them to save room for Vivian.

"Closed," Claudia whispered, inclining her head toward the flower-covered casket at the front.

Ida Mae nodded. She'd expected that, given the way Miss Whittier died. Somehow it seemed more respectful, too. Daphne Whittier had been a dignified person, not the kind who'd want people peering at her up close, either living or dead.

Ida Mae looked at the program. It listed three solos, anthems by two choirs, two hymns sung by the congregation, several messages from ministers, comments from the mayor and other important people, and a time for other people to come forward and say something about the deceased if they wanted to. Ida Mae's own pastor was going to read the scripture. Yes, it would be a fine service. Too bad Miss Whittier couldn't be present to hear the good things people were going to say about her. Ida Mae often thought how nice it would be if people could attend their own funerals. Daphne Whittier would be pleased to know how much she meant to her adopted hometown.

Claudia scooted over to give Vivian a seat, and the younger woman took her mother's hand. Ida Mae knew that Claudia was close to all her children, but Vivian, the oldest, seemed to be a special comfort to her.

"Do you want to speak to the relatives afterward?" Vivian whispered to her mother, pointing to a statement on the back of the program. It said that the family would receive condolences in the fellowship hall after the interment.

"It's up to you, honey," Claudia said, and Ida Mae nodded in agreement.

MORE THAN TWO HOURS LATER, Ida Mae and Claudia made their way down the steps of the church.

Vivian had decided they'd skip the burial and the visitation with the family. She'd gone to retrieve her car, but it looked as if it would be quite a while before she'd be able to pick them up. Many of the mourners were walking toward the cemetery next to the church, but others were headed for home, and the parking lot was in gridlock. Funeral home employees were clearing away the chairs that had been set up outside the church for those who hadn't been able to squeeze inside the building.

"It was a wonderful funeral," Claudia said. "Didn't you think so, Ida Mae?"

"The best I've ever been to," Ida Mae agreed. Claudia's pastor, Reverend Alexander, had brought tears to Ida Mae's eyes and shouts of approval from the congregation when he extolled Daphne Whittier's virtues. Many people had spoken during the service, including the police chief. He praised the murdered woman, his disagreement with her over the drug issue apparently forgotten.

"That looks like Ray and Wayne," Ida Mae said, pointing in the direction of the cemetery. Ray was talking to Reverend Alexander. The other detective was standing a few steps away, looking red-faced and unhappy.

Ida Mae couldn't help feeling sorry for Wayne. The boy was too thin-skinned for his own good. He'd probably taken it personally when Reverend

Alexander called on the police to bring Daphne Whittier's killer to justice.

"We want a speedy resolution, but a fair one," the minister had demanded. The congregation had responded with a thundering *amen*.

BY THE TIME THE FUNERAL was over, Kristin felt thoroughly broiled by the sun. The church was full by the time she arrived, so she had to sit outside. She tried to use her notebook as a fan and sunshade, but it hadn't helped much. The service, which was carried to the overflow audience on the lawn by the church's sound system, seemed to go on forever. As soon as she heard the final words of the benediction, Kristin hurried to her car. She turned the air conditioning on full blast and waited for a chance to pull out of the parking space.

Seeing that she'd be trapped there awhile, Kristin looked back at the people coming out of the church. She spotted Ida Mae and Claudia, two small women in dark dresses, slowly making their way down the steps. When Kristin saw Ray and Wayne, she wondered if they attended the funerals of all murder victims on the theory that the killer might show up, the way the police sometimes did in books.

Buddy Daniels came out of the church and strode toward the cemetery, dressed in a navy blue suit, a white shirt, and a dark tie. How had he managed to change his clothes and still make it to the church in time to find a seat in the sanctuary? Kristin felt sure that before the afternoon was over Buddy would press a business card into the hand of Daphne Whittier's nephew and mention that he wanted to buy the dead woman's property.

Kristin had to stay late at the newspaper office to finish her story about the funeral. She was tired and hungry when she pulled into the York Towne parking lot. Seeing no vacant spaces near her apartment, she muttered angrily at Darren Loflin's new pickup truck, which was straddling a line, taking up two places. There was an empty spot near the manager's office, and the office lights were on. Kristin decided to pay her rent, saving herself a trip there tomorrow when it was due. She scribbled a check and went inside.

"Hi, Kristin! How in the world are you? Hope you've had a great day!" yodeled Tina, York Towne's perpetually perky manager. Her positive attitude, like her elaborate blond hairdo, seemed to hold up no matter what. Kristen had long since decided that the newspaper was right: Drugs were readily available in Oak Hill. Only mind-altering pharmaceuticals and gallons of hairspray could explain Tina.

Kristin gave the manager a wan smile and handed over her check.

"No problems with your apartment, I assume," Tina said, beaming.

Kristin wasn't in the mood to pretend. She wouldn't mention the truck, since it was the first time Darren had hogged two parking places. But she couldn't face another night of interrupted sleep.

"Can you say something to the Loflins? They keep me awake yelling at each other at night."

A tiny frown flitted across Tina's face. "After eleven? The rules say quiet after eleven."

"Oh, yes, way after eleven."

"I'll take care of it," Tina said reassuringly. "The owner wants this to be a nice, quiet place."

The owner? As in one person? Kristin had assumed York Towne was owned by a large corporation. "Who's the owner?"

"Buddy Daniels," Tina said, flashing a thousand-megawatt smile. "Have you met him? He's just the nicest man."

EIGHT

Many of our forebears came from farming
stock. We value our rural roots.

From *Memories of Old Oak Hill*
by Isabel Rowland Everhart

ON FRIDAY MORNING, Claudia had a phone call from
her neighbor.

"I've been thinking about the house where my
sisters and I were raised," Ida Mae said. "It's been
years since I saw the place. I called Vonda this
morning and asked if she'd like to ride out and
take a look at it."

"That sounds like a good idea," Claudia said.
She'd heard all about Vonda's abrupt departure,
and she knew that Ida Mae wasn't just offering
her sister a drive in the country. She was trying
to patch up the quarrel that had sent Vonda to the
Oak Hill Inn.

"Well, *you* think it's a good idea, and *I* think
it's a good idea," Ida Mae said with more than a
little exasperation in her voice, "but Vonda told
me she had better things to do than look at an old
farmhouse that was on its last legs sixty years ago.

Better things to do! Now I ask you, other than romancing Frank Rowland, what is Vonda actually *doing?*"

Claudia had wondered that herself. She and Ida Mae had their apartments to keep clean, laundry to do, church events to attend, family and friends to visit. But how was Vonda spending her time in Oak Hill? It was a mystery.

"I've decided to go without her," Ida Mae said. "I'm driving out to our homeplace this afternoon."

"By yourself?" Claudia wasn't sure how far the Williams homeplace was from town, but Ida Mae was the kind of driver who could get in trouble on any trip, no matter how short.

"I've driven that road many a time," Ida Mae said. "I'll be fine."

"I'm sure you will, but would you mind if I went along with you?" Claudia didn't think a woman of Ida Mae's age and driving habits should be traipsing through the countryside alone. An extra pair of eyes might keep her from ending up in a ditch, or worse.

"Why, that would be nice. I'd enjoy the company," Ida Mae said, sounding much more cheerful. "It's a pretty day. You'll enjoy the drive."

Claudia wasn't at all sure she would. Riding with Ida Mae always made her nervous, and some of their trips to the supermarket had been downright hair-raising. Not that her friend's bad driving

had anything to do with age. Betty Jo had con-
fided to Claudia that her aunt had always driven
as if she were circling a NASCAR track.

"Uncle Odell didn't know," Betty Jo said, "because he always took the wheel when they were
in the car together. I don't think she's ever had a
wreck, but she's probably caused a few."

Later that day, as the old Chevy roared out of
the driveway, Claudia wished she were in the driver's seat instead of Ida Mae. Soon they were on the
highway leading out of Oak Hill. As car dealer-
ships and fast food restaurants gave way to fields,
woods, and farmhouses, Claudia sneaked a peek
at the speedometer. It registered seven miles an
hour over the legal limit. Ida Mae often said she
didn't want to be one of those old fogies who infuriated other drivers by going too slowly. There
was certainly no danger of that, Claudia thought.

"Have you ever been down around Sneed's
Crossroads?" Ida Mae asked, speeding up to pass
another car.

"Yes, but not for years," Claudia said when they
were safely back in their lane. "I go over to the
other side of the county sometimes. I still have
family there, my cousins and Layton's."

"I drive out this way four or five times a year
to put flowers on Mama's and Papa's graves, but
I haven't seen our homeplace for years. It's off the
main road. We sold it after Papa died and Mama

came to live with Odell and me. Mama died in '67." Ida Mae let out an aggrieved sigh. "I don't see how Vonda could let our parents and our sister, Arlene, go to their graves not knowing if she was alive or dead. It would have meant the world to Mama there at the end when she was so sick if Vonda had come home."

Claudia did a little mental math. When her mother died, Vonda had been enjoying Parnell Hatcher's money for almost twenty years. Her son, Harvey, was probably in college, courtesy of his adoptive father. At that point in her life, did the fear of losing Mr. Hatcher and his money keep Vonda away from her family, or had she been away so long they never crossed her mind?

As the Chevy flew along the highway, Claudia's thoughts returned to the questions that had been troubling her for the past few days. Were there other reasons why Vonda stayed away so long, reasons Ida Mae wouldn't want to contemplate? Ida Mae's sister had said she didn't know the young woman who bought the necklace, but what if that was a lie? Vonda had come back to Oak Hill as soon as evidence of the woman's murder was unearthed. Had Vonda been involved in the crime—and returned to make sure her involvement stayed hidden?

Claudia was suspicious of Vonda's relationship with Frank Rowland, too. Vonda claimed to have made his acquaintance the day after she returned to Oak Hill, but could she have known him before she left town? Ida Mae didn't think the two were acquainted back then, but a pretty girl like Vonda could have had male friends her family didn't know about.

"This is starting to look like home," Ida Mae said when they'd passed fields of corn, tobacco, and soybeans. "I've lived in town since I turned seventeen, but I still love the smell of plowed land on a spring morning or the sight of a good crop in the field."

"You can have it," Claudia said. "I milked my last cow the day Layton and I moved to town, and I primed my last tobacco plant not too long before that. I couldn't skedaddle off that farm fast enough."

Ida Mae chuckled. "I said I like to look at it, that's all. By the time I came to town, I'd already done enough farm work to last a lifetime. Working in the mill wasn't easy, but it sure beat dealing with a balky cow or spending a hot summer day in a tobacco field."

As they sped through the countryside, Ida Mae and Claudia reminisced about the farms where they'd grown up. Tobacco was the main cash crop for their families, but they raised corn and sorghum, too. Both families had a cow for milk and butter, a hog or two for meat, some fruit trees, and a big vegetable garden. Both Ida Mae and Claudia could remember when electricity had arrived at their homes for the first time, and they'd both grown up in houses without indoor plumbing.

"We had a bath and a path," Ida Mae said. "The bath was a washtub, and the path went to the outhouse. When Odell and I moved to town, we thought we were living in luxury. We had an electric range, a refrigerator, a bathroom, and a light bulb hanging on a cord in the center of each room. No other electrical outlets. Those came later."

Claudia smiled. "When Layton and I came to Oak Hill, our apartment didn't have a refrigerator, just an old-fashioned icebox, but we knew we were moving up in the world because we had indoor plumbing."

Ida Mae peered across Claudia to look out the window on the passenger side of the car. "The road I'm looking for is around here someplace. We turn right at the sign for Big Hickory Baptist Church."

"You drive, and I'll look for the sign," Claudia said, anxious to have Ida Mae's eyes back on the road. Before long she spotted the church sign and told Ida Mae to turn. After they'd gone a few miles down the side road, Ida Mae slammed on the brakes, backed up ten yards, and turned right again.

"Almost didn't recognize my landmark," she said as they bumped along a gravel road. "That house where we turned, the one with the woods grown up all around it? It used to be a fine place in its day. Looks like nobody's lived there for years."

Claudia detected a note of sadness in Ida Mae's voice. She'd never thought of her neighbor as a sentimental person, but this trip was giving her a different view. Would Ida Mae be upset if her childhood home turned out to be dilapidated and abandoned?

The car slued around on the gravel every time Ida Mae hit the brakes, which she seemed to do on every curve, and the road had more than its share of curves. Then she made an abrupt right turn onto a dirt road, hardly more than a set of tire tracks.

"Our house is up this road a piece," she said.

Then, to Claudia's amazement, Ida Mae stopped, threw the car into reverse, and backed up until she was beside the mailbox. "Thought I'd better see who's living here now." She looked out the window. "Well, how about that!"

Claudia peered past Ida Mae to see the name on the box. She gasped. "R. Tavender. Do you think that's one of the crooked ones?"

"They're all crooked one way or another, I guess," Ida Mae said in an amused tone. Then she shook her head. "My daddy would have a fit, him being so strong against liquor, if he knew some of the biggest bootleggers in Yarborough County were living in the house he built."

Claudia nodded. The name on the mailbox belonged to a family who was legendary in Yarborough County. The patriarch of the clan had been noted for the high-quality corn whiskey he produced, and succeeding generations made good use of his recipe. His descendants also brought in store-bought beer, wine, and whiskey from neighboring counties, which they were able to sell at inflated prices, Yarborough County being officially "dry." According to local rumor, this illegal business had flourished over the years because Yarborough County's sheriffs had been paid, either in merchandise or in cash, to turn a blind eye to the operation.

"No matter who lives there," Ida Mae said, putting the car into forward gear, "I want to see the house. It won't be dangerous unless they're cooking up moonshine out there."

Claudia wasn't so sure. She'd heard that in recent years the moonshining family had branched out into drugs. According to Ray, everybody in the drug trade was dangerous. But before she could object, the car roared forward. Claudia closed her eyes and held tight to the armrest as they bounced over the deep ruts of the road.

"Almost there!" Ida Mae said triumphantly a minute later. "The house is around that curve yonder."

Claudia opened her eyes as they rounded the

curve. But instead of a farmhouse, she saw a doublewide mobile home. It rested on cinder blocks,
and an unpainted wooden porch and a satellite dish
were attached to it. A red pickup truck and a black
SUV with darkened windows were parked nearby.

When the Chevy came to a stop, a yellow dog
crawled out from under the porch and began bark-
ing at them.

"A trailer!" Ida Mae said. "They've replaced the
house with a doublewide trailer."

"You're sure this is the right place?"

"Sure, I'm sure. I've driven this raggedy little
road enough times to know it by heart. This is the
end of the road, so if we haven't found the house
by now, it's not here. See those oak trees? They
were in our front yard. Mama's lilac bushes are
gone. They were right over—"

Ida Mae's reminiscences stopped when the door
of the mobile home opened. A rangy white man in
a khaki uniform stepped out onto the porch and
looked in their direction as he tucked in his shirt
and zipped up his pants.

"Now who's that?" Ida Mae asked. "He looks
familiar, but I can't place him."

Claudia had no idea who the man was, but she
didn't think they ought to hang around to find
out. She was about to suggest leaving when the
man stepped back inside. Then a bosomy plati-
num blonde came out the door. She was wearing

an oversize T-shirt and, as far as Claudia could see, not much else.

"Looks like we picked the wrong time to come calling," Ida Mae said with a chuckle.

The woman reached back inside the door and brought out a shotgun.

"Get us out of here, Ida Mae," Claudia gasped.

Ida Mae threw the car into reverse and gunned the motor. The Chevy went back the way it had come, but backward, much faster, and in a drunken zigzag, running off the road first on one side and then on the other. A flock of blue jays exploded out of the trees and circled overhead, scolding loudly as the car crushed underbrush, crashed through overhanging branches, and careened in and out of the ruts. When they reached the gravel road, Ida Mae backed onto it without stopping to look for oncoming traffic. She slammed the car into forward gear, and they sped off.

A mile or so down the road, when Claudia's heart had slowed down almost to normal, she realized they weren't headed back the way they'd come. "Is this a different way back to town?" she asked.

"A different way? Why, no, it's the same way we— Law me, I'm so addled I've gone the wrong way."

Afraid that Ida Mae might try a high-speed road

turn, Claudia pointed to a house a short distance away. "Why don't you pull into that driveway and turn around?"

A few minutes later, going back the way they'd come, they approached the turnoff to Ida Mae's homeplace again. She slowed the car to a crawl. "I'd love to see the spring. It's a good ways away from the house. I bet I could find it without those people spotting us."

Claudia sucked in her breath. Surely Ida Mae wasn't going back up that road to look for a spring, not after seeing the woman with the gun. She gave a silent prayer of thanks when Ida Mae passed the side road without turning.

Before they'd gone far, a red pickup truck came roaring up behind them. When it sped past them, Ida Mae took one hand off the steering wheel and began rifling through her handbag. She pulled out a ballpoint pen and an old envelope and handed them to Claudia. Then she reeled off a series of letters and numbers, and said, "Write that down."

Claudia was already writing. Those were the letters and numbers on the license plate of the truck that passed them—the truck they'd seen earlier at the doublewide.

ON THEIR WAY BACK TO Oak Hill, Ida Mae and Claudia came close to having their first real argument. It started when they were a few miles from home.

"I just remembered who the man in the red truck was," Ida Mae said. "His mama lives next door to a friend of mine. I met him when he was there cutting her grass. He's a deputy in the Yarborough County sheriff's department."

"Oh, my," Claudia said. "Then he shouldn't have been out at the doublewide with that woman."

Ida Mae agreed. She knew right from wrong, and what was going on at the trailer was wrong. She knew for a fact that the man and woman weren't married to each other. But what made it worse, the man was the law and the woman was from a family of lawbreakers. If that wasn't a crime, it was at least mighty suspicious.

"I heard the Tavenders are selling drugs now, along with all the other stuff they do," Ida Mae said. "Some people say there's a leak in the sheriff's department or the Oak Hill police—somebody who tips them off about raids." Ida Mae took her eyes off the road to glance at Claudia. All she knew was gossip, but Claudia, who did a lot of talking to her grandson Ray, might know these things for a fact.

"I've heard that, too," Claudia said. Her worried expression led Ida Mae to believe that the rumors were true. "As soon as we're home, I'm going to call Ray and tell him what we saw."

"You'll do no such thing," Ida Mae said. "If the

Tavenders find out you told on them, who knows what they might do? If anybody ends up in trouble for this, it should be me."

"If I tell Ray, neither of us will end up in trouble."

Ida Mae snorted. "That doesn't make sense, Claudia. This is my business, and I'm the one who should talk to the law about it. You wouldn't have seen that deputy if it wasn't for me taking you there, and even if you'd seen him, you wouldn't have recognized him."

"Who would you talk to, Ida Mae? According to you, the man in the red truck *is* the law. I can tell Ray because he's my grandson, and I know he's honest. But if a sheriff's deputy was out there at that trailer doing who-knows-what in the broad daylight, there are probably other crooked officers around. What if you tell the wrong one?"

"I'll tell Wayne Henley. I've known his grandmother for years."

Ida Mae had hardly said this when she began to wonder if Wayne was a good bet. More than one of her friends had grandchildren she wouldn't want to trust with her life, and her life could be at stake if she got crossways with drug dealers and crooked lawmen.

To her surprise, Claudia didn't object. "Wayne's all right. You can tell Wayne. Ray trusts him. He and Ray are both upset about the drugs in Oak Hill, and they don't trust the sheriff's department one bit." Claudia smiled. "To tell the truth, I wouldn't want to call Ray today anyway. He's mad at his mother, and I don't want to get in the middle of that."

"Ray's mad at Vivian?" Ida Mae asked, glad to be talking about something besides crime. "I thought they were close."

"They are, usually. But Ray went to dinner at his parents' house last night thinking it would be just family. He didn't know Vivian had invited the new soloist at their church, too, as sort of a surprise blind date."

"Why would Vivian do a thing like that?" Until now Ida Mae had thought Claudia's oldest daughter had good sense.

"Desperation, I guess. She really wants him to find a wife. I tried to talk her out of it, but she wouldn't listen. The way I heard it, Ray was nice enough to the woman, but he called his mother up afterward and gave her what-for."

They were silent for a moment, and Ida Mae's thoughts returned to the deputy at the doublewide. "Do the detectives work on Saturday?"

"Not usually."

"Then I'll phone Wayne at home tomorrow. If any Oak Hill police officers are on the Tavenders' payroll, I don't want them overhearing my call."

NINE

To enrich the lives of our residents, Pleasant Valley Retirement Center offers a variety of intergenerational activities and events open to the general public.

From the brochure, "Pleasant Valley Retirement Center Welcomes You"

KRISTIN STOOD AT THE back of Pleasant Valley's auditorium, looking for a seat. The room was a sea of gray and white heads, with a few more youthful colors scattered here and there. She spotted a broad-shouldered man with a blond buzz cut—Wayne Henley. What was he doing here? There was a vacant space beside the police detective, but Kristin didn't consider taking it. Wayne wouldn't want to spend the evening in her company any more than she wanted to spend it in his.

Vonda's pale gold hair was also easy to see. Ida Mae's sister was seated near the front, talking animatedly to the man beside her. He looked like the white-haired fellow who'd been lunching with her at the Oak Hill Inn, Kristin thought.

Were Ida Mae and Claudia here? Kristin hoped

so. Her research in the old newspapers had yielded nothing, and her investigation into Daphne Whittier's death had been on hold since her lunch with Buddy Daniels. She hoped the two women would be able to tell her something helpful. As old as they were, surely they knew something that would help solve the first murder. Maybe they'd tell her something that would unravel the mystery of Daphne Whittier's death, too.

Kristin's thoughts turned to Buddy Daniels. So far he was the only person she knew, other than Miss Whittier's heirs, who stood to profit from the elderly woman's death. He wasn't likely to be here tonight, Kristin thought, unless some Pleasant Valley residents owned property he coveted.

Her thoughts were interrupted when the house lights dimmed. She quickly slid into a seat near the back of the room. A spotlight illuminated an elderly man in a red jacket at the center of the stage. After a few jokes, he introduced the first act, a tenor, "like everybody on stage tonight, from right here in Pleasant Valley." Dancers, musicians, and storytellers followed, interspersed with more jokes from the fellow in red. Some of the jokes must have been as old as he was, and some of the singers' voices quavered a little more than they might have forty years before, but when the lights came on at the end of the performance, Kristin was amazed at how much she'd enjoyed it.

And the evening wasn't over yet! As the master of ceremonies had instructed them to do, the audience moved from the auditorium to a spacious room nearby, where long tables held an array of refreshments. Impressed by the snowy tablecloths, large floral centerpieces, and crystal punchbowls, Kristin made a mental note to give up journalism for a more lucrative profession. No doubt about it, she wanted to spend her golden years in a place like Pleasant Valley.

As the crowd moved slowly toward the refreshment tables, Kristin heard someone calling her name. She turned and saw Ida Mae and Claudia waving to her.

"Come with us if you want to grab something to eat before all the seats are gone," Ida Mae said when Kristin reached the two women.

Claudia and Kristin followed as Ida Mae elbowed her way through the crowd. Before long the three were leaving the refreshment tables with cups of punch and well-filled plates.

"Now we can enjoy the party," Ida Mae said when they'd taken seats at the side of the room. "There are never enough chairs for everybody at these things, and I like to sit down while I eat."

"I see your sister over there," Kristin said, thinking she might steer the topic of conversation from Vonda to the skeleton and then to the murders.

Ida Mae nodded. "Vonda up and moved out on

me. She's staying at the Oak Hill Inn. That fellow she's with is Frank Rowland, her new boyfriend."

Kristin's eyes widened. Vonda had a boyfriend? The woman must be—well almost as old as Ida Mae. The concept was more than she could deal with, so she turned her attention to the name Ida Mae had mentioned. There'd been Rowlands in the 1946 newspapers. The Treadwells, Rowlands, and Everharts seemed to be the most important people in town back then. Hadn't someone named Rowland accompanied Will Treadwell on his trip to California? The man with Vonda looked as if he might be in his eighties. If so, he would have been in his twenties in 1946, when Vonda was seventeen.

"Vonda was married to one rich man, and now she's set her sights on another one," Ida Mae said with a chuckle.

"Did your sister know Mr. Rowland before she left Oak Hill?" Kristin asked.

"Law me, no," Ida Mae said. "Frank Rowland's family owned the bank. We were lucky to have a nickel or two left from one payday to the next."

"Mr. Rowland was wealthy?"

"Still is, as far as I know," Ida Mae said.

"Isn't that Wayne Henley over there?" Claudia asked, looking across the room.

"Why, it sure is," Ida Mae said. "I need to talk to that boy." She set her punch cup and plate on her chair and bustled off in the direction of the police detective.

Kristin watched as Ida Mae made her way across the room and spoke to the detective. Then the two moved off to a corner of the room and continued their conversation. Why did Ida Mae need to talk to Detective Henley? Kristin felt sure it had something to do with one of the murders. She turned to Claudia, who was sipping punch, apparently unfazed by her friend's sudden departure.

"Some of the people who live here in Pleasant Valley may have been in Oak Hill when that young woman was killed," Kristin said. "Do you think Detective Henley's here as part of that investigation or maybe the investigation into Daphne Whittier's death?"

Claudia looked thoughtful. "You could be right. But more likely he's here because of his grandmother. She was one of the tap dancers. My goodness, weren't they wonderful? The way they moved around, you'd never know some of them are every bit as old as Ida Mae and me."

Kristin had interviewed enough people to know when someone was purposely changing the subject, and she was sure that was what Claudia was doing. As she tried to think of a question that would move the conversation away from the tap dancers and back to the murders, Kristin's attention was diverted by a couple near the refreshment table. A tall woman with snowy hair and ramrod-straight posture was standing beside a shorter man with white hair and a slight stoop. His tie matched the crimson shade of his companion's brocade dress.

"Who's that couple at the punchbowl?" Kristin asked. "The woman looks familiar."

"Adelaide Treadwell and her brother Wilton. They live in Oak Hill, but not here at Pleasant Valley, though they're in their eighties by now, I'm sure. They're still in the big house their daddy, Mr. Carter Treadwell, built. He owned the hosiery mill, you know. Wilton is a lawyer, and Adelaide took over the hosiery mill after her daddy died. There was another brother who went off to Europe. He became a painter or a writer or something like that."

Kristin had stopped listening when she heard the word *lawyer*. Wilton Treadwell was the name on the law office across the street from Myrtle's Grill. Now she knew why the woman looked familiar.

"Is he the only Wilton Treadwell in town? The only one who's a lawyer, I mean."

"Oh, yes, neither he nor Adelaide ever married. They're the end of the Treadwell line, I suppose, unless their brother had children, the one who went to France."

"I think I saw Adelaide Treadwell go into her brother's law office the other day."

"That could be," said Claudia. "You may have seen her at city council meetings, too. A few months back, she was trying to stop the new interstate from going through Treadwell land, but she didn't get anywhere with it. It was all decided in Raleigh."

Kristin shook her head. A few months back, Steve Jacobs had been covering local politics, and she'd been happily writing stories about women who collected salt and pepper shakers and men who made airplanes out of beer cans.

"The only woman I remember speaking at a city council meeting was Daphne Whittier," Kristin said. Then she realized something else. "I saw Daphne Whittier go into Mr. Treadwell's office, too, right before his sister did. I didn't know who she was at the time, but now that her picture's been in the paper, I'm sure that's who it was."

"My, my," Claudia said. "That's strange. Wilton Treadwell wasn't Miss Whittier's lawyer. Grady Wallace was."

Kristin looked at her in astonishment. How did Claudia know that? Between the two of them, Ida Mae and Claudia seemed to know just about everything about everybody in Oak Hill.

"When did you see Miss Whittier at the law office?" Claudia asked.

Kristin thought back. "It was Monday. Monday afternoon. I know it was Monday because Detective Henley was upset about my article in the Sunday paper, the one about Vonda's reappearance."

"You're sure of that?"

"Oh, yes, I'm sure he was upset. His face turned several shades redder than usual and he raised his voice."

"I mean, are you sure it was this past Monday afternoon? Because that was the day Miss Whittier was killed."

"Yes, it was Monday," Kristin said. She wondered if that was significant. Claudia certainly seemed to think so.

Just then Ida Mae reappeared. She took the plate and cup from her chair and sat down.

"There, that's done," she said to Claudia. Then she turned to Kristin. "Claudia and I have been worrying about you. You didn't go bothering Buddy Daniels about the property he's buying on Tabor Street, did you? Because that wouldn't be a good idea."

"Well, I…" Kristin wondered if Ida Mae already knew the answer to her question, thanks to the Oak Hill grapevine. Vonda had been at the Oak Hill Inn when she'd had lunch with Daniels. Though Vonda wouldn't have known who he was, Frank Rowland could have told her, and Vonda could have told Ida Mae. "I did talk to him, yes.

But I...um...I've decided not to pursue that line of investigation any further."

Ida Mae and Claudia looked relieved. Kristin supposed they couldn't believe that Buddy Daniels, someone they might have known all their lives, could be a killer. But Kristin wasn't convinced of his innocence.

"I just realized that I saw Daphne Whittier go into Wilton Treadwell's office the day she died," Kristin told Ida Mae. "Do you think that could be connected to her murder?"

Ida Mae shook her head. "You'd better leave that to the police."

"Ray and Wayne are working hard to solve the case," Claudia said. "If anybody can find the killer, they can."

Kristin could see she was getting nowhere. Obviously these two old ladies didn't want her to investigate Daphne Whittier's murder. But what about the earlier one? Surely that would be safe enough. "Has either of you thought of anything that might help identify the skeleton?"

The two women looked at each other, then looked at Kristin, and shook their heads.

Okay, they'd made their point. They didn't want to talk about the murders. Kristin decided to enjoy the refreshments, chat with Ida Mae and Claudia about the talent show, and leave investigative reporting for another day.

When the crowd began to disperse, Ida Mae looked at her watch. "My goodness, it's getting on toward my bedtime. We'd better be going home, don't you think, Claudia?"

Kristin offered to give the two women a ride to their duplex, but they assured her that the Pleasant Valley shuttle van would take them home safely. A few minutes later, Kristin drove away from Pleasant Valley convinced that Ida Mae and Claudia knew something they weren't telling her.

BY THE TIME THE SHUTTLE van dropped them off in front of their apartments, Ida Mae seemed to have forgotten all about being sleepy.

"Come in for a minute," she said to Claudia. "I want to tell you what Wayne said."

Claudia was eager to know what her friend had heard. The memory of their trip to the country that afternoon had intruded on her thoughts all evening. She hoped Ida Mae had learned something reassuring from the detective.

"We went to a corner where nobody could overhear us," Ida Mae said when they were seated in her living room. "As noisy as it was with all those folks talking, I'm sure not a soul but Wayne heard what I said. I told him everything we saw this afternoon, about the deputy and all. He said not to worry, because he'll keep our names out of it."

"That's good," Claudia said. "I knew Wayne would do right by us."

"That's not all he told me. I thought the deputy was a pure fool to mess with the wife of one of those Tavenders. Well, Wayne told me Rowena Tavender, the woman we saw, is single. She's a direct descendent of the old man who started them off moonshining, and she's the boss of their operation now."

Claudia gasped. "The boss? Oh, Ida Mae, are we in trouble?"

"Wayne said we'll be fine if we keep quiet about what we saw. He told me not to tell anybody." She grinned. "And he said, 'that includes that nosy newspaper reporter, Kristin Grant.' Then he told me that you and I should try to forget about it, but that he and Ray definitely wouldn't."

"I don't know if I can forget about it. Do you think you can?"

"I can do it easier than Kristin can forget those murders. I don't think she paid a bit of attention to us when we told her to leave Daphne Whittier's murder alone." She shook her head. "I worry about that girl. If she even comes close to finding the killers, she could be in real trouble. But I don't think she will, do you?"

Claudia sighed. "I hope somebody finds them."

Ida Mae thought for a moment. "Do you have

any idea why Daphne Whittier would go to see Wilton Treadwell?"

"No. Do you?"

"No. I guess that means we don't know any more than Kristin—which means we don't know anything at all."

Claudia was silent. Although Ray hadn't told her to keep it confidential, she hadn't said anything to Ida Mae about the picture of the woman named Leonora. There was a good reason why she hadn't. She didn't want Vonda to know.

"If I told you something that might be connected to Daphne Whittier's murder, could you keep it from your sister?" Claudia asked.

"Vonda? Vonda's the last person I'd tell. And not just because she's not speaking to me now, either."

"I think Vonda wants to make up with you," Claudia said. "She kept looking in your direction tonight."

"Made up or still mad, I wouldn't tell Vonda anything I didn't want spread around. That woman could talk the ears off a whole field of corn, and she says whatever comes into her head."

Claudia smiled, but thought it wouldn't be tactful to agree. "Ray showed me a picture the police found on the floor at Daphne Whittier's house. A light-skinned black woman. Young, but the picture looked old. The name *Leonora* was written on it. Do you know who it might be?"

Ida Mae pondered this. "Doesn't sound like anybody I've ever known."

"Me, either. I don't know if Ray wanted me to keep it in confidence, but I didn't think I should tell Kristin about it. Anything the police want in the paper, they'll tell her."

"That makes sense to me," Ida Mae said. "Tell you what, Claudia. Anything we find out or think of that might be connected with one of these murders, let's not tell anybody but the police. Not our families, not Kristin, and certainly not Vonda."

That suited Claudia just fine, especially the part about Vonda. Vonda had disappeared about the time one woman was murdered, and she had returned just before another one was killed. Claudia was afraid there might be a connection.

WHEN SHE ARRIVED AT her apartment, Kristin unlocked the door, stepped inside, and reached for the light switch. Then she stopped. Something was different. She stood in the darkness, listening. All she could hear was the hum of the air conditioning. That was it: there were no sounds from next door. She flipped on the lights and walked into her bedroom. It, too, was blessedly quiet. The Loflins must not be home.

The silence was so wonderful that Kristin decided to forgo the eleven o'clock news. She prepared for bed, put her library books on the bedside table, and propped up her pillows so she could read. When she picked up one of the books, the words *mysterious killing* on its dust jacket turned her thoughts to the murders in Oak Hill. She hadn't discovered anything tonight, but she wasn't ready to give up. Maybe if she reviewed everything she knew, an idea would come to her. She'd close her eyes and think…

The ringing of the phone jolted her awake. The lamp was still on, and the clock on the bedside table said two a.m.

She fumbled for the phone.

"Hello," she said groggily.

"You better mind your own business," a muffled voice said, "or you're going to get hurt."

"What?"

"I said, you better mind your own business, or you'll end up as dead as Daphne Whittier."

When she put down the phone, there was silence in the room—far too much silence. Suddenly Kristin found herself wishing for the blare of TV or angry shouts. Where were obnoxious neighbors when you needed them?

TEN

To all those armchair quarterbacks who think they know more about how to fight crime than the police department does, I say back off and let us do our job.

Police Chief Boyd Cates, in a letter to the *Oak Hill Sentinel*

WHEN KRISTIN WOKE UP, the sun was streaming in around the blinds. She squinted at the bedside clock. Nine-thirty. Was she late for work? No, this was Saturday, she was almost sure. She closed her eyes, sank back on the pillow, and tried to figure out why she felt as though she'd been run over by a truck—a monster truck like Darren Loflin's, with fog lights and giant tires.

Then she remembered the two a.m. phone call and the muffled voice saying, "You'll end up as dead as Daphne Whittier."

Kristin was suddenly wide awake. Now she knew why she felt so bad. She'd hardly slept the night before. After she heard the caller's threat, she'd slammed down the phone, turned on all the lights, and checked her doors and windows.

Then she'd lain awake for hours, wondering if she should call the police.

This morning the apartment was still eerily silent. Feeling uneasy, Kristin made another check of her doors and windows. All of them were securely locked.

She quickly showered, pulled on a T-shirt and jeans, and set out for the newspaper office. Bill would know what she should do about the threatening call. He'd been a journalist for over twenty years, so he'd probably received threats himself. Besides, he was usually at work on Saturday mornings, which gave her a perfect excuse to leave her apartment. Not that she was scared, she told herself—just a little uncomfortable, that was all.

As she drove through Oak Hill's peaceful streets, Kristin's anxiety began to fade. By the time she reached the newspaper office, she was sure she'd overreacted to the call. Maybe someone had been playing a prank or had called the wrong number.

"I don't know if I should even mention this to you," she began apologetically when she reached the editor's office.

When she told Bill what the caller had said, he seemed to take it seriously. "Have you told the police about this?" he asked, running a hand through his thinning hair.

"I wanted to talk to you first."

"Your caller was right, you know. Poking around in these murders could get you hurt." He frowned. "You're supposed to report on the murders, Kristin, not investigate them."

"I haven't done much investigating," Kristin protested. "I've talked to Ida Mae Poindexter and her neighbor, Claudia McNeill, but they haven't told me anything useful. I've started looking through old newspapers, too, but I haven't found anything related to the earlier murder."

"That's all you've done?"

"Well, I…um…I talked to Buddy Daniels about the rezoning, as background for my city council stories. When I mentioned Daphne Whittier, he told me I'd better not write anything that sounded like he might profit from her death."

"Did he mention his lawyers?"

"I…yes, I believe he did."

Bill grinned. "Buddy likes to threaten people with his lawyers. He's never actually sued anybody, though a number of people have sued him over the years. I don't think he was your anonymous caller. Buddy likes to see people squirm. It's more his style to make a threat in the middle of a golf game or over lunch at the Oak Hill Inn."

Kristin blushed. There really were no secrets in Oak Hill. "You heard about that? I offered to pay for my lunch. In case it was a conflict of interest, I mean. But he wouldn't let me."

Bill chuckled. "Don't worry about it. Buddy knows by now that to bribe one of my reporters, he'd have to offer a full-course dinner, not just lunch. Anyway, if you're going to write about local politics, you have to know the players, and Buddy is definitely a player."

"I heard he stands to lose his shirt if the Big Mart deal doesn't go through."

Bill raised his eyebrows. "You heard that, too? You must have good sources."

Kristin smiled, but said nothing. Her boss might not be impressed to know that her only sources were a pair of elderly woman.

"You need to tell the police about the threatening call," Bill said. "Not just for your own safety, but because it may tie in with the murders. Call the police department and ask them to track down Wayne Henley or Ray Shelton for you. And be careful, Kristin. Where is it you live? York Towne Apartments? Is it safe there?"

She nodded. "I had dead bolt locks installed when I moved in. Anyway, the walls are so thin, my neighbors will hear me if I yell."

As soon as she'd said it, Kristin realized the thin walls wouldn't be much help. Right now, the Loflins didn't appear to be home. When their TV was blaring, they wouldn't hear her screams, and Mr. Parks, her downstairs neighbor, had told her he took his hearing aids out at night. She'd have to depend on those dead bolts.

After promising Bill that she'd be careful, Kristin left for home. Once she was back in her apartment, she called the police station and asked the dispatcher to have one of the detectives get in touch with her.

"There's no hurry," she added. "It isn't an emergency." This was Saturday, so she assumed they were enjoying a day off. If Ray received her message, he'd be very professional, she was sure. But if Wayne was interrupted when he was involved in some important Saturday activity like washing his car or watching sports on TV, she could just imagine what his attitude would be.

When her phone rang a short time later, Kristin crossed her fingers for luck, hoping the caller was Detective Shelton.

"This is Wayne. What's up?"

She rolled her eyes. Yes, Ray would have been *much* more professional. "I had a threatening phone call. Bill Caldwell thought I should tell you about it."

"Are you okay?"

"Am I okay? Well, of course I am. It happened last night, and it was only a phone call. I didn't know if I should tell you, but Bill—"

"You going to be home for a while?" Wayne

interrupted. "I might as well come by. Where do you live?"

When she told him, he said, "Be there in ten minutes." Then the phone clicked off.

Kristin debated whether she should change her clothes and put on makeup, but decided against it. When Wayne arrived at her door in a wrinkled T-shirt, cut-off jeans, and ratty sneakers with no socks, she was glad she hadn't bothered.

"Nice place," he said, looking around the living room.

"Thanks." Most of the furniture had belonged to her parents. Sometimes it reminded her of their death and made her sad, but most of the time she found the familiar things comforting.

"I've arrested people here a couple of times," the detective said, "and believe me, their apartments didn't look half as good as yours."

Oh, great. She had criminals for neighbors. She resisted the temptation to ask if he'd ever arrested Tammy or Darren Loflin.

He pulled a notebook and a pen from his back pocket. "Okay, tell me what happened."

Kristin told him everything she remembered about last night's phone call.

Wayne frowned. "You haven't been playing Nancy Drew, have you? You're not supposed to be investigating crimes. That's our job. You could get hurt."

That was exactly what Bill had said. What was it with these guys? Come to think of it, hadn't the voice on the phone said the same thing? Kristin gave Wayne a searching look. Would he make an anonymous call to stop her from meddling in a police investigation?

"What are you looking at?" he said, his face reddening.

"I—oh, nothing." She could imagine the explosion if she suggested he might have made the threatening phone call.

"The caller could have been Buddy Daniels," Kristin said. She told Wayne about her meeting with the real estate man.

"He took you to lunch?"

She nodded, glad that he sounded surprised. At least one person in town hadn't heard about her meal at the Oak Hill Inn.

The detective frowned. "I wouldn't hang around with Buddy Daniels if I were you. He's a little too slick for his own good."

Kristin decided to change the subject. "Did you know Daphne Whittier visited Wilton Treadwell's law office the day she was killed?" She wondered if he'd already heard that piece of information via Claudia and her grandson Ray.

"She did?"

"Uh-huh. I saw her go into his office while you

and I were eating lunch in Myrtle's Grill, but I didn't realize who she was until last night. Mr. Treadwell's sister was there, too, but she left before—"

"Whoa! Let me take a few notes. Tell me who, when, and where. Wilton Treadwell may be able to give us the *why* unless it's some kind of lawyer-client privilege thing."

"I don't think Miss Whittier was a client of his. Grady Wallace was her lawyer."

Wayne looked at her suspiciously. "How do you know that?"

"I have my sources," Kristin said, attempting a mysterious smile.

Wayne snorted. "Oh, yeah?"

"I also heard Buddy Daniels will be in financial trouble if the Big Mart deal fails."

"I guess your *sources* told you that, too?"

Kristin nodded.

Wayne grinned. "I think I saw you with your sources last night, chowing down on punch and cookies with the retired folks."

Kristin felt the color rising in her cheeks.

"Hey, there's nothing wrong with tapping into the Pleasant Valley rumor mill," Wayne said. He grinned. "I go out there and check in with my granny at least once a week. Believe me, if the folks at Pleasant Valley haven't heard it, it hasn't happened."

MOST OF THE DAY, IDA Mae had been too busy to worry about her sister. She'd started out early, making a trip to the supermarket as soon as it opened. On the way home, she stopped at the gas station to fill up her car at the self-serve pump, the way Norma had taught her. After that she made a seven-layer salad and a coconut cake to take to Betty Jo's for Sunday dinner.

Next she mopped the kitchen and bathroom floors, vacuumed the carpets, wiped down the kitchen cabinets, and straightened and dusted everything else. Pleasant Valley had people who'd clean your apartment for a fee, and her nieces had offered to pay for it, but she wouldn't let them. She'd done her own cleaning all her life. Why shouldn't she do it now, when she had so little else to do?

By three o'clock Saturday afternoon Ida Mae was tired, but she was pleased with all she'd accomplished. She sat down in her favorite chair in the living room and opened her new crossword puzzle magazine. She'd had the chair reupholstered when she moved to Pleasant Valley. The new cushion didn't fit her bottom as well as the saggy old one had, but when Vonda showed up at her door, Ida Mae was glad she'd had her furniture redone. The chair was a pretty blue that matched the flowers in the sofa. With her new brass floor lamp beside it, the chair was perfect for reading or doing puzzles. Yes, her apartment looked nice, though she knew it couldn't compare with what Vonda had in Atlanta.

Vonda! Now there was a real puzzle! Last night at the talent show, Vonda had spent the evening with Frank Rowland and his friends, hardly speaking to Ida Mae, her own sister, who was right there in the same room. Now that Ida Mae had time to think about it, Vonda's behavior seemed mighty strange. She'd gotten above her raising, that was sure. Vonda had grown up poor, and she'd worked in a hosiery mill alongside her sisters. So how did she get to be so high and mighty?

"You're no more and no less than anybody else," Mama and Papa had always said. "Hold your head high, but not your nose."

Of course, looking back, Ida Mae could see that her parents hadn't held everybody equal. They wanted black people to stand at the back door, hat in hand. Papa didn't think much of Catholics, either, though she doubted he'd ever met one. That was the old days, and times had changed, thank the good Lord.

Vonda thought she was so up-to-date, going to a gym and putting olive oil and those foreign-sounding greens in her salads, but she wanted to spend her time with people like Frank Rowland and the Treadwells, who'd been important in the old days. That was old-fashioned in Ida Mae's book.

Ida Mae sighed. If she kept thinking about her sister, she was going to get herself upset. No use fretting over somebody as silly as Vonda. No, she'd better start a crossword puzzle and forget about her.

About the time Ida Mae filled the first word in her crossword puzzle, Claudia was in the lobby of the Pleasant Valley Nursing Center, looking at the sign that listed the patients' names and room numbers. She'd just spent twenty minutes visiting a friend from her church. Now she had a half hour before the shuttle van took her back to her apartment. Was there anyone else she could visit?

"Mrs. McNeill, is that you?" An ebony-skinned man, skinny, with a fringe of white hair around a bald dome, was moving toward her slowly, using a walker.

"Why, Mr. Haizler," Claudia said. "I didn't know you were here."

"Been here three weeks. I fell and busted my hip. Soon as they let me out of the hospital, I moved in here."

"Were you still living on your farm?"

"Yep. All by myself. Had to crawl to the phone to call the ambulance. I was leaving that old farm anyway, but I didn't mean to go that way."

Claudia nodded. She'd heard that the new interstate highway was going through Mr. Haizler's land, making it possible for the elderly man to sell his farm for more money than he'd seen in a lifetime of hard work.

"When the folks at the hospital told me I'd have to go into a nursing home, I asked where the best place was, and they told me Pleasant Valley." He grinned. "I'll say! Good food, a room all to myself, and pretty nurses to look after me. Only bad thing is, they're gonna kick me out as soon as I get better. But I've signed up for an apartment over there in what they call the Main Building."

"That's wonderful," Claudia said. Mr. Haizler's land must have brought a pretty penny indeed. Apartments in the three-story building at the center of Pleasant Valley were less expensive than the duplexes where she and Ida Mae lived, but nothing in the retirement community came cheap. The cottages, where Vonda's friend Frank lived, were the most expensive.

"If you can spare the time, keep me company a few minutes. We can sit in the lounge," the elderly man said, indicating a large room that opened off the lobby.

"Why, I'd like that," Claudia said. She might miss the van, but there'd be another one coming along. She doubted that Mr. Haizler, a childless widower who must be close to ninety, had many visitors. Besides, she'd thought of something she wanted to ask him.

Mr. Haizler carefully lowered himself into a wing chair, and Claudia took a seat on the sofa beside it.

"So you sold your farm," she said.

The old man nodded. "Lived there all my life. My daddy bought a little bit of land from Mr. Asa Treadwell in 1922, and I added to it. Bought most of it from the Treadwells. They never would sell me the part near their homeplace, though." He paused. "They were smart to keep it. The interstate's going through their land, too."

"You had some wealthy folk for neighbors."

"Not after Mr. Asa and his wife passed. Mr. Asa's son Carter built that big house in town when Miss Adelaide and her brothers were just little tykes. A little later on, when they were teenagers, they used to come back out to that vacant house of their granddaddy's. Did a little drinkin' out there, and a little courtin,' too. I reckon their daddy never knew."

Claudia smiled, thinking of the staid and proper woman she'd seen at the talent show the night before. It was hard to imagine Adelaide Treadwell as a teenager with a wild streak.

When Mr. Haizler paused in his reminiscences, Claudia said, "Those bones they dug up have made me think about the old days, right after the war. I was a young married woman then, and Layton was going to college."

"Right after the war," the old man said. For a moment he seemed lost in his memories—good memories, Claudia supposed, because he was smiling.

"I was out of the Navy then," he said, "and mighty glad to be home. I enlisted as soon as the war started. Lula had to run the farm while I was away. Did a good job of it, too."

Claudia nodded. Lula Haizler, who'd died a few years before, had worked hard all her life. It was a shame she hadn't lived long enough to enjoy the money from the sale of the farm.

"Back then, do you remember hearing of a woman called Leonora?"

"Black woman?"

Claudia nodded. "Light. Maybe straight hair."

Mr. Haizler pursed his lips and wrinkled his brow. "Leonora. Leonora. Only woman I ever knew named that—yep, it would have been along about then. Funny, I can't remember what I ate for breakfast, but I can bring back what happened fifty years ago clear as a bell."

Claudia smiled. She knew exactly what he meant.

"Came down from somewhere north and only stayed here a little while. She used to walk out our way, and sometimes she'd stop and talk. Mighty friendly, considering who she was."

Claudia waited expectantly.

"That little dirt road where Lula and me lived was the tail end of Tabor Street, stretching out into the country. Our nearest neighbors, after the Treadwells moved to town, were those doctors and teachers and such on Tabor Street. Of course, we didn't mingle with them any more than we mingled with the Treadwells."

"Who was she? The woman who used to walk out toward your farm, I mean."

"Who? Oh, that Leonora woman? Why, she was Miss Daphne Whittier's sister."

ELEVEN

It is by remembering the past that we understand the present.

From *Memories of Old Oak Hill*
by Isabel Rowland Everhart

A SMILE SPREAD OVER Ray's face as he tasted the pound cake.

"Great cake, Grandma. Did you make it?"

"My goodness, no. Pound cake is Ida Mae's specialty. I'll tell her you liked it."

"Confess, Grandma," he said after another bite of cake. "Did you invite me over because you felt sorry for me, a good-looking single fellow all alone on a Saturday night? Or do you have something you want to talk to me about?"

Claudia smiled. "I don't feel a bit sorry for you. Not when there are so many nice single women in town who'd like to get to know you better. No, I just wanted to talk to you."

"Please tell me you're not matchmaking. Tell me you haven't thought of some granddaughter of a friend of yours who'd be perfect for me, even though she has six school-age children, two angry ex-husbands, and a nasty temper."

Claudia couldn't believe the woman Ray's mother had tried to interest him in the other day was anything like that. But Vivian's matchmaking was a subject she didn't want to get into. "No, it's something different. I have things I need to tell you."

She decided to start with the easiest one. "Last night after the talent show, Kristin Grant told me she saw Miss Whittier go into Wilton Treadwell's office the day she was killed."

He nodded.

"You knew that already?"

"She told Wayne, and he told me. Did you know Kristin had a threatening phone call last night?"

"Oh, no! Could it have something to do with Miss Whittier's murder?"

"Maybe. I guess somebody thought she was doing a little too much investigating."

Claudia nodded, remembering Kristin's questions after the talent show. The reporter had definitely been trying to find out whatever she could about the murders.

Ray gave his grandmother a stern look. "I heard about that mess you got into yesterday down near Sneed's Crossroads. I want you to promise me you won't go on any more fool trips with that neighbor of yours."

"I wouldn't want to go on any more like that one," Claudia said, shivering at the memory of the woman with the shotgun. "I guess Wayne told you about that, too."

Ray nodded. "Don't tell anybody what you saw there, Grandma. It could be dangerous."

"I won't," Claudia assured him, "and Ida Mae won't, either."

Then she frowned. "You didn't mention my trip to Ida Mae's homeplace to your mother, did you?" Vivian thought it was dangerous for Claudia to ride to the supermarket with Ida Mae. If she learned they'd gone for a drive in the country and had been menaced by a woman with a shotgun, she'd have a pure fit.

Ray grinned. "Don't worry. I have to tell Wayne things. It's part of my job. But I learned a long time ago not to let Mom in on everything I know."

"There's something else I'd better tell you," Claudia said. She recounted her conversation with Mr. Haizler and added, "He's an old man, and his memory may be playing tricks on him."

"You don't remember Miss Whittier having a sister staying with her?"

"No, but I probably wouldn't have known it. That was before Layton started teaching. He and I were just country people back then. We didn't mix with Miss Whittier's sort of folk."

"You say this Haizler fellow is in the Pleasant Valley Nursing Center?"

"Ray, please don't go bothering that old man. If you do, I'll regret I ever mentioned it to you."

Ray took his grandmother's hands in his. "You want the person who killed that woman caught, don't you?"

"Yes, but—" How could she say it without sounding like Jamal, who thought all police officers were racists? "I don't want anybody trying to pin a murder on Mr. Haizler just because he lived near the place where the bones were found or because he thinks he once met someone named Leonora—or because he's black."

"Now Grandma, you know we wouldn't do that. But we'll have to speak with him. We talked to Marcus Whittier, Daphne Whittier's nephew, when he was here for the funeral. He says his father had two sisters. He's pretty sure the other one was named Leonora. No one said much about her, and he had the feeling she'd disgraced the family in some way. He said she died before he was born—of pneumonia, he was told. If that's true, she wasn't the murder victim. So don't you worry about Mr. Haizler."

Claudia was still concerned about her elderly friend. "It wasn't Mr. Haizler's land where those bones were found," she said. "It was Treadwell land. Before you harass poor Mr. Haizler, why don't you ask Wilton Treadwell why Miss Whittier went to see him?"

"Oh, we'll talk to him, all right." Ray looked at his watch. "I'd better be on my way and let you get your beauty sleep so you'll look pretty at church tomorrow."

"There's one more thing," Claudia said. She hesitated, hoping she wasn't about to stir up more trouble by mentioning this. "The other day when I called you about Troy Bandry, you told me he had an alibi, so he wasn't a suspect. That alibi—it wasn't Jamal, was it?"

Claudia didn't want to think that her grandson would lie to the police to get a friend out of trouble. But if he thought his friend was innocent and had been unjustly accused—well, young people sometimes did foolish things.

Ray smiled and shook his head. "It wasn't Jamal. Troy has a lot to thank Daphne Whittier for. When he was arrested on that drug charge, he was fired from his job at Big Bob's Burgers. Miss Whittier talked Big Bob into giving Troy another chance. He was there Monday night, mopping floors and cleaning the place. His mom picked him up around midnight. She's been keeping him on a short leash since his arrest, taking him to work and picking him up afterward. It's bound to be embarrassing for Troy to ride everywhere with his mother, but it took him off our list of suspects."

Claudia smiled with relief.

ON SUNDAY MORNING IDA Mae was in her usual pew at church, the fifth from the front, where she used to sit with Odell. She was trying to keep her mind on Reverend Farley's sermon, but her thoughts kept wandering. And why wouldn't they? He was preaching on the lost sheep, and in Ida Mae's almost eighty years of church attendance, she'd heard just about everything anybody could say about that story.

As the minister described the shepherd spending hours, maybe days, searching for the missing animal, Ida Mae's mind drifted back to the farm where she'd grown up. Molly, their old cow, would never have wandered off like a silly sheep. But once or twice the mules had run off. Catching them and bringing them back had been exciting.

"He never gave up," the minister intoned, interrupting Ida Mae's memories of runaway livestock. She supposed Reverend Farley was going to say that God would go after us no matter how lost we were, just like the shepherd went after that one lost sheep. Where had she heard that first? Probably at Big Hickory Baptist Church when she was just a little thing. Ida Mae's mind wandered back to hot summer Sundays with flies buzzing in through the open windows of the church and her mother fanning her with a cardboard fan that advertised a funeral parlor.

"—our brothers and sisters who have wronged us," Reverend Farley thundered, bringing Ida Mae back to the present. Suddenly she was all ears. Hadn't Vonda wronged her family, first by running off, and then, when she finally came back, by getting crossways with Ida Mae, who'd welcomed her with open arms?

She listened as Reverend Farley said we should never give up trying to make things right between ourselves and others, "both those we've wronged and those who've wronged us."

Ida Mae felt a little guilty. Sure, she'd tried to patch up her quarrel with Vonda by inviting her to ride out to their homeplace. But after Vonda turned her down, she'd left her sister to stew in her own juice. At the reception after the talent show, Vonda had frequently looked in her sister's direction, and each time Ida Mae had started talking to Claudia or Kristin to show how little she cared.

By the time the choir started singing "God Be with You till We Meet Again," Ida Mae had resolved to do better. On her way out of church, she looked Reverend Farley in the eye, shook his hand firmly, and said, "Your sermon brought me up short."

A little later, driving to Betty Jo's house with

her coconut cake and seven-layer salad, Ida Mae thought about how upset Vonda must be with the two of them on bad terms. She became a little misty-eyed as she imagined Vonda apologizing for acting so ugly the day she moved out.

But when Ida Mae arrived at Betty Jo's, Vonda was sitting in the living room like a queen, with Betty Jo's husband, Carson, and his son-in-law, Brian, hanging on her every word. She didn't look the least bit concerned that she and Ida Mae weren't speaking. Ida Mae gave the trio a frosty look and headed for the kitchen, where she found Betty Jo taking a roast from the oven and Betty Jo's daughter, Heather, filling glasses with iced tea.

"Since Vonda's sitting out there talking to the men, I thought you might need some help," Ida Mae said.

"Isn't Aunt Vonda delightful?" Betty Jo said. "She came by my shop Friday and took me out to lunch."

Ida Mae made a sound that was halfway between a snort and a cough.

During the meal Vonda complimented Ida Mae's dress and talked to her as though nothing had gone wrong between them. With Vonda being so nice and Reverend Farley's sermon rattling around in her head, Ida Mae felt much friendlier toward her sister—until Vonda brought up the talent show.

"I talked to Adelaide and Wilton Treadwell while I was there," she said.

Ida Mae's back stiffened. She didn't want to hear about Vonda's upper-crust friends, but she knew she'd have to. When Vonda took hold of a subject, she didn't let it loose.

"Adelaide kept going on about how Oak Hill had changed for the worse," Vonda said. "I finally had enough of it. I told her the town seemed a lot better to me now than when I was working in her daddy's hosiery mill. She stuck her nose up in the air and stalked off."

Ida Mae grinned. Score one for Vonda.

"She'll probably cut me dead at the bridge club," Vonda went on, "but I don't care. The whole club's mad at her anyway. She told them they'd have to start meeting in the afternoon because she didn't drive at night anymore. They were hoping she'd drop out, but she made such a fuss they gave in and changed the meeting time. That made Edith Carvey so mad she quit the club, which is how they had room for me. I'm taking Edith's place."

"You've joined a bridge club!" Betty Jo said. "Oh, Aunt Vonda, I hope that means you're thinking of moving to Oak Hill permanently."

Vonda beamed. "I'm considering it. As Frank says, roots are so important when we grow older. And my roots are here."

Everybody but Ida Mae looked at her blankly.

"Frank?" Betty Jo asked.

"Frank Rowland. He's been trying to convince me I should come to live in Pleasant Valley. He says a cottage will be available soon, and I may be able to get it."

Betty Jo, Carson, Heather, and Brian all started talking at once, encouraging Vonda to move to the retirement community. Ida Mae looked at her sister with a mixture of dismay, astonishment, and admiration. Vonda was a fast worker.

ON MONDAY MORNING, CLAUDIA stood at the shuttle van stop, dabbing her face with a handkerchief and wondering if she'd made a mistake by coming out on such a hot day. When the van pulled up, she climbed inside, greeted the driver and the three other passengers, and sank into a seat, grateful for the air conditioning.

As the van passed the Nursing Center, Claudia felt a twinge of guilt. She hoped Ray hadn't upset Mr. Haizler. On the other hand, the old man might have been glad for the company, even if his visitor was a policeman.

In a few minutes the van reached the Main Building, where a shiny new bus with *Pleasant Valley Retirement Center* in sky-blue letters on each side was ready for the trip to town. When Claudia boarded the bus, the first person she saw was Mildred Pitts, who had taught at the high school with Layton.

"Come sit with me," Mildred said, indicating the empty seat beside her. "Isn't it awful about Daphne Whittier?" Then, without waiting for Claudia's response, she launched into an account of her first meeting with the educator thirty years before. She talked until the bus driver tapped on his microphone for attention.

"We're going to grocery stores and drugstores this morning, folks—Food Lion, Lowe's Foods, Eckerd, and CVS. Remember, it's hot outside. Wait inside the store until I come back for you."

On the trip into town Mildred switched to a new topic. Claudia put in an occasional sympathetic remark as the woman expounded on her recent gallbladder surgery. At the first stop, Food Lion, Claudia exited the bus, glad that her talkative companion preferred the other supermarket.

Claudia didn't need much. Her children and grandchildren kept her well supplied with groceries, and last week she'd ridden to the supermarket with Ida Mae. In ten minutes her shopping was done. Was there somewhere else she could go? Out the store window, she saw a shoe repair shop, a tire store, and a beauty salon—nothing she needed. But if she went through the parking lot of the tire store, she'd be on Main Street, not far from the post office. She could use some stamps, and the walk might do her good. Surely she'd be back in time for the bus.

She set off, her purse in one hand and her bag of groceries in the other. It was hotter and more humid than it had been earlier. Several times she had to transfer her purse to the hand with the grocery bag, so she could take her handkerchief from her pocket and mop her face. By the time she reached the post office, her legs were rubbery.

When she was inside, she set her purse and groceries on a table and leaned against it to catch her breath, telling herself she'd feel better once she cooled off. At a table nearby, a slim young woman with her hair in beaded braids was sticking stamps on a stack of envelopes. She looked familiar, but Claudia was too tired to try to remember who she was.

A few minutes later, Claudia had purchased her stamps and was ready to go back to the supermarket. But when she left the post office, the air was a stifling, soggy blanket, and the sunlight was blinding. After a few steps she was too dizzy to go any farther. She sat down on a low wall outside the post office, closed her eyes, and waited for the dizziness to pass.

"Are you all right?"

Claudia opened her eyes. The young woman she'd seen in the post office was looking down at her.

"Oh, I'm fine, thank you," Claudia said, embarrassed. She hadn't meant to make a spectacle of herself. "I was a little dizzy. I'm feeling much better now." She reached for her grocery bag and stood up.

"Why don't you let me walk you to your car to make sure you're okay?"

"Thank you, but I'm taking the bus from Food Lion. It's not far. I just needed to catch my breath, that's all."

"May I drive you to the bus? I'm Stacy Whittier. I think I've seen you at church, Mount of Olives United Methodist."

Of course. The girl was Daphne Whittier's relative, the one who'd been staying with her. Claudia had seen her at the funeral and at church yesterday morning with her parents and brother. "I'm Claudia McNeill. I'm so sorry about your great-aunt. She'll certainly be missed."

"Thank you. Everyone has been so kind." Stacy gave Claudia a worried look. "Please let me give you a ride."

Claudia started to shake her head, but Food Lion suddenly seemed far away. "Thank you. It would be a help."

A minute later Claudia was sitting in the passenger seat of a lime-green Volkswagen bug with the air conditioning blowing over her.

"How long till your bus comes?" Stacy asked

as she backed out of the parking space. "I could drive you home."

"Oh, no, I don't want to put you to any trouble."

"No trouble. My brother flew back to Boston last night, and Dad and Mom are seeing Aunt Daphne's lawyer this morning. I'm at loose ends until I meet them for lunch. I was running errands so I wouldn't have to spend the morning staring at the walls in the Oak Hill Inn."

Claudia had heard that the Whittiers, Stacy included, were at the inn. She couldn't blame them for not wanting to sleep in the house where Miss Whittier had been murdered. She wondered where Stacy would stay after her parents left town.

Stacy let the car idle before pulling out into the street. She seemed to be considering something. "I think someone in your family mentioned you to me. Are you related to Detective Shelton?"

"Ray's my grandson."

"He was the one who told me about Aunt Daphne's— about what happened to her," Stacy said in a shaky voice. "I still can't believe she's gone."

It occurred to Claudia that the young woman might want to talk to someone. In that case, she'd be glad to listen. "If it's not too much trouble," she said, "I'd appreciate a ride home. But I'll need to stop at Food Lion first to make sure someone tells the bus driver."

A half hour later, the two women were in Claudia's living room with tall glasses of iced tea, and Stacy was admiring the photographs of Claudia's family.

"Such a nice big family. My dad was an only child. We tell my brother it's up to him to carry on the Whittier name." Stacy pointed to a picture of a young man in a cap and gown. "Is that Detective Shelton?"

"His college graduation picture," Claudia said. She wondered if she should mention that Ray was divorced, had no children, and was considering going to law school. Maybe not. Stacy's father was a business executive, quite well-to-do, Claudia had heard. The young woman would probably prefer someone who was already a lawyer, and a successful one at that.

"He and the other detective took me back into Aunt Daphne's house to see if I noticed anything unusual. Everything was the same except for a photograph."

"The picture of a woman named Leonora?"

Stacy looked surprised. "You know about it? The police found it on the floor in Aunt Daphne's living room. I'd never seen it before. I guess the woman in the picture was a relative I never knew I had. My dad recognized the name, but he didn't know much about her."

"She was your grandfather's sister?"

Stacy nodded. "My father's parents died when

I was little. After that, Aunt Daphne was all the family we had on my father's side." Her lower lip began to tremble. "It was horrible, what happened to her. I hope the police find the person who did it."

Claudia patted Stacy's hand. "Ray's working on it day and night."

Stacy looked troubled. "Mrs. McNeill, I wasn't quite honest with your grandson. I didn't tell him that Aunt Daphne and I had an argument the day she died. That's why I spent the night in Greensboro. I feel terrible about it. If I'd been there, maybe she wouldn't have been killed."

"Don't let yourself think that," Claudia said. "You couldn't have been there all the time. If somebody wanted to hurt your aunt, you couldn't have stopped them."

"Maybe so. But I hate it that our last time together was spent fighting."

Claudia wondered if Stacy's argument with her great-aunt was something the police needed to know. She hoped not. She already had Mr. Haizler on her conscience. Would she have to reveal Stacy's secrets to Ray, too?

"I didn't want Mom and Dad to know about the argument. Before I came to stay with Aunt Daphne, they gave me a firm talk about not upsetting her. She was from the old school, you know, and she had pretty strong opinions. I did my best, but how did I know she was going to freak out when I told her about Jeffrey?"

Was Jeffrey the name of Stacy's brother? Claudia couldn't remember. She waited for her guest to continue.

"Jeffrey was my best buddy in high school. Not a boyfriend, just a friend. He lives in Greensboro now, and we've seen each other a little since I've been here. Aunt Daphne flipped out when I mentioned he was white. I shouldn't have argued with her, but I was tired of pretending to agree with her opinions. Anyway, when Aunt Daphne was telling me all the reasons why I should leave white men alone, she mentioned a family member who 'made the same mistake and was lost to us as a result'—whatever that means. I've been wondering, could that person have been her sister, Leonora?"

Claudia was wondering the same thing. She was already convinced from her conversation with Mr. Haizler that the Leonora in the picture was Daphne Whittier's sister and that she'd spent some time in Oak Hill. If Leonora had been involved with a white man, could he have been someone in Oak Hill? Claudia wasn't sure why, but for some reason Vonda's friend Frank Rowland came to mind.

TWELVE

Amateurs can get into a world of trouble when they try to do things best left to officers of the law.

Police Chief Boyd Cates, in a letter
to the *Oak Hill Sentinel*

WHEN KRISTIN FINISHED her presentation to Ms. Barnes's fourth grade class, hands began waving in the air. Some of the children wanted to talk about family members or friends who'd been featured in the *Sentinel*, but others had questions about her job as a reporter.

"Have you ever interviewed a criminal?" a little girl asked, wide-eyed.

The image of Buddy Daniels popped into Kristin's mind. "No. No criminals," she said, wondering if her answer was accurate. She'd written about dozens of people since coming to Oak Hill. Who knew what secrets were hidden in their pasts? For all she knew, she could have interviewed one of the murderers she'd been trying to find, maybe even written a glowing story about him for the *Sentinel*.

Half a dozen questions later, Ms. Barnes called a halt, pointing out that the class was due in the lunchroom in a few minutes. "Let's thank Ms. Grant for coming to talk to us," she said. There was a round of applause.

"We'd love for you to eat lunch with us," the teacher said to Kristin, triggering more applause.

Kristin thought for a few seconds, balancing memories of school cafeteria food against the fun she'd had so far on this visit.

"Sure," she said. A few minutes later she was seated at a child-size table with a tray of pizza, applesauce, and milk in front of her, trying to carry on a conversation above the din of the lunchroom.

When the children finished eating, they began leaving the cafeteria for the playground. Kristin was about to leave, too, when someone tapped her on the shoulder. She looked around and saw a skinny blond boy in a faded T-shirt and jeans. She remembered that he had listened to her presentation in the classroom intently, but hadn't asked any questions. Now he motioned for her to follow him into a corner of the lunchroom where it was a little quieter.

"You came to my street when the old lady was killed," he said. "She lived next door to us."

Kristin felt a surge of excitement. "I remember you," she said. This was the boy who claimed to have seen something on the night of the crime.

"My mom didn't want me to tell you what I saw. She thought the killer was a drug dealer, and he might come back and hurt us," the boy said. "But it wasn't a drug dealer. It was a lady. I saw her."

"Do you know who she was?"

"Nope. I couldn't see her good."

"Why do you think it was a lady?"

"Her hair. It was kind of shiny. Gold maybe, or silver."

"Could you see anything else?"

"She was driving a big black car. After she went in the old lady's house, I heard a noise like a gunshot. Then she came back out like she was in a big hurry."

Kristin hoped the boy's knowledge of gunshots came from television, not from personal experience. "Did you tell the police what you saw?"

He shook his head. "They didn't ask me. Anyway, my mom wouldn't let me talk to them. She said I'd be asking for trouble." He paused. "Are you gonna tell them?"

"Would that be all right with you?"

He nodded. "I want them to find that woman and put her in jail. I don't want her coming around our street and killing people."

No, Kristin thought. She didn't want that, either. She was going to tell her boss the boy's story, and then, unless he told her not to, she was going to tell the police.

AN HOUR LATER, KRISTIN arrived at the police station. "Detective Shelton is expecting me," she said as she breezed by the receptionist.

She knocked on the door of the detectives' office, and Ray's voice called, "Come in."

When she opened the door, she saw he was on the phone. He smiled and motioned her to a seat.

While she eavesdropped on the detective's conversation, which consisted mainly of *Uh-huh* and *I see,* Kristin looked around the office. There were two desks. The unoccupied one had a small wooden sign saying *B. Wayne Henley.* A quick glance at the walls told her Ray had a degree from a four-year college, and Wayne had a two-year degree from a community college. A dozen or so framed certificates attested that both men had attended a variety of law enforcement workshops.

Ray's half of the room held several family photos. In one of them, Kristin recognized Claudia with a man who must have been her husband. The two were surrounded by several generations of people all dressed in the styles of twenty years before.

The other half of the room featured photos of Wayne holding large fish and looking proudly at the camera. There were also two pictures of football teams. Kristin easily picked out Wayne in each one by his husky frame, blond hair, and belligerent expression.

"One of those teams is Oak Hill High School the year they were state champions, and the other's Wake Forest," Ray said, his phone call over.

"Wake Forest? But he didn't graduate?"

"No, he lost his athletic scholarship after he busted his knee," Ray said. "Came back here, went to community college, and joined the police force." He looked at her speculatively. "Wayne's a real nice guy, Kristin."

"I'm sure he is," she said.

"Sometimes he doesn't come across that way."

Kristin grinned. "You can say that again." Then she blushed as Wayne came into the room.

"Kristin wants to talk to us about the Whittier case," Ray said. "She found out something interesting when she was at the elementary school this morning."

Kristin told them the boy's name, Kyle Peters, as well as his mother's name, address, and phone number. "He told me he wanted the police to know about this. Bill Caldwell said I should tell you about it."

Wayne frowned. "You're not planning to put this story in the paper, are you?" His face reddened. "You could be endangering the boy's life just to sell newspapers."

Her temper rising, Kristin held up a hand to stop him. "Of course we aren't going to print the boy's story. I should think you'd thank me for telling you about it. It could be important. At least it lets you know Daphne Whittier wasn't killed by some big drug supplier."

"What makes you think a big drug supplier can't be a woman?"

"You mean one of the local drug kingpins is female?"

"I never said that," Wayne said, glaring at her. "And don't you dare put it in the paper."

IDA MAE WAS WORRIED about Claudia. She knew something was wrong when she saw her get out of the lime-green Volkswagen. Claudia had taken the Pleasant Valley bus to town, so she should have come back on it. From Ida Mae's vantage point at the front window, she could see that her friend was walking more slowly than usual. The young woman with her looked familiar, but Ida Mae was too concerned about Claudia to try to place her. Maybe she was one of Claudia's grandchildren. She had quite a few, and Ida Mae hadn't met them all.

As soon as the Volkswagen left, Ida Mae phoned next door to make sure her neighbor was all right.

"I got a little tired walking from Food Lion to the post office," Claudia told her. "Stacy Whittier saw me there and brought me home."

So that's why she'd looked familiar. Ida Mae had seen Stacy at the funeral, walking up the aisle with the other members of the Whittier family. It would be interesting to know what Stacy and Claudia had talked about, but Claudia sounded tired, so Ida Mae didn't ask. Instead she said, "Let me fix you some lunch. I can carry it over to you."

"That's a kind offer, but I'm too tired to eat. I'm going to lie down and take a nap."

That didn't sound like Claudia. She didn't believe in napping, at least not on purpose. She and Ida Mae both admitted to falling asleep accidentally when they were watching television.

Later that afternoon Ida Mae took a pound cake to friends in her church who'd had a death in the family. Pound cake was her usual bereavement gift. Casseroles were best eaten soon, she thought, and sometimes the bereaved were overloaded with them. A pound cake would freeze and be just as good months later.

When Ida Mae returned home, Vivian's car was parked next door. Ida Mae had a moment of panic. Was something seriously wrong with Claudia? She decided to keep an eye on the window and waylay Vivian when she left. But the car was still there at five o'clock, when Ida Mae started dressing for dinner with her sister.

By quarter of six, Ida Mae was ready. She was wearing a pink flowered dress, one of her favorites, with a white necklace and matching earrings. She had also put on some of the red lipstick she used when she remembered to wear it, plus a little face powder. That wouldn't put her in the league with Vonda, but at least she was trying. Her white purse matched her medium-heeled white pumps.

If she lived long enough, Ida Mae knew she'd probably have to wear low-heeled lace-up shoes even on special occasions, but she wasn't ready to do that yet. She couldn't handle the spike heels her sister wore—how did Vonda do it, at her age?—but she admired her sister's collection of sandals. Ida Mae thought she might buy some for herself. Her toes would enjoy wiggling in the breeze after being cooped up all these years.

Vivian's car was still in Claudia's driveway when Vonda arrived. At least Claudia was in good hands, Ida Mae thought as she sank into the Cadillac's leather upholstery.

Twenty minutes later Ida Mae and Vonda were perusing the menus at the Oak Hill Inn. Ida Mae tried not to let the exorbitant prices bother her. She was her sister's guest, and Vonda had told her to have whatever she wanted. Reminding herself that Vonda drove a luxury car, owned a mansion in Atlanta, and was the widow of a wealthy man, Ida Mae ordered a steak.

The meat was thick and tender, maybe the best she'd ever had and certainly the most expensive. Vonda's meal, which cost almost as much as Ida Mae's, consisted of a tiny piece of fish, some miniature vegetables, and a few wisps of curly green leaves. Some sort of sauce was dribbled over the plate. Ida Mae had seen chefs on the cooking shows on TV fix meals like that. There was so little food on Vonda's plate, it looked more like a snack than a meal. But if Ida Mae were having a snack, she'd have something tastier, like a nice big slice of chocolate cake.

"This is really good, Vonda," Ida Mae said, putting more butter on her baked potato. It was real butter, not the margarine so many places served these days. "Sure you don't want a bite of my steak?"

"I hardly ever eat red meat," Vonda said, shaking her head.

Ida Mae tried not to smile. Best not to mention the second helping of roast beef she'd seen her sister eat at Betty Jo's the day before. Now that she and Vonda were back on good terms, she didn't want to say anything to upset her.

Ida Mae searched her mind for a topic of conversation. They'd already discussed Betty Jo and Norma and their families—so nice, all of them, they'd agreed. They'd also agreed that Pleasant Valley was a nice place, and Oak Hill was a nice town. Nice. Nice. Nice. Ida Mae wanted to hear Vonda's real opinions, something that would help her—what was the word people used so much these days? *Bond,* that was it. She wanted to talk about something that would help her bond with her sister.

Ida Mae looked around to make sure no one was listening. The room was almost empty. Vonda had been right when she said there wouldn't be many people here at six o'clock, Ida Mae's usual supper time. The man at the piano was doing his best to fill up the silence.

"I'm proud of you for telling Adelaide Treadwell what you did the other night," Ida Mae said.

Vonda smiled. Not the polite smile she put on when the occasion called for it, but the deep-down grin Ida Mae remembered from their childhood.

"All that talk about how Oak Hill had changed since the good old days?" Vonda said. "That was to remind me I hadn't been anybody worth knowing back then. I couldn't let her get by with that." She giggled. "Thank goodness she wasn't at the Cut'n'Curl when I was there today. She was there last Monday, so I thought this might be her regular day."

Ida Mae saw that her sister's hairdo had a new flip on the ends. "Your hair looks pretty."

"Thanks. Connie does nice work, doesn't she?" Vonda said, patting her hair. "Adelaide didn't have a clue who I was last Monday, but I recognized her right away in spite of her wrinkles and white hair. She's the same old Adelaide with that haughty voice and that better-than-everybody-else attitude."

"Just like she always was," Ida Mae agreed. "Remember those company picnics and Christmas parties in the old days? Old Mr. Carter Treadwell seemed to enjoy them as much as anybody. But after he died and Adelaide took over, she'd put in an appearance, but you could tell she could hardly wait to leave. Before long, she did away with the picnics and parties."

"I'll tell you, Ida Mae," Vonda said, "after I married Parnell I met a lot of rich people. I mean really wealthy, not like the Treadwells and the Rowlands and the others who looked big because the rest of us were so poor. And some of the wealthiest people I know are just as nice as you'd ever want to meet. Not like Adelaide, always thinking she was better than everybody else." She paused. "Frank's not like her."

Ida Mae smiled. "Are you going to the bridge club with him tomorrow?"

Vonda nodded. "Remember, I told you Adelaide made such a fuss about not being able to drive at night? Well, the night before the bridge club meeting, the first one they held in the afternoon for her benefit, somebody saw her out driving as pretty as you please. Now they're even madder at her."

Vonda started giggling, and Ida Mae joined in.

"Remember how we used to get the giggles when we were little?" Ida Mae asked.

Vonda nodded. "All three of us. And the more Mama told us to stop, the more we giggled."

"And Papa would roll his eyes and say, 'Lord, deliver me from a gaggle of giggling girls.'"

Suddenly Ida Mae didn't feel like laughing. "Vonda, how could you stay away all those years?"

She was surprised to see her sister's eyes fill with tears. "I don't know. I didn't want Parnell to find out I'd lied to him about being a widow. That was part of it. But really, Ida Mae, I don't know why. When I think about Daddy and Mama and Arlene— Oh, Ida Mae, I don't know if I'll ever forgive myself!"

Vonda took a lace-trimmed handkerchief from her brocade purse, but it was no match for her river of tears. Ida Mae unclasped her vinyl handbag and handed her sister a packet of tissues.

"You're here now," Ida Mae said, patting Vonda's hand. "That's what counts."

BY NINE O'CLOCK MONDAY night, Kristin was beginning to think the city council meeting would never end. The meeting room was crowded with citizens eager to discuss what to name the new city park, the pros and cons of changing garbage pickup to one day a week, and the need for a leash law. Kristin scribbled in her notebook until her hands were tired, sure she was missing important nuances she would have caught if she'd lived in Oak Hill all her life.

There were some familiar faces in the crowd. Buddy Daniels was leaning against the wall at one side of the room, and Wayne Henley was standing out in the hall, keeping his eyes on the meeting through an open door.

The issue of rezoning the Tabor Street neighborhood came up last. There was no discussion, and the council voted unanimously in favor of it. Kristin turned to see how Buddy was responding to this success. His expression was impassive.

When the mayor tapped the table with her gavel, saying, "Meeting adjourned," Kristin steeled herself to ask Buddy for his reaction to the vote. In spite of his threats, she had to do her job. But before she could make her way to him, she was besieged by people who'd spoken about the park, the garbage schedule, and the leash law. They all wanted to make sure Kristin would spell their names correctly when she quoted them in the paper.

When the crowd dwindled, Buddy was no longer in sight. Kristin decided to call him the next morning. By the time she reached the parking lot outside City Hall, it was almost empty. Remembering the threatening phone call, she looked around on the way to her car, and she made sure no one was hiding in the backseat.

As she drove through downtown Oak Hill, everything was dark except the *Sentinel* building. When Kristin turned onto the residential street that was one of her favorite routes to and from work, she noticed a white pickup truck in her rearview mirror. There were no other cars on the street, and streetlights were scarce. The trees that lined the road were pretty in the daylight, but now they'd become dark, menacing shapes.

Kristin saw a side street she thought would take her back to a main road. Her heart jolted when the truck turned, too. Was somebody following her? To her dismay, she found herself on another dark, winding residential street. She made another turn, and the truck followed.

Her heart pounded. Should she pull into a driveway, bang on the door of the house, and ask whoever appeared to call the police? Then she saw a familiar name on a cross street. Not sure which way to turn, Kristin made a quick right—and the truck did, too. After what seemed like an eternity, she came to the highway near her apartment.

When she was sure the truck hadn't followed her into the York Towne parking lot, Kristin sprinted up the steps to her apartment. Once inside, she turned on all the lights and began an inspection of the place, including the closets.

While she was checking the bedroom, the phone rang. Kristin's hands were shaking as she picked up the receiver.

"Hello," she said in a quavering voice.

"This is Wayne. Are you all right?"

"Now I am. But somebody in a white pickup truck followed me home."

"That was me."

She couldn't believe this. "What are you, some kind of stalker?"

"Buddy Daniels followed you out of the City Hall parking lot. He quit when you turned off Main Street, but I decided to make sure you got home okay."

"Well, I wasn't okay. I was terrified, and it was your fault."

"I didn't mean to scare you. But maybe you should be scared. Somebody was murdered last week, and the killer is probably right here in Oak Hill. If you don't stop playing investigative reporter, you could be the next victim."

"Is that a threat?"

Kristin heard an expletive from the other end of the line.

"Are you any closer to making an arrest?" she asked.

"Just leave this alone, and let the police handle it."

"Will you let me know as soon as you make an arrest?"

"Believe me, after the killer, you'll be the first to know."

Kristin heard the sound of a phone being banged down, followed by a dial tone.

She collapsed onto her bed, trying to make sense out of the phone call. Had Buddy really followed her, or had Wayne made up that story for reasons of his own? Maybe she should feel reassured that the police were looking out for her, but she couldn't help feeling that the situation had just become a little scarier.

She wasn't any closer to solving the murders, either. Kyle Peters thought Daphne Whittier's murderer was a woman, but the boy seemed to be basing his opinion on the killer's hair. Plenty of men had long hair that could look shiny to a child seeing it in the moonlight. Kyle said he saw a big black car, but any dark-colored car would look black at night. Should she rule out only those people who had small, light-colored cars? But the killer could have borrowed or stolen the car. It was all too confusing, and it was giving her a headache.

Her thoughts were interrupted by Darren's voice from the other side of the wall.

"Just forget about it!" he shouted.

Kristin wished she could take Darren's advice. But with Buddy, Wayne, and an anonymous caller threatening her, it was too late for that.

THIRTEEN

Except for your family, friends are your most important people.

> Tiffany Kearns, age nine, a student at
> Oak Hill Elementary School

BY SEVEN-THIRTY the next morning Ida Mae was at work in the flowerbed in front of her apartment. The sky was a clear blue, the air was cooler than it had been for weeks, and a breeze ruffled the leaves of the oak tree shading her side of the duplex. Best of all, there was nobody in her apartment to keep her from doing her gardening in the cool part of the day.

Last night at dinner when she and Vonda were getting along so well, Ida Mae briefly considered inviting her sister to come back and stay with her. Fortunately, her common sense took over, and she let that idea slide right out of her mind before it popped out of her mouth. There were a whole slew of reasons why living with her sister wouldn't work. Having to tiptoe around in the mornings waiting for Vonda to wake up was one of the most important ones.

Yes, this would be a perfect morning, Ida Mae thought, if she weren't so worried about Claudia. She'd planned to check on her after eating with Vonda yesterday, but the lights were out next door when they returned. So far this morning she'd heard no sounds from the other side of the duplex, and her neighbor's morning paper was still on the sidewalk.

As she snipped dead blossoms and pulled weeds, Ida Mae remembered the lonely days she'd spent before Claudia moved in. She'd never admit it to Betty Jo and Norma, who'd done so much for her, bless their hearts, but her first couple of months in the retirement community had been rough. The people in the other duplexes on the cul-de-sac were nice enough, but she could tell they'd never become the drop-in-anytime kind of friends she'd had on Wendley Street. Dora Nelson, the woman who'd lived in the other half of Ida Mae's duplex, was standoffish. Goodness knows, Ida Mae tried to be neighborly, but Dora was a private person. Ida Mae hadn't even realized Dora had gone into the Nursing Center until a moving van arrived to take her things away.

Ida Mae had known Claudia only three months, but it seemed like they'd been friends forever. The day Claudia moved in, her children and grandchildren had been in and out of the apartment to help her settle in. The next morning when Ida Mae invited her over for coffee, Claudia apologized for the commotion her family made.

"Don't think a thing about it. I like having people around," Ida Mae said, and she meant every word of it. Right away, from that first visit, she'd known Claudia would be a good neighbor, the kind who wasn't nosy and would mind her own business, but would enjoy talking to you, too, and wouldn't shirk if you needed help. She was the kind of neighbor Ida Mae had always tried to be.

Ida Mae clipped off the last dead marigold and stepped back to have a full view of the front of her apartment. The yellow marigolds, bright red salvia, and silver-gray dusty miller looked beautiful against the deep green leaves of the azalea bushes, she thought. Maybe the sunflowers had been a little too much, anyway. Next spring she'd plant them in the backyard where the rules weren't so strict. Now that she knew Claudia better and was sure she wouldn't take offense, Ida Mae also planned to start a flower garden in front of the other half of the duplex next year so both sides would match.

Ida Mae picked up her tools and the low stool she sat on when she did her gardening, and went into her apartment. All was quiet next door. She'd better wait a little longer before calling Claudia. In the meantime there were some marigolds out back that could use some attention.

CLAUDIA HUMMED A TUNE as she rinsed out her cereal bowl and put it in the dishwasher. Vivian was right. All she'd needed was a good rest. Claudia had felt silly lying down while her daughter fixed a meal for her yesterday. She'd felt even sillier going to bed before eight o'clock, but Vivian had insisted.

It wasn't just the walk in the hot sun that had worn her out yesterday. It was the things that were on her mind. First there was the conversation with Mr. Haizler. Then there were the things Ray had told her about the mysterious Leonora. By the time she'd heard Stacy's story, too, Claudia felt weighed down by all she'd learned. She hadn't said a word about any of it to Vivian, of course. She loved her daughter, but telling Vivian would be almost as bad as telling Vonda. It would be all over town before you could turn around.

This morning Claudia's mind felt clearer, and some of the ideas she hadn't been sure about yesterday now seemed to make sense. She wanted to talk them over with her neighbor. Ida Mae had good judgment. Though she liked to talk as much as the next person, she knew when to keep quiet, too. Most important, Ida Mae was trustworthy. If she promised to keep something to herself, you could count on her to do that.

Claudia and Ida Mae had spent a good while talking about the murders, but they hadn't been able to dredge up any memories that might help solve the earlier of the two crimes. As for Daphne Whittier, they agreed she must have stepped on somebody's toes. A drug dealer, Ida Mae thought. Claudia hadn't ruled out Buddy Daniels. The love of money was the root of all evil, the Good Book said, and Buddy must love it a lot, coming from such worthless folk and turning into one of the richest men in the county.

Claudia looked out her kitchen window. It was a pretty day, and Ida Mae was in her backyard looking at her tomato plants. Claudia went out her back door and strolled over to the white picket fence that separated her backyard from her neighbor's.

"Feeling better this morning, are you?" Ida Mae inquired when she saw Claudia.

"Lively as a June bug. I just started a pot of coffee, and I have tea in the refrigerator. Or if you haven't had your breakfast, I could fix you something to eat."

"No, I've eaten, but I'd love some coffee." Ida Mae gestured toward the gate at the back of her yard. "I'll take the scenic route."

The two women had long since agreed that the fences surrounding the backyards of the duplexes were ridiculous. They were far too low to keep out would-be burglars or to lean on and talk, and they were a real nuisance if you wanted to go from your back door to your neighbor's. Claudia watched as

Ida Mae made her way past flowerbeds, tomato plants, and bean plants. At the gate, she stopped, looked at the expanse of grass beyond the back fence, and shook her head. Claudia knew what her neighbor was thinking. Ida Mae often complained that her backyard was too small. She coveted the grassy space beyond the fence for a garden.

A few minutes later at her kitchen table, Claudia told Ida Mae about her dizzy spell at the post office and her rescue by Stacy Whittier.

"Vivian made such a fuss when I told her about it, I was almost sorry I called her," Claudia said. "I had to let her know, though. If she'd heard about my little escapade from somebody else, she'd have been fit to be tied."

"Just the way my nieces were that time I fell when I was changing the light bulb over my basement stairs," Ida Mae said, nodding in agreement. "I didn't tell them about it, but they heard it from one of my neighbors. That made it worse."

Claudia had heard all about the light bulb incident. According to Ida Mae, it had started Betty Jo and Norma's campaign to move her to Pleasant Valley. The battle had escalated when they caught her cleaning her gutters.

"From now on," Ida Mae said, "if you want to go someplace, just tell me and I'll carry you. It's too hot to be out walking this time of year."

"That's kind of you," Claudia said, not ready to

make any promises. Their trip to the country was still fresh in her mind. "Tell me about your dinner with Vonda," she said to change the subject.

Ida Mae launched into a lengthy account of her visit to the Oak Hill Inn, which included the pink tablecloths, the piano music, and the little-bitty dabs of food that constituted Vonda's expensive meal. Claudia could tell by the lilt in her friend's voice that the sisters had reconciled. She was glad for that, despite her suspicions of Vonda. It was a bad thing to have a falling out with anybody, especially your kin. She knew the rift between the sisters had distressed Ida Mae.

Once she finished the story of last night's dinner, Ida Mae inquired, "Did you have a good visit with Stacy Whittier?"

Claudia knew Ida Mae was asking, in as tactful a way as possible, if she'd learned anything about Daphne Whittier's murder. She nodded. "I have things to tell you—things I couldn't tell Vivian. She'd pass them along to her friends, and pretty soon the whole world would know."

"Same thing would happen if I told Norma or Betty Jo. And Vonda?" Ida Mae rolled her eyes. "There's no way that woman could keep a secret."

Ida Mae listened as Claudia told her what she'd learned from Mr. Haizler, Ray, and Stacy, including Daphne Whittier's implication that a family member had been involved with a white man and had been lost to her family as a result.

"Stacy wondered if Leonora, the woman in the picture, could be the relative who had a romance with a white man. If so, the argument over Stacy's friend Jeffrey may have brought Leonora to Miss Whittier's mind. That would explain why she was looking at her sister's picture," Claudia said. She paused, wondering how to proceed. "Vonda still doesn't remember anything about the woman who bought the necklace from her?"

Ida Mae shook her head. "I asked her again yesterday. She just says the person wasn't from around here."

"I've been thinking about that. When Daphne Whittier came to Oak Hill, she had a strong New England accent. Her sister probably spoke the same way. Maybe that's why Vonda thought she came from somewhere away. Did Vonda mention the race of the woman who bought the necklace?"

"No, but—" Ida Mae stopped. Claudia knew what she was thinking. Vonda would have mentioned race only if the person wasn't white.

"Mr. Haizler said Leonora had light skin and brown hair. She may have had hazel eyes, like her sister Daphne. Maybe Vonda thought she was white."

Ida Mae was silent for a moment. Then she said, "You mean Vonda sold the necklace to Leonora

Whittier, and sometime after that Leonora was murdered?"

"Maybe. I've been wondering about something else, too. The newspaper said a latch and hinges from a suitcase were found near the skeleton. I wonder if Leonora was killed when she was about to leave Oak Hill, maybe to be with the man she loved."

"She was going away, only somebody killed her first and nobody ever knew what happened to her!" Ida Mae said. "But if that's so, why did Stacy's father say his aunt died of pneumonia?"

Claudia hesitated. What she was going to say next was speculation, but it made sense to her. "The pneumonia story could have been a cover-up. Stacy's father was born several years after his aunt disappeared, and all he knew about her was what his family told him. Daphne Whittier was a proud woman. She wouldn't have wanted anyone to know her sister ran off with a man, especially a white one. I imagine she let people around here think Leonora had gone back to Boston. When the family never heard from Leonora again, they may have assumed she'd severed her ties with them to spend her life with her white lover, possibly passing for white herself. In order to keep it a secret, they may have told people she died."

"And Leonora was dead all the time, murdered here in Oak Hill, and they never knew," Ida Mae said. "It makes sense, Claudia. But even if it happened that way, we still don't know who killed her. It could have been anybody, I guess. A drifter, just passing through? Maybe one of those serial killers, if they had them back then."

"Or some man from around here who saw her walking down the road with a suitcase in her hand and decided to rob her or maybe rape her," Claudia said.

After she'd said this, Claudia couldn't help thinking about Mr. Haizler. But just as Ida Mae couldn't believe Buddy Daniels would kill for money, Claudia was sure the man she'd seen at the Nursing Center couldn't have a horrible secret in his past. He'd seemed too happy, too at peace in his soul.

The two women sat in silence for a while. Then Ida Mae's face brightened. "I almost forgot. I want you to eat supper with Vonda and me day after tomorrow. I'm fixing pinto beans and cornbread, just a simple country meal."

Claudia shook her head. "Thanks, Ida Mae, but you need some time with your sister without me."

"Law me, Claudia, if Vonda moves into Pleasant Valley the way she's talking about doing, I'll have more than enough time to spend with her. Anyway, I've already told her you're coming. But we'll have to be careful what we say. The things we've talked about today—Leonora, Stacy, Mr. Haizler, and all? And what we've said about Daphne Whittier's death—that it might be related to drugs or that Buddy Daniels might be mixed up in it? We can't mention any of that in front of Vonda."

Claudia nodded in agreement. Telling Vonda would be worse than telling Vivian, and not just because the woman liked to talk. Claudia wasn't ready to trust Vonda—or her friend Frank Rowland.

WHEN KRISTIN ARRIVED AT the police station later that day, she was sure she was going to hear big news about one of the murders, the kind of news that would rate a front-page headline in tomorrow's paper. Ray had called to say he and Wayne wanted to talk to her, and hadn't Wayne promised she'd be the first to know when the police made an arrest?

Anyway, these guys owed her. She'd given them tons of useful information, and she'd done her best to be nice to Wayne, too, which wasn't always easy. Well, okay, she hadn't exactly been nice to him when he confessed to following her home from the city council meeting. But that was his own fault for scaring her half to death.

The detectives were waiting for her in their office. When she pulled her notebook and pen from her purse, Wayne frowned. "Nothing in this conversation is to go in the newspaper."

"We need to go over something you told us earlier," Ray said.

Kristin spirits sagged. If there was no front-page news, what could they want to talk about? Her mind flashed to Kyle Peters. His mother hadn't wanted him to be involved with the police. Had she made him retract his story?

"Tell us what you saw out the window of Myrtle's Grill the day Daphne Whittier was killed," Ray said.

Kristin repeated her story of seeing the African-American woman park her car, cross the street, and go into the attorney's office.

"I thought she looked familiar, but I couldn't remember her name or where I'd seen her. But after her picture was in the paper, I realized she was the woman I'd seen at city council meetings when she spoke against rezoning her neighborhood."

"You're sure that's who you saw?"

She thought for a moment. The woman had been right outside the window, and she'd seen her several times at city council meetings. "Yes, I'm sure."

"What happened after that?"

"After I saw Daphne Whittier? Then Detective Henley came in and asked if he could—"

"Not that part," Ray said, smiling. "Tell us what else you saw outside."

"I saw Adelaide Treadwell on the other side

of the street. She went into her brother's office, stayed two or three minutes, and then came back out."

"But you didn't know who it was at the time?" Wayne asked.

"No, I didn't know until the talent show at Pleasant Valley. She was there with her brother, and someone told me her name."

"You're sure that's who it was?"

Both men were looking at her intently.

Kristin hesitated. "I think so. But she was on the other side of the street. I didn't see her face, so I suppose I could have been mistaken." She looked from one man to the other, but neither face gave her any clues. "Did she say she wasn't there?"

"Yep." Now Wayne's expression had a hint of a smirk. "She wasn't too pleased when we said someone had placed her there. She wanted to know who'd told us."

"Did you tell her?" Kristin imagined the tall, imperious-looking woman berating her, suing her, having her fired.

Wayne grinned. "Don't worry, we didn't tell her."

"The thing is," Ray said, "Wilton Treadwell says no one came in while he was talking to Daphne Whittier. He doesn't have a receptionist in the waiting room, but he was in an inner office with its door partly open. Are you sure somebody went in?"

"Oh, yes, an elderly woman who looked like Adelaide Treadwell."

"And she came out while Daphne Whittier was there?"

Kristin hesitated. "Miss Whittier's car was still parked outside the restaurant. But I suppose she could have left the lawyer's office and gone somewhere else without my seeing her." A wave of embarrassment swept over her. She knew her story sounded shaky.

"Is there anything else you can tell us?" Ray asked.

"No, I guess that's it."

Ray stood up. "Thanks for coming in. You've been very helpful."

Kristin was sure she hadn't been. Both men must think she was an idiot. Ray was too polite to show it, but Wayne's smirk told the whole story.

"Kristin," Ray said as she started toward the door, eager to be gone, "if you've told anyone about seeing Adelaide Treadwell at her brother's office, you might mention to them that you could have been mistaken. Wayne was right, Miss Treadwell wasn't at all happy when we told her she'd been seen there."

Kristin's face blazed with embarrassment as she left the police station. But by the time she was halfway back to the newspaper office, her humiliation had turned to anger. Ray and Wayne had been far too quick to dismiss her story. So what if she hadn't seen Adelaide Treadwell? She'd seen somebody. An elderly woman had gone into the law office, probably while Daphne Whittier was there. With no receptionist in the waiting room and the door to the inner office ajar, the woman could have overheard part of their conversation— and that night Daphne Whittier had been killed.

Kristin reviewed what she'd seen. The woman had been tall, with white hair and excellent posture. She'd worn a royal-blue dress with a matching long-sleeved jacket. Those were just the sort of details the detectives would need to know if they were going to discover who Mr. Treadwell's visitor was. Maybe the woman in blue didn't have anything to do with the murder, but weren't the police supposed to track down every lead?

Kristin knew a good reporter sometimes had to take risks for a story. If she returned to the police station, the only risk was that Ray and Wayne might laugh in her face, which was a small price to pay. With a sigh, she turned around and began retracing her steps.

When she reached the hall that led to the detectives' office, Kristin saw Ray, Wayne, and three other men coming toward her. Ray frowned when he saw her, and Wayne scowled. When Ray said something to the others, all five men ducked into an open doorway and pulled the door shut behind them. Kristin was sure she'd stumbled on something she wasn't supposed to see, but as usual she had no clue what it was.

She sighed. A person would have to spend a lifetime in Oak Hill to understand half of what went on in this town. Fortunately, she knew two women who'd lived here almost that long. She'd go to see Ida Mae and Claudia, and this time she wouldn't give up until she found out what they knew.

FOURTEEN

Oak Hill has its secrets, and some things are best left unsaid.

From *Memories of Old Oak Hill*
by Isabel Rowland Everhart

KRISTIN DECIDED NOT to phone Ida Mae and Claudia before going to see them. A surprise visit in the middle of the afternoon might work in her favor, she thought. Elderly people took naps, didn't they? If she happened to wake them, and if they happened to talk to her before they were fully awake, she might learn something important. Would that be unethical? She pushed the question to the back of her mind for her conscience to wrestle with later. At this point, she was willing to try just about anything.

Her investigations of the murders were going nowhere. So far, she had no clues at all to the first crime, and she knew no more about Daphne Whittier's death than when she wrote the story about it for the newspaper. Marcus Whittier had refused her request for an interview, and he'd insisted that she not contact any other members of his family. The police were no help, either.

Kristin's temper flared as she remembered her conversation with Ray and Wayne. She was particularly angry with Wayne, who'd made her feel like a fool for saying she'd seen Adelaide Treadwell. Nor did she like the way the detectives had avoided her when she went back to the police station. Well, that was their loss, not hers! By ignoring her, they'd missed getting a description of the woman who'd gone into the lawyer's office when Daphne Whittier was there. If she could find that woman, maybe she could uncover some important clues and amaze Bill, Wayne, and all the others who thought she ought to leave the investigation to the police.

When she entered Sunset Court, the cul-de-sac where Ida Mae and Claudia lived, Kristin saw that Ida Mae's car wasn't in her driveway. Okay, she'd go to Claudia's first. Maybe when they were finished talking, Ida Mae would be back. Claudia's driveway was empty, too, but as far as Kristin could remember she didn't have a car.

She rang Claudia's doorbell several times, but there was no answer. Disappointed, she decided to try the other half of the duplex. Ida Mae might be at home even if her car wasn't. The vehicle was old, Kristin remembered. Maybe it was in the shop for repairs.

When there was no answer at that door, either, Kristin started back to her car, ready to give up. Just then Ida Mae's ancient green Chevy roared into the cul-de-sac, turned into the driveway at high speed, and lurched to a stop. The car door flew open, and its owner hopped out. She waved at Kristin and trotted over to her while Claudia made a slower exit from the passenger side of the car.

"I call that good timing," Ida Mae said. "Claudia and I were up at the Nursing Center visiting some of our friends. Come in and have a glass of tea with us."

"Thanks," Kristin said, making a mental note to turn down all offers of cake or cookies. Visits to Ida Mae's were bad for her waistline.

A few minutes later the three women were at the dining table, each with a generous portion of angel food cake and fresh peaches, sliced and heavily sugared. A tall glass of strong, sweet tea stood at each place. As she speared a piece of peach and a bit of cake with her fork, Kristin consoled herself with the thought that today's refreshments were low in fat, if not in calories.

She decided to steer the conversation toward the murders by admitting the mistake she'd made. "I may have been wrong about something I told you Friday night. About seeing Adelaide Treadwell go into her brother's office, I mean. She told the police she wasn't there, so maybe I was mistaken. I hope you haven't told anybody."

"I haven't," Ida Mae said. "Have you, Claudia?"

"I didn't tell anybody but Ray," Claudia said, "and he'd already heard it from Wayne."

Kristin was relieved to hear this. At least the story wasn't on the Oak Hill grapevine with her name attached.

"Ray and Wayne said Miss Treadwell was very upset when they told her she'd been seen at her brother's office." Kristin sighed. "They probably think I'm an idiot."

Claudia frowned. "Ray wasn't rude, was he?"

"Oh, no, he's always very professional—which is more than I can say for Detective Henley."

"Billy Wayne? Don't let him scare you," Ida Mae said with a chuckle. "He just doesn't know how to deal with a pretty girl."

Kristin looked at her in surprise. She'd thought of several reasons why she seemed to upset the detective so easily, but this one had never crossed her mind.

"I've known his grandmother for years," Ida Mae went on. "She told me all about it. Two or three years ago he was engaged, had the wedding date all set and everything, and the girl left him for somebody with more money. Broke his heart. Ever since then, he's been skittish around women."

Kristin was tempted to ask for all the juicy details of the detective's failed romance, which she was sure Ida Mae could supply. But she hadn't come here to find out about Wayne's love life, no matter how interesting it might be. "The woman I thought was Miss Treadwell, the one I saw going into Wilton Treadwell's office, was tall, with very straight posture. She had white hair and was wearing a royal-blue dress with a matching jacket. Do you have any idea who that might be?"

Ida Mae and Claudia looked at each other and shook their heads.

"Nobody comes to mind," Ida Mae said.

"Except Adelaide Treadwell," Claudia said. "I can see how you might have thought that's who it was."

"Could it be somebody who had something to do with drugs?"

"Drugs?" The two women looked shocked. Kristin realized that her question must have sounded ridiculous. But Kyle Peters had said the woman who went into Daphne Whittier's house had shiny hair. Maybe gold or silver, he'd said. White hair could look silver at night, couldn't it? And hadn't Wayne as much as admitted that one of the big drug suppliers in Yarborough County was a woman? Was it too big a jump to think it might be an *elderly* woman? From their incredulous expressions, it was clear that Ida Mae and Claudia thought so.

Kristin switched to another topic. "This afternoon I saw Ray and Wayne at the police station with three men who looked sort of official. They were wearing suits and ties, anyway. When they saw me, all five men hustled away really fast, like I wasn't supposed to see them. Do you think it had something to do with the murders?"

The two women looked at her with expressions of mild interest.

"I suppose it could," Ida Mae said, "though it could be something else entirely."

"Ray and Wayne work on lots of cases," Claudia said. "It didn't have to be one of the murders. And they do things for civic organizations. Maybe the men you saw were working on some kind of fundraising project with them."

Kristin felt sure the five men hadn't been organizing the local United Way campaign or planning a Lions Club pancake breakfast. Had she hit on something neither of these women knew about—or were they just not telling her? She wasn't sure, but from their responses she knew she might as well change the subject.

"Has either of you thought of anything that might help identify the person whose skeleton was found?"

Ida Mae and Claudia suddenly became very involved in eating their cake and peaches.

"I don't think there's a thing I could tell you," Ida Mae said after a moment.

"I'd have to agree with Ida Mae," Claudia said.

"We'd certainly help you if we could," Ida Mae added.

Kristin looked from one woman to the other. They knew something, she was sure, and they weren't going to tell her what it was.

THAT NIGHT, IDA MAE couldn't sleep. Were the coffee and tea keeping her awake? She and Claudia had polished off a pot of coffee—or was it two?—that morning, and she'd had a glass of tea with Kristin in the afternoon and another one with Claudia after Kristin left.

As she lay in bed wide awake, Ida Mae thought about the reporter's visit. She and Claudia had done their best to avoid answering her questions without telling an outright lie. They both believed in telling the truth, and they felt bad about misleading the girl, but they'd done right to keep quiet. That business about Leonora Whittier shouldn't be spread around unless it proved to be connected to one of the murders.

Leonora! Now that was a tragic story. Going to meet the man she loved and being murdered instead—why, the same thing could have happened to Vonda! Was Leonora's lover a no-good skunk like Harvey Dawkins? Ida Mae could have predicted Harvey would turn out to be worthless, but Vonda hadn't been in the mood to listen, being young and in love. Leonora Whittier had probably been the same way.

A long time ago, back when Ida Mae's grandparents were growing up, a young man in Yarborough Country murdered his pregnant lover because he didn't want to marry her. His trial had drawn a huge crowd, and a song had been written about the crime. Was that what happened to Leonora? Not that she was pregnant necessarily, though that could have been true. Ida Mae sighed. Murdering any human being was bad enough, but murdering somebody who loved you was worse. Even Harvey Dawkins wasn't lowdown enough to do a thing like that.

Ida Mae's thoughts turned to the woman Kristin had seen at Wilton Treadwell's office. She and Claudia had told the truth. They honestly couldn't come up with anyone who matched Kristin's description other than Adelaide Treadwell herself. After the reporter left, they'd agreed that the woman she'd seen probably *was* Adelaide. They decided that for reasons of her own—maybe because she was annoyed that somebody had the audacity to mention her to the police—Adelaide had claimed not to have been there.

As for Kristin's idea that the white-haired woman's visit to the lawyer's office had something to do with drugs—why, that was purely ridiculous! Ida Mae grinned at the thought of the Treadwells being involved with something so low-class. She tried to envision Adelaide's Cadillac cruising through Oak Hill after midnight, bringing in a load of illegal substances, and unsavory characters knocking on the door of the Treadwells' white-columned house to make drug buys. No, it was impossible.

That idea just showed that the reporter didn't know anything about Yarborough County's criminals, which was a good thing. Kristin could get herself into a world of trouble messing with those people. Not that Ida Mae herself knew much about criminals, but you couldn't live in a place eighty years without knowing who was on the wrong side of the law.

The other day when she saw the name on the mailbox out where her homeplace used to be, she knew right away no lawman ought to be visiting there unless he was arresting somebody. She was sure the man she'd seen tucking in his shirttail was one of Sheriff Grissom's deputies, and she'd never heard of a deputy having to unzip his pants to make an arrest.

Friday night after the talent show she'd given Wayne the license number of the red pickup truck. By now he must have checked it out, and he'd know if she was right about who the driver was. Whatever happened now was out of her hands. She hoped to goodness she and Claudia weren't going to be mixed up in that business any further.

As Ida Mae drifted toward sleep, all the things that had happened in the last two weeks began to jumble together in her mind...the bones...Vonda's return...Daphne Whittier's murder. Then a thought tugged her back toward consciousness. Was the day Kristin saw someone at the lawyer's office the same day Vonda saw Adelaide at the beauty shop? If so, did that mean anything? Too sleepy to figure it out, Ida Mae tucked the question away to consider another day.

AT FIVE O'CLOCK THE next morning, Ida Mae woke from a nightmare involving drug dealers, a beauty parlor, and her sister Vonda. If her dreams were going to be like that, she'd rather stay awake! She put on her robe and slippers, started a pot of coffee, and padded down her walk to pick up the morning paper. An early start on the day never hurt anybody, she thought—though Vonda probably wouldn't agree.

As she sipped her first cup of coffee, she read the obituaries. When she was sure there were no viewings or funerals she needed to attend, she poured a second cup and turned to the editorial page to see what was on the minds of the people who wrote letters to the editor. Ida Mae had never written a letter to the newspaper herself, though she'd been sorely tempted once or twice.

There were two letters about the dog ordinance and three about once-a-week garbage pickup. Neither issue concerned Ida Mae, since she didn't have a dog, and she didn't generate much garbage. Next she took a look at Bill Caldwell's editorials. One was about litter on the town's streets. He was against it. The other was titled "Local Police Need Help." According to the editor, the Oak Hill police needed to ask the State Bureau of Investigation to help them deal with the murders. "Our local officers lack experience and expertise in cases of this kind," he had written.

Ida Mae frowned. She couldn't help feeling sorry for Ray and Wayne. Claudia had told her how hard they were working, yet Bill Caldwell hadn't included one word of appreciation for Oak Hill's police force in his editorial. Should she write a letter to the newspaper defending them? If she did, people who didn't agree with her would write letters in response, and she'd be in a battle of words in front of the whole town.

No, it would be better to do what she always did for people in distress or trouble. She went to the refrigerator and took out butter and eggs. She was going to make a pound cake.

CLAUDIA COULD TELL RIGHT away that this wasn't going to be one of her neighbor's better driving days. They had a close call while they were still in Pleasant Valley, when Ida Mae didn't brake soon enough for a stop sign and almost collided with one of the retirement center's busses.

"I've been thinking about Daniel Macon," Ida Mae said a few minutes later as she pulled into a line of traffic, ignoring the squealing tires of the cars that had the right of way.

"Daniel Macon?" said Claudia. She couldn't remember ever hearing of anyone by that name. She wondered if he was the cause of her friend's erratic driving. More likely, lack of sleep was the culprit. Ida Mae had mentioned that she'd slept only a few hours the night before.

To Claudia's amazement, her friend began to sing in a reedy, high-pitched voice: "She trusted him and loved him, she thought she'd be his bride, but down beside the river that poor young woman died."

Turning toward Claudia, Ida Mae asked, "Don't you remember that old song?"

Claudia was more concerned about the traffic signal ahead of them, which had turned red. When she was sure they were going to stop without rear-ending the car in front of them, she said, "I believe I do, though I haven't heard it since I was a girl."

"It's called 'The Ballad of Sarah Lewis.' She

was murdered right here in Yarborough County," Ida Mae said. "Daniel Macon was the man who did it. I've been wondering if something like that happened to Leonora. Maybe the man wanted to break off with her, but she threatened to make a fuss, so he killed her."

"It could have happened that way, I suppose," Claudia said. She wasn't convinced that the story she and Ida Mae had concocted was true, but Ida Mae had latched onto it as if it were gospel, and now she was making additions to it. Claudia was still plagued by the suspicion that Vonda and her friend Frank were somehow involved in Leonora's murder or its cover-up. For Ida Mae's sake she hoped they weren't.

"Maybe he lived up north, and the family sent Leonora to spend the summer with her sister in North Carolina so she'd be away from him," Ida Mae said. "But she kept writing him letters, and he was afraid she was going to cause trouble for him. So he told her he was coming to Oak Hill to take her away with him, but he killed her instead."

Claudia tried to think about this, but thinking was difficult with Ida Mae plowing through downtown traffic as if her car were the only one on the street. To Claudia, Ida Mae's theory sounded like something out of an old song all right—or maybe a soap opera.

When they reached the police station, Ida Mae

pulled into the parking lot and stopped in the middle of it. "I don't see any empty spaces, do you, Claudia?"

"No, not a single one."

"Tell you what," Ida Mae said when none of the other vehicles showed any signs of moving. "I'll pull up in front of the building and let you out. You take the cake in while I drive around the block."

Claudia was glad to do it. It was a relief to be out of the car, no longer at the mercy of Ida Mae's heavy foot on the accelerator. When she reached the lobby of the police station, the receptionist greeted her with a smile.

"If that's a cake you have there, Mrs. McNeill," she said, indicating the container Claudia was carrying, "Ray will sure be glad to see you. Is this his birthday or something?"

"No, it isn't his birthday. I didn't even make the cake. I'm just delivering it. My neighbor thought Ray and Wayne might need a little encouragement."

The receptionist lowered her voice. "Isn't it awful the way the newspaper is after us again? Bill Caldwell doesn't think the police department can do anything right."

"Well, maybe Ida Mae's pound cake will cheer Ray and Wayne up," Claudia said, not wanting to offer an opinion about the *Sentinel*. She knew Ray always did his best, and the other police officers probably did, too, but she wondered if Bill Caldwell might not be right. Daphne Whittier's killer should be arrested as soon as possible. Why not bring the SBI in?

When Claudia was halfway down the hall to the detectives' office, Ray came out to meet her, making her suspect that the receptionist had alerted him to her arrival.

"Got some people in my office, or I'd invite you in," he said, greeting her with a hug. "Have you and Ida Mae been doing some more investigating? Those ideas you passed along yesterday were pretty good. We may have to put you two on the payroll."

Claudia wondered if she should say anything about Ida Mae's newest theory or about her own suspicions of Vonda. No, Ray was a smart man. He'd probably already realized that Leonora's lover could have been her killer. If Vonda and Frank were involved in the crime, he'd figure that out, too. Besides, he was busy, and she didn't want to bother him any further.

"We haven't done any more investigating, but Ida Mae's been doing some baking." She held out the cake container. "She made one of her pound cakes for you and Wayne."

"Mrs. Poindexter's a nice lady. You tell her Wayne and I will really enjoy this," he said, taking the container from his grandmother. Then he gave her a look of mock severity. "Please tell me you didn't ride here with her."

"I think I'd better keep silent," she said with a smile. "Doesn't every accused person have that right?"

Ray grinned. "Don't worry. I won't tell Mom."

Claudia hugged him extra hard as she said goodbye. "You be careful, Ray," she said. Compared with the dangers Ray faced on his job, riding with Ida Mae wasn't scary at all.

FIFTEEN

I'm proud to say that Oak Hill is a safe place,
the kind of town where anybody can go anywhere without fear.

Carolyn Powell, mayor of Oak Hill, in a speech
to the Oak Hill Civitan Club

WHILE IDA MAE WAS WAITING for Claudia to come
out of the police station, she started thinking about
buttermilk. She'd planned to make iced tea for tomorrow night's supper, sweet for herself and Claudia and unsweetened for Vonda, who was scared
of calories. But buttermilk would go with the pinto
beans and cornbread even better than tea, and in
her earlier days Vonda had liked buttermilk.

"Do you need to go home right away?" Ida Mae
asked when Claudia slid into the passenger seat.
"I want to buy buttermilk for tomorrow night."

"I'm in no hurry." Claudia smiled. "The meal
you're going to have sounds good to me, but are
you sure Vonda will like it?"

"She said she would," Ida Mae replied. "We'll
see." Vonda had sounded delighted with the menu,

but Ida Mae doubted that her sister had eaten a pinto bean in twenty years.

A few minutes later, when they were walking across the supermarket parking lot to the door of the store, Ida Mae noticed a man putting grocery bags into a nearby car. The vehicle was almost as old as hers, but in much worse shape. It had once been dark blue, but now much of it was covered in primer. The man was stocky, with a receding hairline. His blond hair had been pulled back into a ponytail, and he wore a tank top that showed off his muscles. Both of his arms featured tattoos of writhing dragons.

The man turned and looked directly at Ida Mae. Was he somebody she was supposed to know? She searched her memory for a cute little boy or a likable teenager who could have grown up to look like this. When no one came to mind, she averted her eyes, thinking she might have offended him by staring at his tattoos. She began talking to Claudia about what a pretty day it was, making her voice a little louder than usual so the man could hear her and know she wasn't talking about him.

When they were halfway to the store, Ida Mae glanced over her shoulder. The tattooed fellow was no longer staring at her. He was walking around her car, giving it a careful inspection.

What in the world was he up to? She had a good mind to go back and ask him. Then she remembered that she and Claudia had recently stumbled on a deputy sheriff doing some things he shouldn't. Could this man be one of the Tavenders, maybe a brother or cousin of the woman at the doublewide? Had he found out that she'd reported the crooked deputy to the police? If so, he could be planning to do something to her car in revenge, maybe slash her tires or put sugar in her gas tank.

Ida Mae grabbed Claudia's arm and said, "Don't look around. We need to get into the store as fast as we can."

It was a mark of her friend's good sense, Ida Mae thought, that she did just as she was told. Most people couldn't resist looking around if they'd been warned not to, but all Claudia did was start walking faster. Ida Mae did, too. Both women were almost running when they reached the door.

"You wait over there," Ida Mae said to Claudia once they were inside, pointing toward a display of cake mixes.

With Claudia positioned by the display, Ida Mae pushed her way through a jumble of empty grocery carts to reach the windows at the front of the store. She watched as the tattooed man circled her car, peering in each window. When he grasped the door handle on the driver's side, Ida Mae wished she'd locked her car. Before this, she'd never seen the point. Who would want to steal a car as old as hers?

When the man with the ponytail didn't open the Chevy's door after all, but instead went back to his own car and drove off, Ida Mae trotted over to Claudia.

"I'll go pick up the buttermilk," Ida Mae said. "You stay here and watch for a man with a ponytail and a lot of tattoos. He stared at us in the parking lot, and then he looked at my car a lot closer than he should have. I think he might be one of those—" she lowered her voice "—people from the doublewide."

Claudia gasped. "The deputy?" she whispered.

"Not him. The other ones. You stay here and keep an eye on the door." With that, Ida Mae darted off in the direction of the dairy cases.

WHEN IDA MAE RUSHED AWAY to get the buttermilk, Claudia had a moment of panic. What should she do if she saw the tattooed man? Should she run to the dairy section to tell Ida Mae? Then what would they do? Claudia pictured the two of them dashing into the storeroom at the back of the supermarket and crouching behind giant boxes of paper towels and canned vegetables. The image was so ridiculous she had to smile.

When Ida Mae bustled back with two cartons of

buttermilk, Claudia assured her that the tattooed man hadn't shown up.

"Thank the Lord!" Ida Mae said. After paying for her purchases, she went to the front windows again and looked from one side of the parking lot to the other.

"No sign of him," she told Claudia.

On the way back to the car, Ida Mae asked if Claudia thought the deputy could have recognized her when they were at the doublewide.

"I doubt it," Claudia said. She suspected that to men under forty, a category that included the deputy, all women over seventy looked alike. On the other hand, the Tavenders and their deputy pal could be on the lookout for an old white woman and an old black woman riding together. That wasn't such a common sight. Come to think of it, Ida Mae's car might be a dead giveaway. There weren't many of that vintage on the road.

"He'd only seen you once before," Claudia said, trying to reassure her friend, "and that day at the trailer we were a good distance away from him. Anyway, if he knew we were old ladies, he probably thought we didn't have enough eyesight left to see him or enough memory to remember him."

Though she'd never say so to Ida Mae, Claudia thought the Chevy's wild retreat from the doublewide had probably convinced any onlookers that its driver didn't have all her faculties.

Ida Mae grinned. "Or maybe he was too addled from doing you-know-what with the woman in the trailer to think anything at all. All the same, keep your eyes open on the way home, Claudia. Make sure nobody's following us."

As soon as they were in the car, Ida Mae gunned the motor, and the Chevy roared out of the parking lot. While Claudia craned her neck to look out the back window, Ida Mae made a right turn and then another and another.

Just as Claudia was about to ask why they were circling the block, Ida Mae gave a gleeful laugh. "I saw that maneuver on TV. It's how you know if somebody's tailing you. If nobody's followed us around all those turns, I guess we're safe."

For the rest of the way back to the retirement community, the two women chatted about the weather, their relatives, and the people they'd visited in the Nursing Center the day before. But when the Chevy jerked to a stop in Ida Mae's driveway, she said, "Law me, Claudia. Talk about addled! It's a wonder I even found my way home. That man doesn't have to follow us to know where I live. All he needs to do is give my license number to the deputy, and he can get my address from the computer."

"You're right," said Claudia, who'd already thought of that. "But don't you worry about it. I'm going to call Ray right away."

WHEN KRISTIN LEFT THE newspaper office for an early lunch the next day, the murders were the furthest thing from her mind. But when she was on her way to Myrtle's Grill, the lawyer's office across the street caught her eye. Why not drop in on Wilton Treadwell? If he wasn't with a client, she could ask him what he and Daphne Whittier talked about the day she died. The worst he could do was refuse to answer. After her attempts to obtain information from Ida Mae, Claudia, the Whittier family, and the police, she was used to that.

If he knew she was the person who'd told the police about his sister, he might not be happy to see her. But there was no way he could know that, was there? The detectives hadn't told Adelaide that Kristin was the source of the story, and Ida Mae and Claudia had assured her they hadn't mentioned it to anyone.

She opened the outer door of the lawyer's office and found herself in a small waiting room that might once have been elegant. The chairs were upholstered in a fabric that looked as though it had been expensive, but now it was faded and frayed. The end tables were dusty, and the receptionist's desk was completely empty—no calendar, no phone, not even a pen.

The inner door was a few inches ajar. "Mr. Treadwell?" Kristin called.

When there was no answer, she tapped on the door. Then she tapped again, a little louder.

There were shuffling noises inside. The door opened, and she saw the stooped, white-haired man she'd noticed at the reception after the talent show. Today he was wearing a cream-colored suit with a bright blue tie that matched his eyes, and he seemed delighted to see her.

"Come in, come in, young lady," he said, beaming as he offered her a chair. "What can I do for you?"

One glance around the inner office told Kristin that Wilton Treadwell had few clients. The framed diplomas and the law books on the bookshelves were the only signs that this was an attorney's office. The desk was empty except for a Tom Clancy novel with a bookmark near the middle.

When Kristin introduced herself, the lawyer tapped his ears and said, "You'll have to speak up. These hearing aids aren't much use."

She repeated her self-introduction. When she explained that she wasn't a potential client, he looked disappointed.

"I'm working on a story about Daphne Whittier's death," Kristin said, stretching the truth. She had no new information. Unless the attorney had something to tell her, there'd be no story to write. "I understand that she came to see you the day she died."

"I'm afraid I can't make any comment about that. The police instructed me not to make any statements in relation to the case." He smiled apologetically. "Especially not to the press. It might jeopardize the investigation, don't you see?"

Kristin did see, all too well. She'd hit another brick wall. Well, it hadn't hurt to ask. She stood up, ready to thank Mr. Treadwell for his time and say goodbye. Then she heard the outer door open.

"Wilton, lunchtime," a woman's voice called. It sounded as though she was used to being obeyed.

Kristin's heart beat faster. This must be Wilton's sister, the one who'd been so angry. The reporter put on a confident expression, reminding herself that the woman had no idea who'd mentioned her to the authorities.

When Adelaide Treadwell came into the inner office, Kristin knew she hadn't been mistaken in what she'd told the police. This was the woman she remembered. Tall, with perfect posture and snow-white, carefully coiffed hair, Adelaide Treadwell wore a teal linen suit, a white blouse, and pearls.

The older woman looked at Kristin in surprise. "I'm so sorry. I didn't realize Wilton had a client." She turned to her brother and said in a louder voice, "Sorry. I'll wait outside."

"Oh, I'm not a client. I was just leaving," Kristin said, making a move for the door.

"I'm Adelaide Treadwell. I don't believe we've

met," the other woman said, clearly curious about who Kristin was and why she was there.

"I'm Kristin Grant, a reporter for the *Sentinel*."

"A reporter? Here to interview Wilton?" Adelaide said, frowning.

To Kristin's amazement, Adelaide's brother said, "Miss Grant is thinking of doing a series of articles on the old families of Oak Hill. She thought we might be able to help her."

Adelaide's frown changed to a smile of pleasure. "Why, of course." She sat down and gestured for Kristin to take the other chair. "The Treadwells have been prominent throughout Oak Hill's history."

Kristin wasn't sure, but it sounded like the beginning of a lecture. While Adelaide looked down at her hands, as if considering where to begin the saga, Wilton gave the reporter a conspiratorial wink. Thoroughly bewildered but willing to play along, Kristin took her notebook and pen from her purse.

In the next half hour she filled a large portion of her notebook with the exploits of the Treadwells as city councilmen, mayors, bankers, and entrepreneurs.

"Wilton chose the legal profession," Adelaide said when she reached the current generation. She nodded in the direction of her brother, who seemed to be dozing in his desk chair. "Top of his class in the law school at Chapel Hill."

Many, many years ago, Kristin assumed.

Wilton opened his eyes. Apparently he'd been following the conversation after all. "Adelaide managed Treadwell Manufacturing for twenty-seven years. She did an excellent job."

"When we sold the company, the buyer promised to keep it going," Adelaide said with a trace of anger in her voice. "Within five years the plant was closed."

"You two were the only Treadwells in your generation?" Kristin seemed to remember Claudia saying something about a brother.

"Just the two of us and our brother, Holt. He died many years ago," Adelaide said, rising from her chair. "Now, Miss Grant, if you have no other questions, I need to take my brother to lunch. He tires easily these days."

Kristin felt like whooping with joy. She'd thought Adelaide would never stop talking.

"THIS IS WHERE JAMAL'S friend Troy works," Claudia said as Ida Mae maneuvered her car into the parking lot of Big Bob's Burgers.

"I haven't been here in a right long time," Ida Mae said. "A hamburger would taste good. Those refreshments didn't go very far."

Claudia was of the same opinion. The two

women had just spent more than an hour at the Oak Hill Senior Center, where a local banker had shown slides of her recent trip to Japan. The refreshments were green tea and rice cakes—healthful, and certainly in keeping with the theme of the program, but not very filling, Ida Mae and Claudia agreed.

Claudia smiled as Ida Mae skillfully squeezed her car into the gap between a black SUV with tinted windows and a battered pickup truck filled with paint buckets and ladders. She had no complaints about her friend's driving today.

Claudia had been in a quandary when Ida Mae offered to take her to the Senior Center. She knew it might be safer to go there on Pleasant Valley's bus with the others from the retirement community, but Ida Mae's suggestion of lunch at a restaurant had been appealing.

Before accepting the invitation, Claudia asked how Ida Mae had slept. When her friend replied, "Like a baby," Claudia decided to take a chance on riding with her. Sleep did Ida Mae's driving skills a world of good.

Big Bob's pine-paneled walls were decorated with signs advertising patent medicines and other products of bygone days. The restaurant featured hamburgers in a variety of sizes, plus meals of the home-cooking variety.

"I'm so hungry, I feel like I could eat one of

those Monster Burgers," Ida Mae said when they found seats near the back of the restaurant, "but I think I'd better settle for the senior citizen plate."

Their waitress was a young woman with long brown hair, jeans, and a tight-fitting T-shirt. Ida Mae, who knew her from church, introduced her to Claudia as a rising senior at Oak Hill High School.

"Is Troy Bandry working today?" Claudia asked when the teenager had taken their orders.

"No, ma'am. He comes in at five o'clock. I could give him a message. Are you his—" The girl gave her an appraising look. "Are you one of his relatives?"

"No, he's a friend of my grandson, Jamal Harris. You can tell him Claudia McNeill asked about him."

"You're Jamal's grandmother?" The waitress was clearly impressed. "He's like, super smart. Popular, too. He'll probably be student council president this fall and valedictorian when we graduate."

Claudia smiled. She already knew, thanks to frequent reports from her daughter Francine, Jamal's proud mom, that he was a big man on the local high school campus.

Ida Mae grinned at Claudia when the waitress left. "Now that girl was tactful. Did you hear how she didn't want to ask if you were Troy's grandmother, in case you weren't old enough for that?"

Claudia chuckled. "More likely she thought I was too old to be his grandmother. She was probably trying to figure out how many greats I was."

As they waited for their food to arrive, Ida Mae tapped her fingers on the tabletop in time to the music from the jukebox. Claudia hated to dampen her friend's good mood, but she needed to return to a topic they'd talked about on the way to the Senior Center. She took a slip of paper from her purse and gave it to Ida Mae.

"These are Ray's home phone and cell phone numbers. He said to call him any time, day or night, if you think you're in danger. He said you were right about that man."

"The one at the grocery store?"

Claudia lowered her voice, though she felt sure no one could hear her over the jukebox and the buzz of conversation in the restaurant. "No, the other one, the man we saw at the trailer. The license plate number you gave Wayne belongs to the man you thought it did."

"What about the one with the tattoos?"

Claudia shook her head. "He said your description didn't fit anybody he or Wayne knew. He's definitely not one of that bad family."

"Then I'm not going to worry about him," Ida Mae said. "Tell you what, Claudia, maybe I'll forget about those folks and take up Japanese gardening instead. What would you think if I turned my backyard into a garden that was nothing but rocks, like the lady showed us this morning?"

Claudia laughed. "I'm not going to worry about that. You love flowers and fresh vegetables too much to settle for a yard full of pebbles."

SIXTEEN

Oak Hill is a warm, friendly town. Newcomers are welcomed and strangers soon become friends.

From the Chamber of Commerce brochure,
"Welcome to Oak Hill"

ONCE SHE'D ESCAPED FROM the Treadwells' clutches, Kristin was in no mood to eat at Myrtle's Grill. It would be too easy for Adelaide to follow her there and pass along more tidbits of family trivia. Instead, Kristin retrieved her car from the *Sentinel* parking lot and headed in the direction of the fast food places on the outskirts of town, confident that she'd be safe from the Treadwells there. Adelaide didn't seem the type who'd stand in line for a sandwich or eat off a plastic tray.

A few minutes later, Kristin turned into the parking lot of Big Bob's Burgers. Big Bob employed waitresses, so his establishment wasn't exactly a fast food spot, but she didn't think giant burgers and loud country music were the Treadwells' style. The music wasn't her style, either, but the hamburgers were.

When she arrived at the restaurant, Kristin saw Ida Mae and Claudia in a booth near the back. Fortunately they were too busy chatting to notice her. After her half hour with Adelaide Treadwell, Kristin wasn't ready for more talk. Careful not to look in their direction, she made her way to a seat where she'd be out of their view. She was hoping for a quiet, solitary lunch.

But that was not to be. She'd just taken the first bite of her Monster Burger when she heard Ida Mae say, "Well, look who's here."

The two women had money clutched in their hands and were obviously on their way to the cash register, but at Kristin's halfhearted invitation they slid into the seat across from her in the booth. She didn't bother to broach the subject of the murders. She knew it was a lost cause. Instead she concentrated on eating while they talked about Japanese gardens and rice cakes.

After a few minutes, Ida Mae asked, "Who have you been interviewing this morning, Kristin? Somebody interesting, I bet."

Kristin was glad she could tell them about the nice young woman she'd interviewed for the "Volunteer of the Month" column in the newspaper. She knew better than to mention her encounter with the Treadwells. She remembered all too well that Ida Mae had a family saga as long as Adelaide's. She'd probably want it in the paper, too.

When Ida Mae and Claudia began talking about their friends who volunteered at the soup kitchen, the reporter's thoughts turned to Wilton Treadwell. Why had he told his sister that Kristin was writing about the old families of Oak Hill? Did he want the newspaper to do a series like that? It didn't seem probable, since he'd appeared to be bored by his sister's account of their family's history. Had he been trying to keep Kristin from mentioning Daphne Whittier's visit to his office? Maybe he knew that subject would make Adelaide angry. Or had his mind gone the way of his hearing, causing him to say things that made no sense at all?

Kristin knew a series of articles on the town's old families would be a nightmare. She'd infuriate the ones she left out, and the ones she included might not be satisfied. She could imagine Adelaide Treadwell's indignation if the newspaper confused her uncle John, the factory owner, with her greatuncle John, Oak Hill's first doctor. She was going to forget the whole idea. She hoped Wilton and Adelaide would, too.

Kristin tuned back into Ida Mae and Claudia's conversation in time to hear Ida Mae say that Frank Rowland was a volunteer at the elementary school. "He's a reading tutor. Vonda says she may try it, too. Tutoring kids isn't something Vonda would pick up on her own, so I guess it's a sure sign she's in love. They're dating right steadily, you know."

Kristin put down her hamburger to contemplate Vonda's love life. The idea of people Vonda's age dating and falling in love was unsettling to her. Besides, it was unfair. Vonda had acquired a steady boyfriend in her first two weeks in Oak Hill, yet in six months here Kristin hadn't had a date. By the time Vonda was Kristin's age, she'd already married twice, but Kristin hadn't even come close to being engaged.

One thing was sure, she was going to have to stop hanging out with old people and meet some single men her own age. But were there any in Oak Hill? While Ida Mae and Claudia speculated about the probability of marriage between Vonda and Frank, Kristin glanced around the restaurant. She saw families with children, groups of teenagers, and a few silent couples who looked as though they'd been married forever. On the other side of the room, she spotted a blond, muscular man seated alone. The next time she glanced at him, he was looking her way.

When Kristin finished her hamburger, she told her companions she had to be going. The three left Big Bob's together. While the others headed for Ida Mae's car, Kristin stood outside the restaurant trying to decide if she had time to go back to the newspaper office before her next interview. When the door opened behind her, she stepped aside to make room for the person leaving the restaurant.

"Excuse me," a deep male voice said.

It was the man she'd noticed while she was eating! Close up, with his long ponytail and dragon tattoos, he looked amazingly like someone she'd met when she lived in Raleigh, a guitar player in a band that had been popular there. But what could he be doing in Oak Hill?

"Are you one of the Vicious Slime Invaders?" she asked.

He recoiled as though she'd slapped him.

"I'm sorry," Kristin said, blushing. "I know that sounded weird. It's a band."

He looked at her apprehensively and shook his head. "Never heard of them." Then he smiled. "I'm into country rock, myself. Possum Creek. Dancing Palomino. Groups like that."

Kristin nodded as if she knew what he was talking about, though she was as ignorant of Possum Creek and Dancing Palomino as he was of the Vicious Slime Invaders.

"Do you mind if I ask you something?" he asked.

"I—well, I guess not."

"Those two women you were sitting with, the ones who just drove off in the green Chevrolet? I was wondering who they were, especially the white one who was driving the car."

His smile was so disarming that she answered without thinking. "She's Ida Mae Poindexter."

"Know where she lives?"

"Pleasant Valley. You know, the retirement place. In a duplex on Sunset Court."

"Thanks, ma'am. I appreciate it." With that, he strode off into the parking lot.

A wave of anger and embarrassment swept over her. *Ma'am?* He'd called her *ma'am?* Why, he had to be older than she was. He was losing his hair, and he had wrinkles around his eyes.

Then she realized what she'd done. She'd given Ida Mae's name and address to a total stranger, just because he had a nice smile, great muscles, and looked like someone she'd known briefly several years before.

"Hey, wait a minute," Kristin called after him. But her words were drowned out by raucous music as a car filled with teenagers drove past her. Then a van paused by the restaurant door, blocking her view. A mob of children swarmed out of the vehicle and into Big Bob's, almost sweeping Kristin along with them. When the van moved on, she saw the blond stranger again. He was in an old car, one that looked ready for a paint job. Its windows were open, and as it passed her, the driver's tattooed arm gave her a friendly wave.

As she drove downtown to interview a couple who'd recently opened a martial arts studio,

Kristin wondered what she ought to do. Try as she might, she couldn't convince herself that the man's questions were innocuous. True, this was Oak Hill, where most people knew each other. He could have been trying to remember who Ida Mae was so he could greet her by name the next time he saw her. On the other hand, he could be a con man, someone who pulled scams on the elderly and was lining Ida Mae up to be his next victim. Or he could be… Kristin shuddered, wondering if she'd just met a serial killer of old ladies.

By the time she arrived at the martial arts studio, Kristin had made up her mind. No matter how embarrassing it was, she had to warn Ida Mae about the man with the dragon tattoos. She reached for her phone.

When Kristin told the older woman about her encounter with the stranger, Ida Mae seemed to have a hard time taking it in. "He wanted to know what?" she asked. "What did you say he looked like?"

Kristin repeated the information, apologizing with every other breath.

There was a pause. Then Ida Mae said, "He probably just wants to sell me encyclopedias or vinyl siding."

Kristin was quite sure that wasn't the case. "Does he sound like somebody you know? Or somebody you've seen before?"

There was another pause. "No, I don't know him," Ida Mae said. Then her voice became more cheerful. "Don't think another thing about it, Kristin. I'm sure there's no harm done."

When the doorbell rang that evening, Kristin had just changed out of her work clothes and was looking in her freezer for an instant supper, something that would require only a few minutes in the microwave. She went to the door and looked through the peephole, half expecting to see the blond, tattooed man outside her apartment. The skewed face she saw there looked a lot like Wayne's. She opened the door a few inches and peered out.

The detective scowled at her. "Don't you have a chain lock? People can push right in if you open the door like that."

"Of course I have one," she said, "but I knew it was you. What are you doing here anyway?" Then she blushed, realizing she'd been rude. She opened the door wider and said, "Come in."

Wayne was in his shirtsleeves, and he'd loosened his tie. He looked so hot and tired that she couldn't help feeling sorry for him.

"Would you like something to drink?" she asked, motioning him to a seat on the sofa.

"Got any tea?"

She'd lived in North Carolina long enough to know he meant iced tea, not something that required a cup and saucer. Fortunately she'd made some that morning before work, strong and sugary, using a recipe from a colleague at the newspaper.

He accepted the glass with words of thanks that sounded heartfelt. Then he drained half its contents without stopping.

"Good tea," he said.

Kristin smiled, glad she hadn't failed this test of Southern hospitality.

"Mrs. Poindexter called me," the detective said after declining a refill. "She said some guy had been asking you about her."

Kristin nodded, surprised that Ida Mae had called the police. She must have been more concerned than she'd admitted on the phone.

While Wayne took notes, Kristin recounted the conversation she'd had with the stranger, skipping the part where she'd mistaken him for the guitar player from Raleigh.

When she'd finished, Wayne frowned. "You'd never seen this guy before?"

"No."

"And you gave him Mrs. Poindexter's name and address?"

"Well, yes. I just told you that."

He shook his head. "What did he look like?"

Kristin gave him the man's description without mentioning that he looked like the lead guitarist for the Vicious Slime Invaders. That would be meaningless to Wayne, she was sure. He looked more like the Possum Creek type.

"Did you see what he was driving?"

"An old car."

"How old?"

"I don't know."

"What make?"

She shrugged. "I don't know much about cars. It was a big one. It was dark blue, mainly, but with dull-looking gray paint in a lot of places."

"You mean primer?"

"Is that the stuff that goes on before you paint it?"

Wayne's expression made it clear that he couldn't believe the depths of her ignorance. "I guess you didn't get the license number."

"No."

The detective scowled.

Kristin was growing tired of his attitude. She might not know anything about cars, but she was pretty sure that in ordinary circumstances her encounter at Big Bob's wouldn't have warranted this much police interest.

"This has something to do with the murders, doesn't it?" she asked. "Maybe with Miss Whittier's death? Maybe with drugs?"

Wayne's face became impassive. "I can't comment on that."

Kristin gave an exaggerated sigh. "Because it might jeopardize the investigation, I suppose."

He shrugged. Then he glowered at her. "Don't ask Ida Mae Poindexter about it, or Ray's grandmother, either."

"Don't worry, I won't ask them." Why would she? Ida Mae and Claudia hadn't told her anything useful yet. There was no reason to think they would now.

He rose to leave. "Don't put any of this in the paper, either."

"I won't," she repeated. How could she, when she had no idea what was going on?

SEVENTEEN

Some of our family's happiest times were
spent at the supper table, talking about anything and everything that came to our minds.

From *Memories of Old Oak Hill*
by Isabel Rowland Everhart

IDA MAE SET THE BUTTER plate on the dining table
along with a plastic container of the low-fat margarine Vonda liked. Then she turned to her guests,
who were sitting in the living room. "Claudia,
could you help me in the kitchen a minute?"

Ida Mae hoped the request sounded more nat-
ural to Vonda and Claudia than it did to her. She
was perfectly capable of serving a simple meal—
or a complicated one for that matter—by herself.
She never liked to ask company to help. But there
was something she needed to find out from Claudia, and she didn't want Vonda to hear.

After Claudia followed her into the kitchen, Ida
Mae whispered, "Have you talked to Ray?"

Claudia nodded. "That's why I was late. He
called just as I was about to go out the door. He
said—"

"Can I give you a hand, Ida Mae?" Vonda said from the kitchen door.

"Why, thank you. You can put this on the table," Ida Mae said, handing her a basket of cornbread. She should have known her sister wouldn't stay in the living room by herself. She liked to talk too much for that.

"I'll tell you later," Claudia murmured when Vonda left with the basket.

Ida Mae nodded. With Vonda around, there wouldn't be much chance for private conversation. They'd have to talk after she left.

A few minutes later, the three women held hands while Ida Mae asked the blessing. She made it shorter than usual because the cornbread had been out of the oven a good while. She didn't want it to get cold.

There was no problem keeping Vonda away from the subject of the murders. They seemed to be the furthest thing from her mind. All the other two had to do was suggest a topic, and Vonda was off and running. When Claudia asked about Vonda's son—a subject Ida Mae wouldn't touch, not wanting to start another argument—Vonda had news.

"Harvey's coming to Oak Hill next week. He wants to meet the family he's never known." She sounded thrilled by this, as if she hadn't been spitting mad at him the week before. Vonda was as changeable as the weather, Ida Mae thought. Harvey had probably learned long ago that when a storm came up, all he had to do was hunker down and wait for it to be over.

"I told Harvey I want to move into Pleasant Valley," Vonda continued. "He was delighted, of course. He's wanted me to sell my house for quite a while. I told him I wasn't ready to sell, though. I'll just close it up, maybe hire a caretaker, in case I change my mind."

Ida Mae wondered if her ears were working right. Vonda was going to move into Pleasant Valley and keep her house in Atlanta? The woman must be made of money. Even the wealthiest residents of the retirement community sold their homes before moving here. Did this business about changing her mind have anything to do with Frank Rowland? As flighty as Vonda was, she might tire of him and move back to Atlanta. Or worse, what if he tried to break off with Vonda before she was ready to be done with him? Ida Mae could just imagine the fireworks if that happened.

"I cooked the cornbread in the same iron skillet I've used for fifty years," Ida Mae said as she poured Vonda a second glass of buttermilk. "I bet you haven't had a meal like this in a long time."

"Not since I left Oak Hill," Vonda said. "But it's good—simple, but healthful."

Ida Mae suppressed a grin. She knew better

than to mention the bacon grease she'd put in the pinto beans. Vonda had a fat phobia, like so many people these days. In Ida Mae's opinion, if you didn't put a little fat in food, it didn't taste right.

"You were always a good cook, Ida Mae," Vonda said. "I never was."

Ida Mae wondered if her sister had cooked at all, once she landed Parnell Hatcher. If Vonda moved here, she'd probably eat all her meals in the Pleasant Valley dining room, a swanky place with a professionally trained chef and starched linen tablecloths. It was the Oak Hill Inn all over again, except that there wasn't a piano player, and all the diners were up in years. Yes, Vonda would fit in just fine at Pleasant Valley.

"I think I could be happy here," Vonda said, echoing Ida Mae's thoughts. "Connie is a genius with my hair, and there's a gym in town that's adequate, at least for the time being."

An unkind thought flitted through Ida Mae's mind. If Vonda hadn't been able to find a gym and a hairdresser that pleased her, not to mention a wealthy suitor, would she have any interest in settling down near her sister and nieces?

"I'm in the process of developing a proposal for a fitness facility at Pleasant Valley," Vonda went on. "There's room for a building in that empty space behind these duplexes. I'll pay for the construction and furnishings—a pool, a weight room, a sauna, the works—if Pleasant Valley will hire the staff."

Ida Mae's eyes widened. Parnell Hatcher must have been quite a catch. With a husband that rich, no wonder Vonda was able to forget her family in North Carolina. But had Harvey heard about the fitness center? If he was counting on inheriting his mother's wealth, he might be upset to see it spent on weight rooms for the elderly.

After Vonda had chattered about the fitness center for a while, Ida Mae changed the subject. There was something she wanted to find out, if she could do it without Vonda's noticing.

"Vonda saw Adelaide Treadwell at the Cut'n'Curl the first time she went there," Ida Mae said to Claudia. "She recognized Adelaide right away."

"Yes, the first Monday I was in town," Vonda said. "Connie was finishing Adelaide's hair when I arrived for my two o'clock appointment. That's how I knew Connie was a good stylist. Adelaide always wanted the best."

"She was all dressed up, I bet," Ida Mae said. "I've never seen her without a nice dress, earrings, and maybe a string of pearls."

"That's Adelaide, all right," Vonda said. She launched into a description of Adelaide's jewelry and her blue dress and jacket. "As she was leaving, she made a point of mentioning that she was going to Wilton's law office—as if he really practiced law these days! Frank says the only reason Wilton goes there is to escape from Adelaide. Now that he can't see well enough to drive, she really has him under her thumb."

Ida Mae bit her lip to keep from smiling. Vonda had told her what she wanted to know. If Adelaide left the beauty shop for her brother's office at two o'clock, and if she was wearing the outfit Vonda described, she must have been the woman Kristin saw.

Vonda was already moving on to a new subject, her plans for furnishing her future cottage in Pleasant Valley. "I'm going to simplify my life. I'll have the things I need to be comfortable, but no more than that. Frank says that at our age too many possessions are a burden."

Across the table, Claudia's eyebrows rose slightly. Ida Mae wondered if her friend was speculating about the number of possessions Vonda had in her house in Atlanta. Or was she thinking, as Ida Mae was, that the fewer things Vonda and Frank had in their cottages, the easier it would be for them to combine their households, should they decide to marry.

"How about some dessert?" Ida Mae asked. "I have homemade blackberry pie and vanilla ice cream to go on top of it."

As she fixed their dessert plates—no ice cream for Vonda, of course—Ida Mae could hardly wait for the meal to be over and her sister to leave. She and Claudia had things to talk about.

After Ida Mae's guests turned down second helpings of dessert, Claudia asked if they could help with the dishes.

"No, no. You're my guests," Ida Mae said. "We'll just let them sit. In fact, I may not do them till tomorrow." She covered her mouth with a hand, feigning a yawn. "I must not have slept enough last night. I'm a little tired."

"Then we shouldn't keep you up," Claudia said. She picked up her plate and Vonda's. "I'll just take these to the kitchen, and then I'll be on my way."

Before long Claudia left for her apartment, and Vonda drove off into the twilight, whether to the Oak Hill Inn or to Frank's cottage, Ida Mae didn't know. She felt a twinge of guilt for hurrying her guests away. Then she grinned. It was probably Claudia's offer to help with the dishes that hustled Vonda off. Vonda's hands didn't look as if they'd spent much time in dishwater. After a supper of pinto beans, buttermilk, and cornbread, she probably was afraid Ida Mae would bring out a tin dishpan and lye soap to wash the dishes.

Claudia's mind was in a whirl when she reached her apartment. Vonda was going to build a fitness center next to the duplexes! Claudia pictured it as a building the size of a high school gymnasium, towering over their apartments. That was even more incredible than Vonda's plan to live in Pleasant Valley while keeping her house in Atlanta.

Claudia smiled, remembering that Vonda had said she'd have only a few possessions in her cottage. In the early years of their marriage Claudia and Layton had little more than a bed, a table, two chairs, and a few dishes and cooking pots. Vonda would never settle for that! She probably had more clothes in the suitcases she brought to Oak Hill than they'd had between them when they married.

When the phone rang, Claudia wasn't surprised to hear Ida Mae's voice, nor was she surprised that Ida Mae didn't sound the least bit tired.

"Isn't Vonda something?" Ida Mae said, chuckling. Claudia had to agree. "Yes, indeed. But I think you've lost your chance for a bigger garden, Ida Mae. Vonda's going to take all that space behind our backyards for her fitness center."

Ida Mae laughed. "I may have to give up gardening and take up lifting weights."

The women talked about Vonda's desire for a simpler life. Neither of them gave it much of a chance. Then they moved on to her romance with Frank Rowland, which they thought had better odds of surviving.

Ida Mae brought up Adelaide Treadwell. "I guess you put two and two together like I did. From what Vonda said, Kristin was right about seeing her."

"But why would she lie to the police?"

Ida Mae chuckled. "Because she was eaves-dropping on her brother and Daphne Whittier and didn't want to admit it."

"Do you think we should tell Kristin? Or maybe Ray and Wayne?"

"Yes, especially Wayne," Ida Mae said. "We ought to make him apologize to Kristin. That boy needs to learn some manners."

Claudia remembered that she had something to tell Ida Mae. "Oh, about Ray's call. He said he and Wayne still don't know who the tattooed man is, but with him asking Kristin about you, we'd better be careful. He offered to stay in my apartment a few nights to make sure nobody bothers us."

"Law me," Ida Mae said, "I forgot all about that other mess when I was listening to Vonda's big ideas. I don't think Ray needs to do that, do you?"

Claudia hesitated. That had been her first response, too. But maybe Ray knew something he couldn't tell her. It was Ida Mae's car the tattooed man had been looking at. If he came after anybody, it was likely to be Ida Mae—and if her friend was in danger, Claudia wanted her to be well protected.

"We didn't make a decision about it," she said. "He's going to call me back tonight."

"If it's me he's worried about, tell him I'm fine," Ida Mae said. She laughed. "As soon as these dishes are done, I'm going straight to bed and dream about doing exercises in Vonda's fitness center."

EIGHTEEN

The safety and security of our residents are of utmost importance.

From the brochure, "Pleasant Valley Retirement Center Welcomes You"

CLAUDIA HAD HARDLY hung up the phone from talking to Ida Mae when it rang again. It must be Ray, she thought, calling to ask if she wanted him to stay in her guest room. She still didn't know what to tell him.

To her surprise, the caller was Jamal. "Troy wants to see you," he said. "He wants to thank you for talking to Ray for him last week."

"There's nothing to thank me for, honey. The police weren't going to arrest him anyway. But I'd love to see Troy. I haven't seen him since—why, it must have been when you and he were in fifth grade."

"Is tonight all right? About nine-thirty? That's as early as he can leave Big Bob's. We won't stay long. I had to promise his mother he wouldn't be out late. Anyway, Mom will be on my case if I'm not back by eleven." He paused. "Mom thinks

Troy's some kind of criminal so I'm not going to tell her I'm taking him to see you. Unless she asks, of course. Then I'll tell her the truth."

"I'll tell her the truth, too...but only if she asks."

"Thanks, Grandma. You're the best."

Claudia turned on her outside light for Troy and Jamal. Then she turned all the inside lights off and sat down in the living room to rest until they arrived.

IT WAS AFTER NINE O'CLOCK, and Ida Mae was still washing dishes. She hadn't meant to leave them sitting, but after she and Claudia finished their phone call she remembered she'd seen a Japanese beetle on her bean plants earlier in the day. Those bugs would eat every leaf if she didn't stop them. She went out to spray the bean plants, and then she decided to water the tomatoes and the flowers. The truth was, she just liked being outside on a summer night, especially one like this when there'd been a break in the hot weather.

Ida Mae swished the dishes with a sudsy dishrag. Her nieces urged her to use the dishwasher, but unless she had a crowd for a meal she didn't bother with it. She was thinking about Ray's offer to stay in Claudia's apartment. Surely that wasn't necessary. She'd been a little perturbed when she heard that the tattooed man had asked Kristin about her, but having supper with Vonda and

Claudia had put things in perspective. Unless she had whiplash from watching Vonda jump from one outlandish idea to another, she'd be just fine.

But what if she was wrong? What if she and Claudia really were in danger, and Claudia got hurt? Ida Mae would never forgive herself if that happened. She felt safe, but that didn't mean anything. Daphne Whittier had probably felt perfectly safe the night she opened her door to her killer.

The thought of Daphne Whittier reminded Ida Mae that she hadn't locked her doors. Betty Jo and Norma wanted her to keep the place locked up all the time, but who could do that? To please her nieces, she tried to make sure the doors were locked by dark. She'd do that as soon as she finished the dishes.

As Ida Mae put the last dish away, she thought she heard the front door open and close. She stood still and listened. Her ears must be playing tricks on her. She knew they weren't what they used to be. Maybe she'd heard a noise from the street or a sound from Claudia's apartment.

Then the kitchen became slightly dimmer, as though a light had gone out in a nearby room. Ida Mae wondered if it was one of the lamps in the living room. She hadn't replaced a bulb since she moved in. As she bent down to take a new bulb from the cabinet under the counter, the room became even dimmer. When she looked around, she realized the light in the dining area had gone out, too.

Ida Mae had never been a scaredy-cat. When she was a girl on the farm, she'd killed many a snake, including a rattler or two, and when Odell worked the third shift, she'd stayed by herself at night, sleeping like a baby. She'd lived by herself since his death, never once checking her closets or under her bed to see if anybody was hiding there—but now her heart was pounding.

"Claudia, is that you?" she called out.

She wasn't surprised when nobody answered. Claudia wouldn't walk in uninvited. Neither would Betty Jo or Norma. The person who was in her apartment was up to no good. Where had she put that fool thing Norma gave her for protection? She opened a drawer, took out a small object, and dropped it into her apron pocket. Then she tiptoed to the alarm button by the phone and pressed it hard. You were supposed to use it if you needed medical help, but right now she'd take any kind of help she could get.

Ida Mae started edging toward the back door, keeping her eyes on the murky shadows of the dining area. She was sure someone was there. A human hand had turned off those lights.

"Stop where you are," a low voice said. Ida Mae squinted into the darkness, trying to see who it was.

Just then the phone rang. Ida Mae had been expecting it. When you pushed the alarm button, someone from the Nursing Center was supposed to call you back to ask what was wrong.

"Don't touch that phone," the voice said from the darkness. "Turn off the lights in the kitchen and go sit down in the living room. If anybody comes to the door, just keep quiet till they go away."

A figure stepped out of the shadows. Seeing a gun in the intruder's hand, Ida Mae decided to do as she was told.

A FEW MINUTES LATER Claudia fumbled her way to her bedroom in the dark, trying not to make any noise. She found the flashlight she kept beside her bed for emergencies, dialed Ray's number, and prayed that he would answer.

"Something's happening in Ida Mae's apartment. All the lights have gone off over there," she whispered when she heard his voice.

"Grandma, is that you? I can hardly hear you. Are you all right?"

"I'm fine," she said in a slightly louder voice, "but I don't think Ida Mae is." She explained how she'd heard a sound outside and had gone to the door, thinking it might be Jamal and Troy. "I saw somebody go into Ida Mae's apartment without

ringing the doorbell or knocking on the door—
and then her lights went out."

"I'll be there in five minutes. Meanwhile, you
stay put. Are your doors locked?"

Staying put was the last thing Claudia wanted to
do. She had a feeling that whatever was happening
at Ida Mae's involved her, too. Right now, the intruder might think nobody was home at Claudia's
because the apartment was dark. If she turned
on a light, she'd be in danger. But the darkness,
which usually seemed so peaceful to her, was now
frightening. She made her way to the back door
and slipped outside.

Claudia made a wide half circle around her part
of the duplex, careful to avoid the area illuminated by the light at her front door. When she
reached the sidewalk, a car entered the cul-de-sac
and headed in her direction. Claudia hurried toward it and waved it to a stop. But instead of Ray,
two lanky teenagers got out.

"Jamal?" she whispered. "Troy?"

"Good to see you again, Mrs. McNeill." The
voice was an octave lower than the one she remembered, but it was Troy's.

"What's going on, Grandma?" Jamal asked.

In a hurried whisper, Claudia told them what
she'd seen. "Ray's on his way. I don't know what's
going on in Ida Mae's apartment, but it's not good."

"Take it easy, Grandma. Let Troy and me check it out."

"Don't you go in there!"

"Hey, we'll be cool." Jamal put his arm around her and gave her shoulders a squeeze. "You stay here. We'll sneak up and take a look."

"No, don't!" But before she could stop them, the two boys took off across Ida Mae's lawn. When they were close to the house, they dropped to the ground and started crawling like soldiers in a war movie. They skirted the flowerbed and disappeared behind the azalea bushes beneath Ida Mae's living room windows.

NOW THAT IDA MAE knew who her visitor was, she didn't feel quite so afraid. Adelaide Treadwell wasn't the world's nicest person, but as far as Ida Mae knew the only harm she'd ever done was to snub people she didn't consider her social equals. But why was Adelaide here with a gun? Did it have something to do with the murders? Or, if Kristin's farfetched theory was right, with drugs? Or had Adelaide come down with Alzheimer's, like some of the people who lived in Pleasant Valley?

"I want to know what you told the police about me," Adelaide said.

It was Alzheimer's for sure, or some other kind of mental derangement. Ida Mae had heard that medications sometimes affected people her age in strange ways. Maybe Adelaide had started a new prescription and had gone haywire. The best thing to do was to try to calm her down and, if possible, talk a little sense into her.

"I believe you're mistaken. I haven't talked to the police about you," Ida Mae said in what she hoped was a soothing tone. "Maybe you've confused me with someone else."

"No, I haven't," Adelaide snapped. "You're Ida Mae Poindexter, aren't you? Your sister pointed you out to me at the reception after that silly talent show. You were talking to a police detective. I didn't know who he was at the time, but he showed up on my doorstep not long after that. I want to know what you told him and who else you told."

So that was it. Adelaide had seen her with Wayne and had jumped to the wrong conclusion. But how could she convince her of that? She couldn't tell Adelaide what she and Wayne had been talking about. If word of that conversation spread around, she'd be in bad trouble, and maybe Claudia would, too.

"I talked to him, but it didn't have anything to do with you," Ida Mae said.

"That's a lie! What did you tell him?"

Ida Mae had never been a liar, and she didn't like being called one. "None of your business," she said, forgetting that she was trying to calm a deranged woman.

"I saw you at the police station, too. Were you talking to that detective about me again? And don't try to tell me you weren't there. You pulled out of the parking lot right into the path of my car. If I hadn't slammed on brakes, I would have hit you. Your driving is worse than my brother's, and I had the Department of Motor Vehicles take his license away."

That was more than Ida Mae could take. Norma and Betty Jo could complain about her driving—that was their right, because they were family—but not this person who didn't even know her.

"You come into my home uninvited, you threaten me with a gun, and now you insult my driving? Believe me, Miss High-and-Mighty Treadwell, you're not as important as you think you are, and you never have been. I'll thank you to put that gun away and get out of my house."

"Shut up!" Adelaide shouted. "One woman has already died for sticking her nose into other people's affairs, and you're going to be next if you don't tell me what I want to know."

Ida Mae gasped. Had Adelaide been on some kind of murderous rampage tonight? All she knew for sure was that she had to separate her visitor from the gun. But how could she do it?

There were footsteps outside. Then the doorbell rang. While Ida Mae was wondering if she should shout for help, the front door opened, and someone switched on the overhead light. Two women in nurses' uniforms stood there looking at Ida Mae with concern.

"Mrs. Poindexter, your alarm went off," one of them said. "We phoned you, but you didn't answer, so we came to see if—"

She stopped, seeing the gun. Adelaide was now pointing it at the newcomers.

"Get out," Adelaide said. "Right now."

The nurses started backing out the door. This was Ida Mae's chance. She fumbled for the object in her apron pocket, but before she could take it out, there was a sudden movement in the dining area. Something flew through the air and hit Adelaide. She staggered, lowering the gun.

Then Ida Mae aimed her pepper spray canister and pushed the button.

CLAUDIA WAS IN JAMAL'S car with the doors locked and the windows rolled up. Her grandson had told her to keep her head down, too, but how could she, with such terrible things going on? She had to know what was happening.

Minutes before, Jamal and Troy had come running back from Ida Mae's apartment. "When Ray gets here," Jamal said, "tell him there's somebody in your neighbor's apartment with a gun, threatening to kill her. We're going around back."

"No, don't—"

But before she could stop them, they'd hustled her into the car and locked it. Right after that, Claudia had seen car lights coming into the cul-de-sac. Praying it was Ray, she began fumbling with the door, trying to get out. But when the vehicle passed her, she realized it was a Pleasant Valley van. When women in nurses' uniforms exited the van, Claudia rolled down the window to warn them not to enter the duplex, but she was too slow. After they went in, she saw the living room light come on. Ray drove up just as the nurses stumbled back out.

Now Ray was talking to the nurses, who were gesturing wildly toward Ida Mae's apartment. Sirens began screaming, and two police cars pulled up, followed by an ambulance. By the time Claudia managed to unlock the car door, police officers and paramedics were swarming into Ida Mae's apartment. When Claudia saw Troy and Jamal talking to Ray, she decided to stay where she was. The teenagers could tell him more than she could.

Before long, all the duplexes on the cul-de-sac were blazing with light. A crowd of onlookers gathered in Ida Mae's front yard. When two people were carried out of the apartment on stretchers, a band of fear tightened around Claudia's heart. Was one of them Ida Mae?

Claudia couldn't stay in the car any longer.

When she opened the door, Jamal hurried over to her.

"Are you all right, Grandma?"

"I'm fine. What about Ida Mae?"

"Ida Mae will be fine," said Ray, who'd joined them. "Both of those ladies had a bad encounter with pepper spray. They'll be in the hospital overnight, but they should be okay by tomorrow. The Pleasant Valley nurses had a little whiff, too, but not as much."

Pepper spray! That was bad stuff! But—thank you, Jesus!—at least nobody had been shot.

Then Claudia realized he'd said *both of those ladies*. "Who was there besides Ida Mae?" she asked.

"Adelaide Treadwell."

Claudia gasped in disbelief. "Was she the person I saw sneaking in?"

"I don't know. Ida Mae hasn't been able to tell us anything yet. But Troy and Jamal say Adelaide was threatening Ida Mae with a gun." Ray put his hand on his grandmother's shoulder. "I want you to be somewhere safe. I called Mom, and she's on her way. She's going to take you home with her for the night."

"Thank you, Ray," Claudia said. Right now the idea of being taken care of sounded wonderful, and no one could do it better than her eldest daughter.

A few minutes later, Vivian's car screeched to a halt in the spot the ambulance had vacated. Claudia went to meet her.

"I'm all right, and Ray is, too," she said, giving her daughter a hug. She knew these were the things uppermost in Vivian's mind.

"Thank God for that! What in the world happened? Ray didn't tell me a thing on the phone," Vivian said. "Is that Jamal over there? And who's that with him?"

"Yes, that's Jamal and his friend Troy Bandry. They were on their way to see me when all this happened."

Claudia gave her daughter a brief account of the evening's events, which Vivian punctuated with gasps, an occasional *Oh, my God,* and, when she learned nobody was seriously hurt, a fervent *Praise Jesus!* Then they went into the apartment, where Vivian insisted that Claudia sit down while she collected her medicines and several days' worth of clothing.

"You're going to stay with me till this mess blows over," Vivian said.

As THEY STARTED BACK to the car, Vivian spotted the nurses, who were talking to Wayne. She insisted that they take her mother's blood pressure, saying, "It's probably sky-high after what she's been through tonight."

It turned out to be normal, but one of the nurses asked, "Would you like to stay in the Nursing Center tonight, Mrs. McNeill, just as a precaution?"

"She's not staying anywhere in Pleasant Valley," Vivian said. "She was minding her own business when all hell broke loose in the apartment next door. Who knows what else might happen here?"

Claudia wasn't about to contradict her daughter, but she knew she hadn't been minding her own business. In fact, she'd meddled in several other people's affairs—Mr. Haizler's and Stacy Whittier's, to name two. She shivered. Someone had threatened Kristin for investigating the murders. But she and Ida Mae had been doing the same thing with their speculation about Leonora Whittier—and look what had happened to Ida Mae. Claudia wished they'd left everything to the police.

NINETEEN

Our seniors are our greatest resource. Where would we be without their lively minds, warm hearts, and wealth of experience? We need to listen to them.

> Carolyn Powell, mayor of Oak Hill,
> at the dedication of the Oak Hill Senior Center

WHEN IDA MAE OPENED her eyes, everything looked blurry.

"Aunt Ida Mae?" she heard Betty Jo say.

"Can't see." It came out as a croak that made her throat hurt.

"Oh, your glasses. They're right here."

After Betty Jo helped her put the glasses on, Ida Mae saw both her nieces looking down at her anxiously. Where was she? She was on a bed, but it didn't feel like her own. The walls of the room were pale yellow, not the blue of her bedroom at home, and wires and tubes were attached to her body.

"Hospital?"

Betty Jo nodded.

Ida Mae tried to wiggle her fingers and toes.

She wasn't sure, but she thought they were working. Maybe she wasn't as bad off as she felt.

"As soon as the doctor okays it," Betty Jo said, "we're going to take you to the Nursing Center at Pleasant Valley."

Ida Mae closed her eyes, hoping this nightmare would be over when she opened them. She didn't want to go to the Nursing Center. When she visited friends there, she always told them what a nice place it was. She meant it, too—for them, but not for herself. Sometimes people went into the Nursing Center and never came back out. She wasn't ready to give up her apartment, her flowers, her tomato plants. Besides, she wanted to go home so she could talk to Claudia. They'd figured out something they needed to tell the police, she was sure, though at the moment she couldn't say just what it was.

Then she remembered. "Adelaide Treadwell," she said, opening her eyes and raising her head off the pillow.

"She's here, too," Betty Jo said. "But don't worry, Aunt Ida Mae. She's going to be all right. She had a little more of the pepper spray than you did, but fortunately the ambulance arrived right away."

Pepper spray? Ambulance? Ida Mae had no idea what her niece was talking about. She didn't think pepper spray or an ambulance had anything to do with the thing she and Claudia needed to tell the police. She closed her eyes again and tried to sort through her jumbled memories...Adelaide in her living room...nurses coming to the door...

Ida Mae shook her head. What she remembered didn't make sense, and it was far too complicated to try to tell her nieces.

"Oh, Aunt Ida Mae," Norma wailed, "I should never have given you that pepper spray. Lloyd told me it was a bad idea. What in the world made you use it? Did somebody break in while Miss Treadwell was visiting you?"

Ida Mae tried to remember. Somebody else had been there...somebody who'd thrown something at Adelaide...

"The sugar bowl," Ida Mae croaked. "The one from Betty Jo's store. It got broken."

Her nieces looked at each other in a way that made her realize she'd better start making more sense, no matter how fuzzy her brain was. If they thought her mind had flown south, they'd pack her off to the Nursing Center for sure.

"Excuse me, ladies," a voice said. It was Ray, and Wayne was with him. "We need to talk to Mrs. Poindexter alone for a few minutes."

Ida Mae watched with relief as Betty Jo and Norma trooped out the door. She'd never thought the day would come when she'd be happier to talk to the law than to her own kin, but right now she was glad to have her relatives out of the room. Once she talked to Wayne and Ray, maybe she'd feel better. Then she'd tell her nieces that she wanted to go home, and she wouldn't take no for an answer.

Ray smiled down at her. "Are you able to talk to us, Mrs. Poindexter?"

Ida Mae nodded. "Kristin saw the blue dress. Vonda, too." Then she stopped, realizing she wasn't explaining it right.

The two detectives looked at her as though she'd made perfect sense.

"My grandmother called me a little bit ago," Ray said. "She told me Miss Treadwell really did go into her brother's office while Daphne Whittier was there. She explained how you two figured that out."

Ida Mae was glad to hear this. For one thing, it meant Claudia was all right. She hadn't been involved in the mess that landed Ida Mae in the hospital. And if Claudia had told the detectives about the blue dress and the Cut'n'Curl, Ida Mae wouldn't have to try to explain something her mind seemed too confused to handle.

"Why don't you tell us what happened in your apartment last night after your supper guests left?" Ray said. "We know bits and pieces of it, but you're the only one who knows the whole story.

Start at the beginning and take all the time you need."

Ida Mae smiled. That was the way she liked to tell a story, especially one as complicated as this. She felt sure she'd be able to remember everything if she went slowly and told things in the order they happened.

"I started to wash the dishes," she said. "I've never been one to let work sit undone. But then I remembered the Japanese beetles. They're bad on beans, you know. So I—"

Ray held up a hand to stop her. "Wayne and I had better sit down," he said. "We'll need to take a few notes."

"BILL WANTS TO SEE you right away," the receptionist said when Kristin arrived at the newspaper office the next morning. She made it sound so important that Kristin went directly to the editor's office without stopping to leave her purse and coffee cup at her desk.

Bill was on the phone. "We won't sensationalize it. I can promise you that." His tone was serious, but Kristin could see he was amused. "The best thing for all concerned would be for us to put the full story on the front page. All kinds of rumors are going around—a burglary gone wrong, a home invasion, a gang war. Believe me, all those stories will be a lot worse for Pleasant Valley than the truth.... Uh-huh.... Uh-huh."

Bill winked at Kristin as he listened to the person on the other end of the line.

"Tell you what," Bill said. "We've had a little trouble getting the police department to talk to us. Why don't you call Chief Cates and ask him to have one of his detectives brief us?...He should talk to Kristin Grant, the reporter who'll handle the story.... Thanks. That'll be a great help."

Kristin could hardly wait for the phone call to end. Some kind of crime had occurred at Pleasant Valley, and the police were going to give her the whole story! Maybe it had something to do with the murders. Maybe it was a murder. But then Bill wouldn't be smiling, would he?

When he hung up, Bill said, "That was George Willis, the head honcho at Pleasant Valley Retirement Center. There was some kind of altercation out there last night involving Ida Mae Poindexter—the woman you wrote about, the one whose sister reappeared—and another woman, Adelaide Treadwell. You've probably heard of her. The Treadwells are prominent locally, or at least they used to be. Both women were zapped with pepper spray. My informant says they both ended up in the hospital, but they'll be fine."

Kristin felt a stab of guilt. Could Ida Mae's attacker have been the man with the blond ponytail?

She quickly pushed her concern aside. Something Bill said had caught her attention.

"You have an informant in the police department?" she asked.

He grinned. "No, in Pleasant Valley. The former editor of the *Sentinel* lives there—on the same cul-de-sac as Ida Mae Poindexter, as a matter of fact. He keeps me up-to-date on the stories, true and otherwise, that circulate there. He says two African-American teenagers, apparently not the perpetrators, were at the Poindexter apartment. He was afraid the neighbors who saw them might jump to the wrong conclusions. I embroidered on that to make George think all kinds of rumors were flying, because I wanted him to talk to Chief Cates for us. George will do just about anything to keep Pleasant Valley from having bad publicity, especially the kind that makes it sound as if it's dangerous to live there."

A few minutes later Kristin was back at her desk, her mind churning with questions. Why would somebody attack two old ladies with pepper spray? Was the attack related to Daphne Whittier's death? How long would it be before she heard from the police? She hoped Wayne would be the one who called. When he was angry, he sometimes blurted out details he didn't mean to share, and she was good at making him angry.

A half hour later, Wayne called. Sounding almost as professional as Ray, he told Kristin that Ida Mae had used the pepper spray in self-defense.

"Miss Treadwell threatened her with a gun. She also threatened two Pleasant Valley nurses who came to the apartment in response to an alarm."

"Was the man with the dragon tattoos involved?"

"Who? Oh, him. No, nobody's mentioned that he was there."

Kristin was relieved to hear this. "I understand that two teenage boys were involved," she said, thankful for Bill's informant in Pleasant Valley.

"You understand wrong," Wayne said with a touch of his old belligerence. "I mean, they didn't commit any crime. One of them helped disarm Miss Treadwell."

"He overpowered her?"

"No. He…uh…I believe he threw a sugar bowl at her."

"A blue pottery sugar bowl?" Kristin asked, remembering the one on Ida Mae's dining table.

"How did you know that?" Wayne said, sounding suspicious.

"Oh," Kristin said, "I have my sources."

IDA MAE WAS LYING IN the hospital bed, wondering how long it took to die of boredom, when Vonda appeared at the door. She was carrying a huge basket of flowers with balloons attached.

"Aren't they pretty!" Ida Mae said. As she

thanked Vonda for the flowers, she could see that
her sister was upset.

"What's the matter?" Ida Mae asked. Had
Vonda been in another argument with her son?
Or, even worse, was her romance with Frank Row-
land on the rocks?

"Oh, Ida Mae, it's all my fault," Vonda said, her
eyes brimming with tears.

"What is?"

"This." Vonda made a sweeping motion, indicating her sister and the hospital room.

Ida Mae felt a prickling of unease. A tiny part
of her mind had wondered about Vonda ever since
she returned to Oak Hill. Could her sister have
been involved in something bad before she left
town or since coming back—something that was
related to Adelaide's strange behavior last night?

Ida Mae pushed her doubts away. This was her
sister, raised by parents who had a strong sense of
right and wrong. Vonda might be stubborn, a little
selfish, and as quick to flare up as a brush fire, but
Ida Mae couldn't believe she was a bad person.

"Don't be silly, Vonda," Ida Mae said. "I'm here
because Adelaide Treadwell came after me with
a gun, and I shot her with pepper spray. So blame
Adelaide or me, but not yourself."

Vonda dabbed her eyes with a handkerchief.
"That's just it, Ida Mae. I told Adelaide you didn't
lock your doors. Well, actually I told the whole

bridge club. I was just giving an example of how much safer it is here than in Atlanta. Adelaide came in through an unlocked door, didn't she?"

Ida Mae had an answer ready for this, the same one she was planning to give Betty Jo and Norma if they raised a fuss. "Locked or unlocked wouldn't have made a lick of difference. If Adelaide had rung the doorbell, I would have let her in. Anyway, the back door being unlocked saved my life. That's how Claudia's grandson and his friend came in, the one who beaned Adelaide with the sugar bowl."

Vonda didn't look convinced. "All the same, I want to make it up to you, Ida Mae. Is there anything I can do for you?"

Ida Mae's first thought was to ask her sister to bring her a sausage biscuit and a hot cup of coffee. The hospital breakfast had been meager, and the coffee had been tepid. But she knew what Vonda's response to that would be—a lecture on cholesterol and caffeine.

Then Ida Mae had an even better idea. "Yes, there *is* something you can do for me. Call Betty Jo and Norma and tell them I'm just fine, and I need to go home."

IT TOOK A LOT OF TALKING, but Ida Mae was able to go straight home from the hospital, bypassing the Pleasant Valley Nursing Center.

"They had to make sure my brain was working before they'd let me out," she told Claudia the next day. "They asked me what day it was and who the president was, and they wanted me to count back from a hundred by sevens."

"Did you pass?"

Ida Mae laughed. "Just barely. I messed up somewhere around sixty-five. Tell you what, Claudia, we'd better practice that subtracting, just in case."

"They should have put your picture in the paper this morning, along with Jamal's and Troy's," Claudia said.

"I'm not as vain as Vonda, but I wasn't about to let them take a picture of me the way I looked in that hospital bed. Anyway, Jamal and Troy are the heroes, not me."

A photo of the teenagers had been on the front page of the *Sentinel* that morning, along with a story by Kristin, headlined "Youths Prevent Tragedy in Retirement Community." The article quoted a police spokesperson, Detective B. Wayne Henley, as saying that Adelaide Treadwell would probably be charged in the incident. The newspaper article made it clear that Miss Treadwell was not a resident of Pleasant Valley Retirement Center, and it stated that she was now at a private psychiatric hospital for evaluation.

"I had some time to think, laid up in that hospital bed," Ida Mae said. "When Adelaide was waving the gun at me, she said a woman was dead because she'd meddled in other people's business. I told Wayne and Ray about that, but they said not to mention it to Kristin because it might jeopardize a police investigation. That made me wonder if Daphne Whittier was the meddler and the Treadwells were involved in her murder."

Ida Mae paused, expecting Claudia to look shocked or at least surprised. When she didn't, Ida Mae continued. "According to Vonda, Adelaide's brother can't see or hear a bit good, so I doubt he could drive to Tabor Street even in the daytime. That would make Adelaide the one who killed Miss Whittier, though, for the life of me, I can't figure out why."

Claudia nodded. "I've been thinking about Leonora. The Treadwells could have been involved in her murder, too."

Ida Mae considered this a moment. Then she said, "How about a piece of pound cake, Claudia? We have some thinking to do."

WHEN THE TWO WOMEN HAD combined all their ideas into one theory and had tested it up, down, and sideways over slices of cake and glasses of tea, Ida Mae suggested that they go to the police station.

"Let me call Ray," said Claudia, who doubted

that a dose of pepper spray and a night in the hospital had improved her friend's driving skills.

As Claudia hoped, Ray insisted that the two women stay where they were. "Wayne and I will come there," he said. "We have something to tell you."

"Bet you a nickel they've arrested Adelaide," Ida Mae said when Claudia told her what Ray had said. "They need to, the way she was carrying on the other night. I'll tell you, Claudia, I didn't know I could be that scared."

But Wayne and Ray hadn't come to talk about Adelaide.

"The SBI arrested some of the county's big drug dealers today, including the woman you saw out at Ida Mae's homeplace," Wayne said.

"And the deputy, too?" Claudia asked.

"Yes. But don't worry, there was plenty of other evidence to implicate him without mentioning you two."

"What about that fellow with the dragon tattoos? Was he arrested, too?" Ida Mae asked.

"No," Ray said. "Nobody's come up with any local bad guys who fit that description."

Ida Mae didn't know what to think about that. It made her feel safer, but a little foolish, too. Had she been wrong about him? Could she have been as confused as Kristin, who thought Daphne Whittier's death was drug-related, or Adelaide, who thought Ida Mae had reported her to the police?

"Kristin saw some men with you at the police station the other day," Ida Mae said. "I guess they were from the SBI."

Ray grinned. "You guess right."

"She thought she'd stumbled on something you didn't want her to see," Claudia said.

"She was right," Wayne said. "For once."

"What I want to know is," Ida Mae said, "when are you going to arrest Adelaide for Daphne Whittier's murder?"

Ray looked perfectly calm, but Wayne's face began to redden.

"You might as well tell us," Ida Mae said. "We've near about figured it out anyway. We know Adelaide had something to hide. Otherwise, why did she come after me with a gun to find out what I'd told you?"

The detectives were silent.

"Here's what we think," Ida Mae continued. "Holt Treadwell, Adelaide and Wilton's brother who went to France to live, was Leonora Whittier's lover—and her killer. Maybe they planned to run off together, but he changed his mind. Or maybe all he wanted was a short, secret fling, but she threatened to raise a ruckus when he tried to break off with her. The Treadwells found out he'd killed her and kicked him out."

"We think Daphne Whittier knew Holt was her sister's lover," Claudia said, "or at least strongly suspected it. When he disappeared from Oak Hill at the same time her sister did, she thought they'd gone away together. All these years, she never said anything to the Treadwells or to anyone else. Then when the bones turned up and the newspaper said Vonda sold her necklace to somebody in 1946, she realized that her sister might not have gone to France with Holt Treadwell after all. Maybe she even remembered seeing her sister with the necklace."

"We think Miss Whittier went to see Wilton Treadwell to try to find out what happened to her sister," Ida Mae said. "Adelaide overheard them talking and decided to kill her before she went to the police."

"Have you told anybody else this theory of yours?" Wayne asked.

Claudia shook her head. "Ida Mae and I agreed we wouldn't tell anybody but you and Ray."

"We won't tell," Ida Mae said, "but we want to know if we're right."

The two men looked at each other.

"Okay, you can tell them," Wayne said to Ray, "but don't blame me if the story spreads all over town and spoils the case against her."

TWENTY

Sometimes life seems too confusing for us
to understand. But other times, things begin
to fall into place, and we praise God for it.

The Reverend Douglass Alexander, pastor of
Mount of Olives United Methodist Church

CLAUDIA WAS PROUD OF Ida Mae for asking the detectives to tell them the truth about the murders, and she was pleased that Ray was willing to share what he knew. That meant he trusted her and Ida Mae. From Wayne's frown, she knew the other detective wasn't so sure.

"You were right," Ray said. "Miss Whittier went to Wilton Treadwell's office to ask him about Leonora. Wilton said he was completely surprised by her story. He told Miss Whittier he'd never heard of her sister, but he was sure Holt hadn't gone to France with a woman. A private detective hired by the family traced Holt's journey and found him there. After Holt left, he wouldn't take any Treadwell money. He even turned down the inheritance left to him in his father's will. Wilton said the Treadwells never understood why Holt went away or why he refused to have anything to do with them."

"Did you believe his story?" Ida Mae asked.

Ray shrugged. "We know Wilton didn't kill Leonora. He was off touring the country with his friend Frank Rowland that summer. Rowland backs him up on that."

Ida Mae's eyebrows rose at the name of her sister's suitor. "How do you know Frank's telling the truth?"

"We checked it out," Wayne said. "Wilton wrote articles for the newspaper while they were traveling. In July of 1946 they were in California."

Claudia tried to think this through. "If Wilton was in California," she said, "Holt could have had an affair with Leonora and killed her, and Wilton wouldn't have known it. But if Holt Treadwell was as bitter toward his family as you say he was, it's more likely he was planning to run off with Leonora, but somebody, maybe one of the Treadwells, killed her first."

The two men looked at each other.

"All right, go ahead," Wayne said, but he didn't look happy about it.

"Adelaide has been confessing right and left," Ray said, "ever since we questioned her in her hospital room. She says she killed both of the Whittier sisters, and we believe her. The gun she was waving at Ida Mae was the one that killed Daphne

Whittier. It was a German pistol, World War II vintage. Wilton told us his brother brought it back from the war. A couple of years ago when there was a rash of break-ins in town, Adelaide thought they ought to have some protection, so Wilton cleaned and oiled the gun. He's kept it loaded ever since."

"I just realized why Adelaide opposed the new highway," Ida Mae said. "She knew those bones were there, and she was afraid they'd be discovered."

Claudia thought about Daphne Whittier, who'd opened the door to her killer. Maybe she assumed that Adelaide, who'd fought the coming of the interstate highway, wanted to join her in opposing the rezoning of Tabor Street. If so, the conversation hadn't turned out the way she expected. Claudia pictured the two women sitting down in the living room, and then—

"Were Adelaide's fingerprints on the picture of Leonora?" Claudia asked.

The detectives looked at her in surprise.

"How did you know that, Grandma?" Ray asked.

"I can see how it might have happened. As a young woman, Adelaide may have found the picture in her brother's room and made up her mind to stop the affair. Then, years later, she taunted Daphne Whittier with the picture before she killed her."

All four were quiet for a moment. Then Ida Mae broke the silence. "For so many years we thought Adelaide was just a silly snob—but she was a cold-blooded killer all along."

A FEW DAYS LATER, AS Ida Mae was rereading the article in the *Sentinel* about Adelaide's arrest for murder, her doorbell rang. Vonda was on the doorstep holding a flower arrangement, the third one she'd brought her sister since her encounter with the pepper spray.

"They're beautiful," Ida Mae said when she opened the door, "but you can't keep bringing me flowers. People will think I'm sick, or maybe dead."

"I want to do something for you," Vonda said, "and you turned down the other thing I tried to give you."

Over her sister's protests, Ida Mae had refused her offer of a gym membership, saying she'd wait and do her exercise in the fitness center Vonda was going to build in Pleasant Valley. Ida Mae had never been able to turn down flowers, however, and these would look perfect on her dining table.

"Thank you, Vonda," Ida Mae said, feeling a rush of affection for her sister. "I do love flowers."

Once the floral arrangement was in place at the

center of the table, Vonda perched on the edge of the sofa and gave her sister an earnest look. "I hope you don't think that Frank—well, that he had anything to do with those awful things Adelaide did. He was a friend of the Treadwells, but he wasn't even in Oak Hill when the first murder happened."

"I'm sure you're right," Ida Mae said with a reassuring smile. She'd heard all this from the detectives, of course, but she and Claudia couldn't admit to knowing more about the crimes than they'd read in the newspaper.

"Frank says Wilton didn't know anything about the murders, either."

"I'm sure he didn't," said Ida Mae, who'd heard this from the police, too.

Vonda smiled and settled back on the sofa, apparently relieved that her sister agreed with her. "Wilton is selling his house and moving into Pleasant Valley. Frank says he would have done it years ago, but Adelaide wouldn't hear of it."

Ida Mae let Vonda talk for a while. Then she said, "Let me tell you about the dinner I'm planning. I'm doing it to thank Claudia's grandson and his friend Troy for saving my life. I'm inviting Ray and Wayne, too."

"Oh, Ida Mae, could I come?" Vonda asked. "And Frank, too? I know he'd like to."

"Of course. I'd love for you and Frank to be

there." The idea was such a good one, Ida Mae
wondered why she hadn't thought of it herself.
Vonda would enliven any party, and it was appropriate for Frank to be there, too. The purpose of
the meal was to thank people Ida Mae felt grateful to, and Frank was one of them. If not for him,
Vonda would probably be back in Atlanta by now.

"Just don't tell our nieces," Ida Mae said.
"They think I'm too old to cook for a crowd."
She grinned. "Betty Jo and Carson are going to the
beach next week, and Norma and Lloyd are going
to Gatlinburg. I'll have this meal while they're
away. With any luck at all they won't find out
about it till it's over."

The next day, Vonda's son, Harvey, arrived for
a short visit. Ida Mae had lunch with him and her
sister at the Oak Hill Inn. Vonda was on her best
behavior, though her mouth tightened into a thin
line each time Harvey mentioned his new wife.
During the meal, nothing was said about selling
Vonda's house in Atlanta or about the fitness center she intended to build in Pleasant Valley.

Ida Mae couldn't help liking her newfound
nephew in spite of the fact that he'd left his first
wife, depriving Vonda of her grandchildren's
company. Harvey wasn't the spitting image of his
mother, but his wavy brown hair, blue eyes, and
warm smile reminded Ida Mae of Vonda when
she was young.

After the meal Vonda and Harvey dropped Ida Mae off at her apartment, declining her invitation to come in.

"I'm going to show Harvey one of the cottages here in Pleasant Valley," Vonda said, "the one I'm thinking of taking."

Ida Mae knew that the only vacant cottage in the retirement community was right across the street from Frank's. She wondered if Vonda had told her son about her new boyfriend yet.

After Harvey and Vonda drove off, Ida Mae went to the phone to give Claudia a full report. When there was no answer, she remembered that her neighbor was spending the day with her granddaughter Lisa and the new baby.

Ida Mae had just changed from her good dress to an everyday pantsuit when the doorbell rang. As she looked out the living room window, the first thing that caught her eye was the car parked out front. The large swaths of gray primer looked familiar. She peered out the corner of the window to see who was on her doorstep.

Her heart skipped a beat when she saw the writhing dragons on the muscular arm nearest the window. The receding hairline, the blond ponytail—yes, that was the fellow she'd seen before! Thank goodness she was keeping her doors locked in the daytime now. She'd just slip into the kitchen and call the police.

But it was too late. The man was looking straight at her. When he reached toward his pocket, she made a quick step to the left so she was behind the door, hidden from view. But when he tapped on the window, her curiosity overcame her caution. She inched closer and saw that he was pressing a small rectangle of paper against the glass. It looked like a business card.

Ida Mae was fairly sure that a hit man wouldn't show her his card before shooting her. She moved nearer the window so she could read it. *J. B. Kimrey, Classic and Antique Auto Restoration,* it said.

"I want to buy your car," the man called from the other side of the glass.

Ida Mae shuffled through her memory bank of names. Yes, she knew some Kimreys. She opened the door a crack, bracing it with her foot so he couldn't push it open.

"Who are your people?" she asked.

"Bedford Kimrey's my daddy, ma'am. And Ward Kimrey's my granddaddy."

"Ward Kimrey who married Essie Blackburn from down around Sneed's Crossroads?"

"She's my grandmother, ma'am."

Ida Mae had known Essie all her life, which made her feel a little better about the man. Of course, she wouldn't trust some of her friends' grandchildren any further than she could throw them, but this one had a printed business card. Surely he was all right.

Ida Mae opened the door wider. "Come in and let's talk. Would you like a glass of tea and a slice of pound cake?"

A WEEK LATER CLAUDIA was at Ida Mae's, helping her prepare for her guests.

"Have you decided about selling your car?" Claudia asked as they pulled the dining table apart to add extra leaves. She knew the streets of Oak Hill would be safer without Ida Mae's Chevy careening through them, but she doubted her friend was ready to give the car up yet.

"No. J. B.'s called me twice, offering a little more each time. The way I figure, if I wait a few more years my car will be antique instead of classic, and he'll give even more for it." She laughed. "Which do you think we are, Claudia—classic or antique?"

Claudia smiled. "I don't know, but either way we ought to be worth a lot."

"I have a whole passel of folks coming tomorrow," Ida Mae said as they added the last leaf to the table. "You, me, Ray, Wayne, Kristin, Jamal, Troy, Vonda, and Frank. There's still room for Stacy. Are you sure Ray doesn't want me to invite her?"

"No. He said he didn't want us matchmaking for

him. He made me promise there wouldn't be any women here we hadn't told him about. He said he's gun-shy from the time he went to his mother's for a family dinner and found that woman from the church fluttering her eyelashes at him."

A few minutes later the women were at the kitchen table with glasses of tea, resting up from their work.

"Where's Stacy staying for the rest of the summer?" Ida Mae asked. She'd heard that Stacy's father had agreed to sell Daphne Whittier's house to Buddy Daniels as soon as the estate was settled. She didn't think Stacy would want to be there in the meantime.

"She's living in Greensboro with that white fellow, her friend from high school. Ray says they're just roommates. She's paying him rent, and they have separate bedrooms." Claudia shook her head. "It sounds strange to me. A man and a woman living in the same apartment, without—well, you know what I mean. But Ray says that's not uncommon these days."

"Maybe so, but I don't understand it," Ida Mae said. Then she chuckled. "But what do we know, Claudia? We're antique, or at least classic."

"Are you doing a little matchmaking of your own by inviting Wayne and Kristin?" Claudia asked.

Ida Mae grinned. "Could be. Kristin is convinced he doesn't like her. She says she makes him mad without even trying. It reminds me for all the world of a little boy who was sweet on me in the third grade. He didn't know whether to be nice to me or torment me."

"I'm glad you're inviting her. Maybe it will make up for our being so closemouthed when she was trying to investigate the murders."

Ida Mae nodded. "I feel bad about that, but I feel worse about the one thing I *did* tell her. I should have known better than to mention Buddy Daniels. I can't believe he'd call her in the middle of the night and threaten her, but still…"

Claudia nodded. Somebody had threatened Kristin, and she and Ida Mae didn't think it was Adelaide. Adelaide hadn't suspected Kristin of investigating the murders any more than Kristin had suspected Adelaide of committing them.

"Are you sure Troy and Jamal will like what I'm fixing for dinner tomorrow?" Ida Mae asked. "They're not the kind of teenagers who'll eat only hamburgers and pizza, are they?"

"Jamal eats anything and everything. If my memory is correct, Troy does, too."

"You're sure Troy can take a night off from Big Bob's without any problem? I'd hate to cause him trouble after all he did for me."

Claudia smiled. "Big Bob thinks Troy's a hero. He put a framed copy of the newspaper article about Troy and Jamal beside the cash register with the part about Troy working at Big Bob's underlined in red."

"Troy and Jamal are both heroes, and you are too, Claudia," Ida Mae said. "You were the one who called the police. If it weren't for you and Troy and Jamal, I'd be in the cemetery beside Odell now. Remember, you're a guest of honor tomorrow."

"Guest of honor or not, what time shall I come over to help you? It'll be too much for you, doing it all yourself."

"I swan, Claudia, you sound like Betty Jo and Norma! I'll be fine. But come over any time. I'd appreciate the company."

TWENTY-ONE

I have confidence that if we strive to do our best and treat others with respect and kindness, we can accomplish great things.

Daphne Whittier, at the opening of
Oak Hill High School

CLAUDIA BIT BACK A GRIN as her friend prayed. The more guests Ida Mae had, the longer her blessings went on. She'd already mentioned Jamal and Troy, "who delivered me from danger," Ray and Wayne, "who solved crimes that were a blot on our community," and Stacy "who has suffered a great loss."

As Ida Mae gave thanks for Kristin, "whose writing adds so much to our lives," Claudia opened her eyes a tiny bit to peek at the other guests. Ray was across the table, sitting beside Stacy. He'd called Ida Mae the night before to ask if he could bring her after all. When Ida Mae's guests joined hands for the blessing, Claudia had been pleased to think of Ray's hand closing around Stacy's.

Jamal and Troy were on either side of Kristin, with their eyes tightly closed. When they arrived in T-shirts and baggy shorts, Claudia was concerned that they weren't properly dressed, but they assured her that Ida Mae had said they didn't need to dress up.

Vonda was next to Troy. Now there was a woman who was *always* dressed up. Today Vonda wore a cornflower-blue linen dress and gold jewelry. Frank was beside her in a navy jacket and tie. He looked like the kind of man who wouldn't be comfortable in casual clothes.

By now Ida Mae had thanked God for Vonda "my dear sister who's back with us after all these years," Frank, "a newcomer to this table we hope we'll see here again," and Claudia, "my good and dear friend." Sensing that the end of the prayer was near, Claudia tucked her head down, closed her eyes, and joined the others in echoing Ida Mae's *amen*.

The table held an abundance of food—roast beef, baked chicken, five kinds of vegetables, a relish tray, hot rolls, biscuits, three kinds of homemade pickles, and two kinds of homemade jam. The guests began passing the serving dishes around, and before long their plates were heaped high. After the first few bites, they showered Ida Mae with compliments.

Then Frank turned to the detectives. "I want to congratulate you gentlemen on solving Daphne Whittier's murder in such a timely manner. Her death was a great tragedy for our town."

Vonda beamed at Frank as though he'd just uttered a profound truth, but Claudia wondered what he meant by *timely*. From her point of view and Ida Mae's, too, she was sure, it would have been much better if Adelaide had been arrested a couple of days sooner. Of course, Claudia didn't blame Wayne and Ray. She knew they'd done their best.

"My great-aunt Leonora's death was a tragedy, too," Stacy said. "Her only mistake was to fall in love with Holt Treadwell. If he'd had more courage, he would have brought her killer to justice sixty years ago. Then Aunt Daphne wouldn't have been killed, and Mrs. Poindexter's life wouldn't have been threatened."

Jamal and Troy looked up from their plates and regarded Stacy with expressions of interest. They seemed to be waiting to hear what she would say next.

"True," Ray put in smoothly, "but we have to be grateful to Wilton Treadwell. He's been most helpful in our investigation."

Claudia tried to look as though she hadn't heard this before. The other guests appeared genuinely surprised by the news. Kristin seemed so excited by this revelation that Claudia almost expected her to pull out her notebook and start writing an article for the paper.

Ray smiled in the reporter's direction. "Kristin

has been a great help, too. Wayne and I appreci-ate her assistance."

Wayne, who was sitting beside Kristin, stopped piling strawberry jam onto a roll long enough to turn toward her and say, "Yeah, that's right."

With everyone's eyes on her, Kristin couldn't help blushing. She hadn't expected public thanks from the detectives. It had been enough when they'd appeared at her desk a few days before to apologize for not believing her. They hadn't men-tioned the man with the tattoos, and Kristin hadn't brought the subject up. Since Ida Mae appeared well and happy, Kristin assumed he hadn't caused her any trouble.

Kristin looked around the table. What a wonder-ful opportunity to find out more about the mur-ders! The detectives had given her only a bare outline of the story to put in the paper. With Stacy apparently willing to talk, surely she could learn something new.

Kristin was sorry she'd tried to pry informa-tion out of Ida Mae and Claudia. Apparently they hadn't known anything at all. The detectives had told her that Adelaide's visit to Ida Mae's apart-ment was simply a mistake on the part of the killer, who was confused and possibly deranged.

Now, with Ray smiling at her and Wayne look-ing less unfriendly than usual, Kristin remem-bered something she'd been meaning to tell them.

"Do you remember the anonymous call I had? The person who said I'd better mind my own business or I'd end up dead?"

Everybody stopped eating and looked in her direction.

"It didn't have anything to do with the murders. It was my neighbor in the next apartment. He was mad because I complained about their noise. When his wife found out what he'd done, she made him apologize to me."

"Do you want to press charges?" Wayne asked.

"Oh, no. They're moving out anyway."

Wayne frowned, but before he could say anything further Ida Mae urged everyone to have more to eat.

"Just help yourselves," she said to Ray, Wayne, Troy, and Jamal, whose plates were almost empty. All four did as she suggested.

A few minutes later, the conversation turned to the murders again.

"Adelaide Treadwell will probably spend the rest of her life in a plush psychiatric facility instead of prison—or death row," Stacy said.

Ida Mae heard the bitterness in the young woman's voice, and she couldn't blame her for it. "It doesn't seem fair," she agreed, "but if it's any consolation, I thought Adelaide was as crazy as a bedbug the night she almost shot me. She would have done it, too, if it hadn't been for these two young men."

"It was Troy who saved your life, not me," Jamal said as he helped himself to another slice of roast beef. He grinned. "It's a good thing he plays baseball. Now me, I would have tried to slam-dunk that sugar bowl on her head like a basketball, and she would have shot me dead."

"I'm sorry about your sugar bowl, Mrs. Poindexter," Troy said.

"Don't worry about it," Ida Mae said. "A sugar bowl's not much to lose when your life's at stake." She nodded toward the pink pottery bowl that was at the center of the table, flanked by matching salt and pepper shakers. "My niece gave me a whole new set. She sells them in her store."

Vonda beamed at Troy and Jamal. "You both are heroes." Then she gave them a speculative look. "You'll be high school seniors this fall?"

"Yes, ma'am," they said in chorus.

"Are you planning to go to college?"

Jamal said he hoped to go to his parents' alma mater.

"I want to go to college, too, but I'll probably have to work a few years first to earn the money," Troy said. "I've been thinking about a career in law enforcement or maybe becoming a lawyer."

As Ray and Wayne began telling Troy about law enforcement careers, Ida Mae noticed her sister's face. Vonda was looking at the teenagers with the same intent expression she'd had when she talked about her plans for a fitness center at Pleasant Valley. Was she thinking about helping Troy, and maybe Jamal, too, with college expenses? That wouldn't surprise Ida Mae a bit. She'd do the same if she had the money. But since she didn't, she'd offer them a home-cooked meal from time to time. Maybe she'd invite their families, too. That was the least she could do, considering that they'd saved her life.

"We haven't mentioned the other recent victory for local law enforcement," Frank said to Ray and Wayne. "The arrests of the drug dealers and the deputy sheriff were very impressive. I'm sure you fellows had a part in it."

The detectives smiled, but said nothing.

"Frank explained to me," Vonda said, looking fondly at her gentleman friend, "that the woman who was arrested was one of those Tavenders who were selling whiskey when I was a girl."

"She's a direct descendant of the original Tavender moonshiner who set up his first still over a hundred years ago," Ray said. He began giving Stacy the capsule version of the family's history as moonshiners, bootleggers, and drug dealers.

None of this was news to Ida Mae, but she could see that it was to Kristin, who seemed to be listening intently. It was amazing how much the girl didn't know! Now that the murders were behind them, Ida Mae thought she might invite her over for a meal and tell her all about Oak Hill and Yarborough County.

Well, not *all,* Ida Mae reminded herself. She wouldn't tell Kristin that she and Claudia had helped the police solve the murders, and she surely couldn't mention tipping them off about the corrupt deputy, either. Come to think of it, she'd better be careful about anything she told Kristin. The girl seemed to want to investigate things, and there were some things that were best left uninvestigated.

As the others discussed the Tavenders, Ida Mae looked around the table. She was pleased with the way the meal was going. So many people, all enjoying the food she'd prepared, and all getting along well, too. There was plenty of food left, and some of the plates had empty spaces that needed to be refilled.

"More candied yams, anybody?" she asked. "Green beans? Squash casserole? Start the chicken and roast beef around for us, Wayne."

As the serving dishes went around the table again, Ida Mae was happy to see that everybody took something—even Vonda, who put a carrot stick and a piece of celery on her plate.

Ida Mae smiled. She could hardly wait to offer her guests dessert. She'd fixed three different things, and all of them were good.

* * * * *

IDA MAE'S POUND CAKE

(Recipe from the Greensboro Daily News, 1946)

3 cups flour
2 sticks butter
1 cup milk
¼ tsp. salt
½ cup Crisco
1 tsp. rum flavoring
¼ tsp. baking powder
2 cups sugar
1 tsp. lemon flavoring
5 eggs

Sift flour, salt, and baking powder together three times.

Cream sugar, butter, and Crisco. Add eggs one at a time, mixing well.

Stir flour mixture and milk into sugar and shortening mixture, alternating ⅓ milk and ⅓ flour, beginning with milk.

Add flavoring.

Put into greased and floured tube pan. DO NOT PREHEAT OVEN. Bake at 330 degrees for 1¼ hours.